THINKING
SCIENTIFICALLY

THINKING SCIENTIFICALLY

John Fraser

AESOP Modern Fiction
Oxford

AESOP Modern Fiction
An imprint of AESOP Publications
Martin Noble Editorial / AESOP
28a Abberbury Road, Oxford OX4 4ES, UK
www.aesopbooks.com

First paperback edition published by AESOP Publications
Copyright (c) 2021 John Fraser

www.johnfraserfiction.com

A catalogue record of this book is
available from the British Library.

First edition 2021

ISBN: 978-1-910301-81-4

CONTENTS

1

THE OPERA

'WHAT A CROWD! Who's paying? Some without instruments – Singers! Their tool's in their head! Some are truly appetising – no, I mean the women *and* the men. See, the instrumentalists cluster round in families, like sparrows and crows – brass with brass, fiddles with each other. Who sings louder gets to fuck more females – same with trombones....'

'And you, Hervé?' I ask. 'You've no family. Being a critic can't take all day.... Why not put yourself in harmony?'

'No voice,' he says. 'But I've a scarlet rump and a red flag on my crest.'

There's a movement of disquiet, fragments of discontent. The percussionist says – 'Our parts. They're empty – nothing to play...? Or do we improvise?'

There's Giselda, looking red and moist, stuck in a corner, explaining absences – 'The machine,' she wails. 'It printed nothing out.'

Hervé laughs. 'Mine's an easy piece to write,' he says. 'Three acts of acufene, a drama of deaf-mutes....'

*

It isn't true. It's opera. The singers know their parts. The rest – will fit. In time.

'My subject, Hervé,' I tell him, as he pulls to get away, 'It's how once work made us; it filled our adult years with comrades

7

and our politics. Now, these middle years are full of triviality –
of family, fathers who failed, then lovers who don't love, or not
enough and not exclusively.... And then you die, just like
before.... Except you've had no politics, no mates, and nothing
that you've done remains....'

He stares at me. 'You don't like what's real and here to stay?'
he asks. 'You're in the right trade: opera. Nostalgic bourgeoisie!
– you've found your champion in my friend ... his silent music,
quite unplayable – the hired hands in their penguin suits will sit
and strum, then take a bow. Then, silent applause, from never-
dirtied hands.'

*

'I have to get away – can we begin?' asks a sturdy lad, Dromy.
'The protagonist,' I say. 'I don't see her.'

'Oh, she works bars in Haskovo,' says Dromy. 'Maybe she
missed the bus to here. Anyway, my part is high. Who am I?
Am I a trans?'

'If you can't do the part,' I say. 'You should have said –
someone else....'

'I need the money,' Dromy says. 'I'll make out.'

'Need's not a criterion here,' I say, 'Not on this earth.
Everybody knows it.'

'We'll call it off,' Giselda says, recovered. 'The original parts
aren't here....'

'They were copied late,' I say. 'Give the band some cash,
tomorrow we'll all come....'

That isn't possible – tomorrow is another country, other laws
and different people.

'Can you write something, Hervé?' I ask. 'A puff? An
exclamation, not what you'd call critique.'

'Oh yes,' says Hervé. 'Mine's not content, it's just style. Say
what you want – music has no country, exists in no space, the
words don't matter – I'll tell my public how good, how difficult,
how awful it all is.... No one needs hum along....'

Everybody leaves: they're all busy, say they are, have futures
determined somewhere else, everything will happen some time,
but ... we can't re-schedule....

Of course we can't. For things to happen, everybody has to organise, all serve perfection, exactly similar – that's why there's hordes of angels. 'Hosts', they're called, but they're not hospitable, don't have a place to entertain....

Dromy says, 'My club – it's not for gentlemen. It'll wind you down....'

I'm fascinated by what seems to be – an adam's apple. 'It's a goitre,' Dromy says. 'If it goes on, it will throttle me. Your gig and my swan song ... will meet up in space, like every genre....'

'It'll still happen, some time,' I tell him. 'Just – without you. It's better so....'

*

'You need relax,' says Dromy, as we leave the theatre: 'My club.... You can do anything you want....'

'So anyone can do it to you,' I say, joking.

'Exactly,' he says. 'You're punished, but once you take the hit, you can do anything you want to anyone – murder is out, of course, they need live bodies to pay the fees....'

'Just for some drinks,' I say, 'and stuff.'

'There's lots of stuff,' says Dromy, 'so bring a lot of cash.'

*

The punishment's with sticks. I guess they're wrapped to blunt the hurt ... there's curtains, and the arms come out.... The stick leaves a purple welt across my hand, and then behind my ear. It's like the rabbit hole: someone says 'Take this', and there's a pill, could be a demerol, so you can take more hurt. 'Hey,' I shout to Dromy, who's being beaten hard – 'It's like TV.'

'No stars, no plot, and no one watching,' Dromy shouts. 'You take it on the flesh, so's you can give it out, and double up your pain....'

'This is my last time,' says Melissa, laughing a little. She's been knocked around, her badge is torn.

'It's my first,' I say. 'But I guess you are a prize, and not a punishment. That's what makes going on worthwhile....'

'Oh no,' she says. 'I'm not a tart. People say that I'm a bitch, but that's not at all the same – a tart gets paid, a bitch is yours for ever, or as long as you can endure.... Dearer than coke, but I don't harm your nose.'

Dromy has disappeared – maybe everyone gets a Mel or a Melissa, some get both. There's a sticky jug passed round: manhattans – better than a demerol.

'I'm a surface,' says Melissa. 'You can stick to me. This extinction talk – should make us cleave to one another, value the flower, the industrious ant. Not so – we're scared, indifferent. I'm a floor – you can lie on me and gather strength. Love, if you wish.'

'Are you a customer or an employee here?' I ask. 'It's clumsy, asking, I know....'

'Read the books: we're always both,' she says. 'Work's crap. They pay you so you can spend. Or if you like, you starve, but still you're paid. They call it humanitarian. It just shows – you live a complicated life – you need people to clear it all away and spruce you up, defend you and punish you. It goes to battleships, electric chairs, electric cars. You can live well without paid work – but you'll find you can't. Being with me – is free. It's all the rest, the drinks, silk panties.... You must pretend to work, get paid.

'It's like you can be a doctor – kill or cure. A soldier – much the same.'

'And all in this club,' I say, marvelling; and wondering how a dumb lump like Dromy found it....

'You can't stay here,' she says. 'No one can. It seems an easy way – you think you'd turn some tricks, be dealer, spin the wheel – live for a hundred years. It can't be so. Here, you know the secret – then you're outside again. Do what you've always done ... only you'll have had to pay. It's like that for me too,' she says, handing me a stick, pulling me behind the curtain, and I feel her body, all of it, pressing, urging me on to take aim, hit – some fat guy – and I catch him just behind the ear, he staggers, and Melissa ... she's naked underneath her smock, her nipples are erect, they press into my chest, all is more vivid and immediate – 'Go on,' she says, 'hit, hit again, they expect it, you hit now, soon it will be their turn, all's paid and reimbursed, and then we leave ... these stcks – they wound, but nothing permanent, they cripple, even blind, but you don't feel it mostly, just take care, and be judicious....'

*

'Where'd Dromy go?' I ask Melissa.

'Who is he?' she asks – 'You want another on this bed?'

'No, no – I'm a creative. I do shows, not sex. Dromy, he's an extra. Signed me in....' I say.

I'm excited, aroused as I've ever been, and yet – libido comes and goes, it's like a schooner in high waves, down goes the poop, then up the masts appear, the tattered pennant.... 'Maybe it's the drink....'

'Oh, first time's always like this, it hits everyone – doing what you want ... we're not prepared for that,' she says.

'How much longer do we have?' I ask Melissa – there's no way of telling time ... she must have been here earlier, perhaps another time ... often ... for years....

'Oh, you're signed in,' she says. 'Time's nearly up. We can come back when we want. You don't want being hit again – you need to watch your eyes, your prick, your teeth – a bad strike..., and she laughs. 'You're out!'

*

We're both outside, I hug Melissa, she hugs back, it's happened all exactly as I thought.

'Looking for Dromy?' she asks me, quite mischievous,

'Oh no,' I say. 'He's a singer, we get any number of them – they don't have a proper instrument, not in a case,' and I tell her how my opera stalled.

'Well, opera doesn't sound so great – a bunch of guys in makeup sing along, kind of a gay choir ... it doesn't seem it's worth a grieve if you can't put them on a stage....' she says.

*

Dromy calls. 'Hey,' he says, 'How'd you make out? I got beaten bad.'

'I'm healed,' I say. 'But after my punishment, I don't seem to have done a crime. Just life – better than usual, but more uncertain....'

'I thought the opera was off,' says Dromy. 'I want to ask you for a bigger part.'

'Yes, Dromy,' I say. 'It's off – so you can have the biggest part you want.'

'Thanks – I've noted that,' he says. 'And did you get the review from that guy, your friend Hervé?'

I tell him, 'Hervé said it was a rowdy silence – voices of musicians, white noise. It's been done before – "I can attest," he says, "That Jimbo's nothingness is better than the earlier nothingnesses that we know so well."'

'You're called Jimbo?' Dromy asks, 'I didn't know.'

'I'm not,' I say. 'It's Hervé making sure no one will recognise. If ever it's re-scheduled, I'll let you know....'

He says, 'Enjoy Melissa,' and rings off.

*

Later, I call back, my duty to commiserate: 'Tell me about the opera,' he says, 'Since I'm the heroic principal....'

'That's not exact,' I say. 'It's about everything, not you. There are no principals. Or – there are principal parts, not principal singers. The stage revolves, and singers have a part *in nuce,* a cluster. They elaborate it, then someone takes it up, but not by chance or grab – the story runs around the proscenium arch in lights....'

'It doesn't sound much, put like that,' he says. 'I'd take it all in hand. Improvising is the easy part for me – it's following the written stuff....'

'That's why I hinge it all on written stuff,' I say. 'You would be Jedermann, but everybody is: all start off like that ... can be again, briefly ... all differently.'

I'm not committed to interpretation, or to meaning – art is like that, it surpasses reality, but has the real already in its bag; and better still, it wriggles out of contracts, people don't show, and so it doesn't pay its bills, and in the end it's always that monster, public, that doesn't show. Sometimes the monster is a mammoth or a dinosaur, sometimes a sea of jelly-fish, sometimes a bird-limed mask bewitched, bewitching, in a grove....

*

'Forget your opera,' says Hervé. 'Find a woman, or a man, who's difficult and tantalises. Then, when you're dumped, you have the inspiration in your craw. Use it – go hunting, go to war, invent a pair of shoes that fly you round the world....'

He takes me to the races – it's his passion, life – his hobby. 'I'll wait outside,' I say. 'Enjoy it, it's too complicated to know who's won: – the horse, the jockey, owner, punter or the bookmaker. Football's a bore, but at least it's cretinous....'

'No, no,' he says. 'You bring me luck, the idiot always does. We'll eat those tiny eggs in the expensive bar – the plovers go extinct but there's a store of eggs, the same with quails – then there'll be wrens, hedge-sparrows too....'

There's dogs and horses, donkeys too, jockeys on saddles or in carts and chariots, sideshown jaguars to try to set a record for a sprint, hippos for the laughs. 'O fuck,' says Hervé. 'The favourite's a grey. They always lose. I think they're dead. *They* think they're dead. Jimbo – you'll have to pay for everything today .... I wagered everything – my mistake ....'

'It's not what I envisaged, Hervé,' I say. 'There's a smell of *déjà vu*. I had the world, had it in nutshells, made into a necklace, with earrings, a *parure*. I held it all – luck of the world – and then the focus slipped.... Now – it's fleeting. My fortune – rode off on Fortuna's spotty back....'

'Oh come,' says Hervé. 'Forget the music. It's another fiddle – worse, a fiddle-faddle – we'll go into town, some drinks....'

Melissa doesn't answer when I call. She rarely does. She still emits a strong charge, of sex adventurous; abundant life, mysteries resolvable by long research, sauced up with sweaty interludes of copulation....

'We're a pair, Melissa,' I have said....

'Of course,' she says. 'We beat them all, we are two pairs of hearts or swords – or maybe cups.... Be patient, Jimbo dear, my love, my excess, my rhino horn, my horn of Siegfried ... I must stop, I'm panting with desire for you....' and off she goes, she has appointments she can't miss....

*

'Let's try your club, my friend,' says Hervé.

No, I think, what if Melissa's there, and this time – who knows, if I was assigned a crime I must commit, what could it be?

'You know my backer, Hervé,' I say, turning him away from my Melissa. 'Have them pay what's owed, and an advance to come....'

'I don't know your backer,' Hervé says. 'Nothing to do with me. I floated names and themes around, no more. It would be improper to butt in to the finance: – more important, it's a risk I wouldn't take. Yours is a merchandise that's slippery, a bubble, bladder – a boil, a beauty-spot, a bangle or a bang, a smirk that lasts a lifetime or a grin – a trifle or a punch, to hide a fart, death-rattle ... a twist in the trachea, in your case.... And in song: – what plot can you have found out that will not happen, or has already happened, to us all?'

'You may be right, Hervé,' I say. 'It's all arrangements.'

We drink, and migrate from bar to bar, as Hervé likes; a new country, new ethnic, demographic, landscape with figures, in each one. There's someone looking like an elephant-man – he, or his brothers, comrades, children – seems to follow us. I know you shouldn't evoke those poor elephants: it's just a medical condition, after all. We all have one of those: a face, a thorax, knee, a body looking like a plank or carrion.... But, this guy is a creation, an original, the most ... a book to his credit, photos, many lookalikes, a party theme....

With each reappearance of an elephant-man, Hervé says, 'A revelation! Symbol – we in the forest, what are we? Lemurs, ghosts – and him – that trunk! Borne with such careless dash – see how he swings it, dangles it into his drink – a super-penis!

'He forgets! He is denatured, his instincts shot, desalinated with a pharmakon. It's us who are the memory of his species now, we are the cemetery he's been trudging to since birth, we lie here like open graves, and he, his troop of lookalikes – we are his destination.

'Clearly, it's time for us to recompense the beasts we have extinguished, hunted to oblivion. It's our turn – take on their face, their pelts, their diet. Be the tigers and the toads. The elephant.'

'It's true,' I say. 'We start to look like animals, we play the part, we squeak and roar, pee in the sawdust, scratch and scrabble on the bar – "only a sleeping beast knows who you are" – I should music that, you know....'

'You should find out about your sponsor,' Hervé says. 'You've spent their money, no records, no receipts. You could be in deep .... and no performance either.'

He's part concerned, part gleeful....

We do noisy things, carouse and row with other people, takes us days to remember all of it. There comes no follow-up, no summons, but I don't feel like doing music till I've remembered everything I did. It doesn't look as if I shall.

*

'Here I am,' Melissa says. 'You can stop being anxious.'

'I did call,' I say.

'Yes; lots,' she says. 'I was nowhere, doing nothing. Everything is so precarious. Work. Not work.'

'The club,' I say.

'I've seen Giselda,' says Melissa. 'Your vice.'

'I know,' I say. 'I felt ashamed. Pissed off. We didn't start the singing. I should have apologised, or perhaps she should.'

'I missed you, Jimbo,' Melissa says. 'I get wet thinking of you,' and she giggles.

'We saw the elephant-man,' I say. She hasn't heard of him. 'Hervé and me,' I say. I don't mention we were drunk.

'Well,' she says. 'This has been quite lovely ... seeing you, all that....'

'Melissa!' I say. 'Stay!'

'Oh yes,' she says. 'We could do something, if you've time.'

'Let's not go to the club,' I say. 'It's too much like – imagination. Free flight.'

'I spend time, lots, with Giselda,' Melissa says. 'It's almost work, looking for work, for me, for her. We're not commodified, not merchandised, just looking. It's creative, and inventive. Free time. I hope we never find work, Jimbo. Toil. Labour. It never satisfies, it loses you – work nowadays, does not give that single hour the body needs of satisfaction, of delight....'

'I know,' I say. 'It's commonplace....'

She's offended, says, 'I should tell you – Giselda thinks you are a fink, your music crass, pretentious, rackety and void. Against nature – you slice voices like you're slicing eggs.

'She has a thing for that guy Slick, and his trombone – it's very sexual, the slide. The valve trombone you use on horseback instead – it's true perversion: soliloquy, orgasms inside your pants, like in the olden days – Mussolini, Bonaparte: – unconfessable.... At least, that's what Giselda says....'

'My work.' I say. 'It has a part of parody, pastiche – it all depends on who directs. That opera – can last for hours, or finish in five minutes. It depends – the time musicians have, the time you think the music fits. Of course – it covers everything; and that has no time, no lapse specific, no limit ... when you make a work of art, it can be quick or very slow ... a miniature, a Ring. You must avoid the repetition, though, the mouldy tales, stock heroes, puffed like bags of popcorn....'

'I understand all that,' Melissa says. 'If it's too long, it bores. Too short – there's nothing to enjoy.'

'We musicians – all walk the natural way,' I say. 'The passacaglia: walk of the quail. Nature, art, that knows exactly where it wants to go, and where it left its nest. It all begins with Webern and his opus one. Myself – I like a joyous sound – all the noise that's tolerable, and all the instrumentalists you can afford. Enough the japonnaiseries of pluck and splat – the stories of a note that goes for little limping walks.. I'm a putter-in. Leaving out – it ends in emptiness. I must assert. Voices that overcome their limits, like soldiers on invasions and retreats....'

'There's people who suggest,' Melissa interrupts. 'If I can't find better – there's a tiny farm, a big smallholding. If it suits – we could try running it. Live off it. Nature. No sticks, no club, no punishment. Perhaps a village dance on Saturday – the carmagnole, I bet that's done ... Slick and Giselda – they could visit us....'

'We'd see about that, Melissa,' I tell her. 'But it sounds delightful. I have a worry too – paying back my sponsor, if I knew who.... We could lie low....'

'Paying Giselda too,' Melissa says, pinching my hand so hard the blood clots purple on the back. 'Poor soul.'

It's a prospect that enthralls, incites, excites.

'Don't forget your oath to me,' Melissa says. 'When they call you to the army – keep your fingers crossed when you are made to swear – and think of me. I shall prevail.'

There is a puzzle here. 'Service is voluntary, Melissa, paid,' I say. 'That takes the sting out, and it means that nothing matters much – certainly not your life. You don't need loyalty to anything imaginable. Work. That's important, and that's all. Doesn't matter what. That's why the club ... is an exception, but not one we should repeat.'

'Oh we, we,' Melissa says, and snorts. 'You include yourself in everything, so really there is only you.'

*

The farm – more of an allotment – is very small. The soil is black – you can grow leeks, and not much else.

Melissa's already in the bed, a linen spread pulled up to her neck, held tight in her pink mousey paws.

It is wet, the bed. I sleep at once, and wake in minutes. It's so damp, we're shivering. We cannot, dare not, light the stove – it's modern, there's a tube, a pipe, we're afraid of suffocating – the fuel looks like black cobble-stones.

'Let's get up and dig,' Melissa says.

It's done. At dawn, a guy passes, says – 'If you bury all the grass, it will shortly rise again.'

*

It's Saturday – the dance. The band has never heard of
Carmagnole. Giselda doesn't speak to me, but sits beside and
stares, while Slick takes Melissa, and they dance, entwined.

Giselda and Slick take to our bed. 'Dig!' Melissa tells me –
and we do. We dig up all the grass all night. I think I ought to
leave.

Melissa says, 'The people ... I was hired to dig their patch.
We did it twice, and now it's like it was when we began. Slick
and I will hide the grass somehow – but the pay ... I can give
you bus fare, Jimbo, and when the leeks come up – a bundle,
more than you can lift, and more than you will want to eat...
And back in town, I'll make it up to you....'

I hear Slick's practice arpeggios as I run off, down the
slope....

*

Hervé says, 'At least – she knows you are a genius. The music –
never lies.'

'It's strange,' I say. 'Melissa says I'm great, but she can't
hold a note, let alone a tune. Maybe she hasn't tried, or
thought....'

'The virgin eye....' says Hervé. 'Maybe she's mad or on the
make ... or has an old affliction, eighteenth-century stuff like de
Sade and Byron had: indiscriminacy. Doing the first thing. Over
and over.'

'It's the virgin eye,' I say. 'But everything is that way,
always. Each time, a first time. Pathways are infinite, the brain
is sandy desert, the bones are never human, till you find a heap,
and that's your family. Down you lie, on top, and hope the
notices are good: – "a pioneer, explorer; the innovations not
quite new ... a little soiled, in fact. A merited neglect; derivative
– deserving all he got...."'

'Oh, boohoo to you,' says Hervé, laughing. 'Let's do the
round of pubs.'

*

We never see the elephant-men, never again.

*

The first pub is empty. 'Maybe they've been snatched,' I say. 'In jail, deported. Every drinker, taken up. And it's us two to do resistance.'

'All the pieces are in the box to make dictatorships,' says Hervé. 'Of every kind – party, people, persons ... they're just not assembled yet.'

'It's super-lego, that's for sure,' I say. 'It's always so – the moment isn't when things multiply, it's when they coalesce, when all the systems fuse, and work as one. Who isn't in the squad is a conspirator, denying till the end: screaming meat you put your fork in....'

'Oh,' Hervé says. 'It's not modern, to bang up your opponents. You put the weak sheep in detention, people who have no one, who don't threaten – and the job is done. The rest think you're strong, follow you, and they're protected. You put off the challenge; have a base supporting you, and the prisons for the opposition have been built....'

'When?' I ask.

'Tomorrow. Never,' he says. 'Listen: – it happens when it serves. You should wonder what lists your name is on. Anyway, it's become a minor thing, man against man. Now – mass suicide! That's what the latest contest is – mankind versus nature: better, against destiny – pleading, raping, burning, blaming....

'Now, I have a contact with a patron. He wants a genius to do his work. I thought of you. Your music? – write it when you have spare time – the longer you can leave it, the more contemporary it seems. You may write, but without employing hangers-on, it's cradle-dead. The writing part matters least – you've found that out....

'You are the most ingenuous and the most sceptical person that I know. Total innocence, but suspicious. You know every-thing, set it to music: but you can't communicate. What you need is cash. That's like rat-poison – it makes blood flow as loose as schnapps.'

'What's his interest?' I ask, depressed.

'Like you – everything. Especially,' says Hervé, as he moves us on to another empty bar, no men or women animals: 'Futures. He knows about pasts, as he's a leftie. He makes his cash from futures – some may be very short. There's futures short, and futures long, you realise ... it applies to nature and to wars. How do we adjust? – the longs and shorts of it – existence.... See? Without people, except for barmen, we manage perfectly well.'

'Opera doesn't come in at all....' I say.

'Crap!' says Hervé. 'It *is* opera. There's no better vessel – just cut the instruments, cut the sound, the singing, do it like silent film. Two revolving stages, different speeds....'

'That's prehistorical,' I say. 'There's virtuality now....'

'It all is,' he says. 'Till you must show your ticket at the door.'

*

'Soft bones,' says the genius, Mithat. He has a gopher, Delinda, sat close beside him. All his arms and legs are plastered – he can't move, he is his statue.

'There is a story not yet to be told,' he says. 'How I broke everything. For the moment – there's an advantage. Sex. Delinda here....' and she's impassive. 'Knows how I enjoy my state: a fly, a spider – all its limbs pulled off – and yet, sex, induced, with Delinda – unique, magnificent.'

'Just while you're impotent, dismasted,' says Delinda, signing unlikely names on Mithat's chalky arms: Karl and Groucho, naturally, but also Sasan, Arsaces. A man of infinite referents, refinements.... Delinda, probably his master – mistress too.

'Sponge them off, Delinda,' Mithat says. 'I know I was an idler before this impotence, but it annoys – you, scribbling your knowing-all upon my leg. I know the names except – this Groucho. Was he a founder too?'

'Maybe he is to come,' Delinda says. 'Ask Jimbo – he knows about the futures –'

'No, I say. 'I don't know the future. It changes as the history proceeds. Future's like mowing grass. In front you cut it down to size – behind, it grows immense.... Everything's in flux. I know nothing – I threw away the past, or tried to, when I wrote my opera, fixed it in the score. I am the future, Mithat.... It is I, unknown ... nothing, spirit, mayhap. Growing behind, cut down but growing into what is, was, to come....'

'And, Jimbo,' he asks. 'The future. Does it work?'

Each thinks up some answer; I suspect that none is smart enough. There is embarrassment instead.

'You need a someone like Delinda,' Mithat goes on. 'But you're just another fashionable gay. All that will pass. Who cares? Who cares about your granny's skin, if it was black or white? If she worshipped trees or ghostly things?'

'All interest in belief is gone,' I say. 'We all believe the same thing; believe in panic and uncertainty. And how there's only bad things anyone can be remembered by. If we don't manufacture genocides, what else? A telephone?'

And we all laugh. I've struck the right note with those two....

The project – future. If you wait, the future's less, becomes the past. Or maybe there is more. Or just the same, an intuition, elaborated more intelligently.

*

'Melissa!' I say. Her call again: it's not a good surprise. How to react?

'This farming is a paying thing!' she says. 'These little unkempt plots proliferate, and they all need first aid. Oh, how I missed you, lovely Jimbo – and I've found a double nest, where we can snuggle in, before we go and dig....'

'Look, Melissa,' I say. 'Don't play the sex card to get my help, it isn't indicated. I'm in a project now. I see the same thing happening there too: sex. Sex is the grease, the *feu follet,* it lubricates and warms the world, and makes it wander, but – it's humiliating for all....'

'Oh, what a grump you are,' Melissa laughs. 'I'm not a body-snatcher – that's a primal fear ... grow up, reach your own conclusions, live your own life....'

'I understand all that,' I say. 'You're right. It's just – the digging. It is not my thing.'

I think she says 'too bad'.

*

'What are your thoughts?' Delinda asks. 'Mithat requires that you have a plan....'

'Futures,' I say, as though I'd thought. It's true, I'd thought a lot about Delinda.... I explain: 'Finance and risk – those bonds you'll never loose, thirty years, then thirty years, you re-invest and wait for two per cent. Slow time. Then – there's these cartoon games: you go in them, and stay, like the fish took to the sea, and others climb and trip on land ... except you are not real, not really anywhere ... moving like the light ... which, naturally, is not a thing that moves.... There's time – that doesn't move, except – game over, and you're at the start, again, and yet – there's nothing moved....'

'Yes,' says Delinda, 'We non-fish ... we're the animals in the bars and in the porno clubs. I approve, of course, of those, of them, and what they do ... it's quite irrelevant, anyway, what I think. You can't disapprove of fish. Or elephants, or porno bars: but go on, Jimbo.'

'Weapons and viruses. For years people have designed them – extermination. It didn't start with all this heat, the idea of ending everyone....' I say. 'You can't think usefully about one life that ends, like your own, without thinking of them all; of one life ending, and inferring – everyone's. With all the means we have to close the show, kill everyone, imagine someone starting everything again; inventing sin and guilt, begetting, shields and spears and cuniform....'

'Mithat wants more than that,' she says. 'It's trivial, what you've cooked up.'

'There's ethics, naturally,' I say. 'Coexistence, movements, and sects – and how you measure all this stuff – variable metre, or none ... times stratified, some fast, some slow, the stone age men still stuck in *lento*, us seemingly *con brio, presto* ... and yet, all contemporaneous....'

'It won't do, Jimbo,' says Delinda, mock stern. 'It's bits and pieces. Mithat's not interested in what people think – only in what *he* thinks. He's stuck – he needs a push. He can guess as well as you ... he needs you to be a wall to bounce his balls off....'

'I see all that,' I say. 'I could get there, where he wants – but it takes time: and dropping my creative stuff....'

'If it's cash you seek,' Delinda says. 'There's people doing gardening, and growing stuff in soil – they pay you to pull up the weeds and bottle things....'

'The life-world – tell Mithat I'm exploring that. Marx and phenomenology....' I say.

'It's vieux chapeau,' she says, 'but maybe he'll not remember that.'

'Clubs,' I say. 'To live for, find desire unlimited and not find gratification, not at all.'

'Porno clubs,' she says. 'Mithat and I – yes, we frequent. Is that your future? Vision? Refuge?'

'Oh no,' I say. 'I think it's all gone by – but maybe, people thought....'

'Mostly they don't,' Delinda says. 'Don't think. Won't in a future either. That's Mithat's principal idea. If he had thought, he'd not have broken all his limbs at once....'

'It's my fantasy, of course,' I say. 'Those places, with innocent people flailing, hitting out, holding each other close ... and only desire, burning: just desire. No end, full in, of, itself. For a person, it would mean pursuing wholeness, arms and legs all sound.'

'Don't dwell on it, Jimbo,' says Delinda, stroking my hand, quite kindly. 'It seems you went bee-hunting, got a bonnetful, and stung. The more you talk about it, the more naive you seem. Mithat is a blob – he doesn't talk about that, his disarmament, and I don't press. Emotions? – they may evolve, but you don't know what from.'

'Why should you talk, expose yourself, Delinda,' I say. 'You're all of a piece, curated, all you say's thought out, and every step is flawless....'

I mean to say, that dressing up, having clean hands and well-matched makeup, raises your social class by a whole category. Maybe Delinda's is already near the top....

Here, it's birth decides your future: in modern places, it's your job. And yet – in those modern places, they shout at you in the street, insult you, run you down and rob you....

*

'Everything was new,' I tell Mithat. 'We shuffled off the past, and then we dumped the new and invented more – and so the new, novelty, it died. And we didn't live in the new, but in the bed-hollows we had made; the warmth, Mithat. And the old tales – that what was good survived, that corruption was insidious, always looking for a chink, a way in.... That's what Ibn Khaldun and Ibn al-Khatib maybe wrote: the mystic rose.... Ah, the beauty and the peace: the eternal garden afternoons of el-Andalus – that was our way forward, blocked for ever by a fall of rocks.'

'I read about that too,' says Mithat. 'You can't make money there. No bets taken on dead horses.... Movements decline, paradise finishes in a spat, a tweet.... Eternal renewal? It's milk, Jimbo – fresh every day; if you leave it, it goes sour. That's an observation. I can't do anything with spare remarks: not risk and not enjoyment.'

I remember what Melissa said – 'I'm sure it hurts, Jimbo, but it must. Love, pleasure, and today. Never consummate. Not ever. It will destroy everything. If it satisfies, it's dead. If it doesn't, it's dead. Believe me, desire me, need me. I shan't be there, not ever.'

Mithat stares at my silence.

'Of course,' Mithat continues. 'There's false voices too. An industry. It used to be devils who deceived – now, they tell the truth, it's angels who tells lies.'

'I think they always did,' I say.

'Cheap shot, Jimbo!' says Mithat, laughing. 'I love it!'

'There's the song, Mithat,' I say. '"Everybody dies, chasing after time...."'

'Yes, yes,' he says, irritated. 'Plangent but irrelevant. And your sages, the *ulama*, they've been sent packing.'

*

Dromy calls, possibly he didn't mean to....

'Dromy,' I say, 'I can't talk now. Learn your part – it may be useful. When? – I – we – no one can tell. I've moved on meanwhile.'

He says, 'I want to tell you – I've found work, an interim. With Slick, and women too – we're a team. It's not fuck gardening – it's farming, growing food for anyone who wants.'

'I'll let you know,' I say.

It's noble work, they say.

*

'We could carry Mithat, but it's hard, getting him through doorways, into cabs,' I say.

'If you're inviting me, Jimbo,' Delinda says. 'OK. A porno club, I bet.'

I can't find Dromy's haunt, the club we went to. 'They're all different,' she says. 'The clubs, the ethic, before you get stuck in.'

This one spirals down: there is a tiny bar, like where Gréco started out: deserted. 'You confess, or not,' she says. 'The judge will question you – if they believe you, you go down. If not, it's up.'

'Up into the street?' I ask. 'Or on to someone you don't know? Better than you?'

'Mithat's a convincing type,' she says. 'Sometimes he'd lie, and sometimes he had done those deeds. We were questioned separate, so I don't know where he went.'

'You must have known the truth....' I start.

'You silly,' says Delinda, laughing heartily. 'It isn't real, they're not real judges – it may be that if you lose you don't get the chance to go with anyone. Truth doesn't count, conviction does. But – what is lose? And a conviction: – is that what you believe, or what you get? And think – we're all complicit – that's what they say: flying in planes, or burning coal. Universal death. Or then there's selling arms and cheating charities, and foreign aid, and anything you don't suspect how bad it is. And fish. I feel guilty for the fish.'

'Yes, I do too,' I say. 'Maybe I should have found you here, not brought you: instead, I stand to lose you in the game.'

'Well, that's a risk,' she says. 'And risk is always future-oriented – your task. You might confess to something not yet

done, and take the rap, do porridge – then when you're out, do
the deed and get away with it....'

'You don't seem the type, Delinda – that dreary slang....' I
say. 'I know you're not an innocent, but prudent, avoiding
capture and – yes! I spent years, shut in my room to serve out
time, writing that opera.... They say it is creation, but it's work
as well, leaving its trace on you, hopes unrealised, and vanishing
completely...'

'I know,' she says: 'It's time: unprofitably spent until they
give you cash – and then? And then?'

'Oh, then, it's done,' I say. 'Performed. That becomes the
story, the success. Your time's paid off. It's the consummation –
makes the wanting and the hope worthwhile. Brings different
scenarios, at least.'

'You get more than that from jail,' she says. 'When you get
out. Freedom's better than watching your own opera – probably
done bad: then over, forgotten, thrown on the pile with all the
rest....'

'Mithat must have faith,' I say: 'He seems to beat the tricks in
places rigged like this....'

'He discounts the present. Tomorrow, and tomorrow – all
will resolve, and you will grow and prosper,' says Delinda. 'Or
maybe not. You start again, the future's full of chance....'

'Did they send him down, for winning here? Being believed?
Down the stairs – he fell...?' I ask.

'Oh, what a simple heart you have, poor Jimbo,' says
Delinda. 'He's plastered, cruciform, like a saint, the mark, his X
the signature of huddled masses ... and don't you see? – the X
on treasure maps. He is his treasure chest, my dear....'

The trial begins, before I can object.

*

The court – they put on masks – tigers and pelicans.... The judge
says I must plead – 'Oh, I've done nothing, judge,' I say. 'But
I've imagined everything, the massacres, vendettas, the
improvidence that's put the future into doubt – I have been
ignorant like all the rest, but....'

Delinda seems to take my part. She wears a cloak with wings and silver claws: 'This guy,' she tells the court, 'Is idle. He has bet his life on emptiness – spinning a tune that doesn't bind, that straggles round the universe, that says it's everything, but that is true of anything. It all connects, the parts are parts of all the rest, and parts make up the everything. He is an idler.... Innocent, through incapacity and sloth....'

I cannot see the judge's face, nor judge her gender from his voice. I'm an innocent, dissatisfied.

They put me in the street; 'not proven'. What will Delinda say?

I shout down: 'I want a re-trial, judge!'

The voice says, 'Maybe you haven't understood. You must plead guilty of doing something. Not doing anything? – how can we judge what you've not done. We don't know you – you're just a punter, dropping in for booze and sex, probably some recompense, free lodging in a cell, marrying and growing old, losing your mind, needing a person paid to hose you down; or hung up by a foot or stoned – and paying for each stone; having your heart and brain removed and given to another customer, the head to hold their lust in check, the heart to pump the longing out....'

'Yes, now I understand,' I say. 'I don't want her, Delinda, as my lawyer, though...'

'Oh, we can't stop her, defending is quite voluntary,' says the judge. 'We don't know you, we can't say if you, your lawyer, anyone, is truth-telling or a fantasist ... indeed, your first confession was: – 'I am a fantasist', creating out of naught. That's how you want to live and gain acclaim....'

*

It all starts over – no one bothers to be masked this time.

'I lust,' I say. 'That is my crime, its root and branch. If I can't have Melissa, I'd make do with my free advocate, Delinda here. I work for Mithat – if there is a way to leave him crippled, have him enjoy himself alone – that's fine. I will his exit, somehow, anyhow. I fantasise, not in music, but on sex. Mithat's an obstacle – have him spun out into a duration, a carriage-clock,

tick-tock – he watches while you cuckold him ... The time is
fold on fold, it makes a tutu or a serviette, let him be sutured in
them for a period indeterminate.... Jealousy, milord: I plan
vendetta.... That's my crime.'

*

There is applause: not much. It's a performance, grudgingly
received, misunderstood, and happily dismissed. The jurors –
waiters, barmen ... they wear faces familiar, as though it's
Dromy, Slick, Giselda ... filling in their vacant night with
service in the club, moonlighting without a sky, without
illumination....

I say, 'I want you, not to have you, dear Delinda, just to
want...' but she is off, down a red corridor, a lair, a throat. Is
that my wish? Granted – deferred?

How I desire her, how I detest my task ... examining the
future, discounting totally what I am living through ... my
everyday ... my every day....

*

I look for Delinda, find Mithat. He's solid again, it seems, arms
and legs spread wide, like a table flattened on the floor, one of
those early robots made to look unlike us, in case they take our
place....

'Now it's the spine,' he says. 'My affliction – it has spread –
I'm too flexible. I should drink milk. Delinda's, for choice, but
she is barren, beauties always are.'

'Where is Delinda?' I ask.

'Oh, down the club,' he says. 'I don't pay her, so she works
there in reception and godspeed.....'

'This work of mine,' I say. 'I'm Faust, seeking my Mephisto
... if it is you, speed up the search!'

'Oh yes,' says Mithat, 'the Gauguin masks you were to bring
me back – tigers and pelicans....'

'No,' I say. 'That was the club. My project is to seek the
future before it comes about and shows if I was right or wrong.
Everything seems to follow after everything – like those

monkeys, each tied to the one in front, the long-dead leader, our species mother, responsible for millions ... all straggling along, tied to a string that disappears in clouds ... the future following some enormous kite, up there, maybe in the hand of God....

'Maybe there's politics, that I've left out. There's been none in my quest.'

'Nonsense,' he says. 'It's all political. Draw the conclusions. Never apologise. Did you?

'Expect nothing permanent. Do you? Don't theorise, don't try to talk to people who are chained up in that sinking boat.... Have you made all those mistakes?'

'No,' I say. 'None of those. I just explain what has been done, and what's the awful thing you are about to do.'

'Yes, yes,' says Mithat, dismissively. 'That is the two steps back. Remember the one step forward, before it's cancelled out....'

'Forward to what?' I ask. 'It's all been downhill since we left the garden, and we went forth and multiplied enormously, and began to fear the snakes.'

He laughs, '*My* epic starts a ways before that one,' he says. 'Only after millennia, there was your story of the garden, and of God. Those tall buildings they erected ... does it upset you that babies were buried in the foundations to make the walls and towers secure?'

'They mostly fell down anyway,' I say, judiciously. 'If I die tomorrow, should you grieve, Mithat? If it's you that's gone, should I?'

'You want too much,' he laughs. 'Two bites at one apple – it's too much. Enjoy your knowledge – and your ignorance. Two doses of the evil, the poison of the second guess – too much, it makes you mad! Sink the hole deep, forget the baby, that is my advice.'

'Who can we trust, Mithat?' I ask, unsettled.

'I'm a table, but my top is flexible,' he says. 'Trust my legs, don't put a weight on my spine, that's all.'

'That is a commonplace,' I say.

'You want judgment?' Mithat asks. 'Take Delinda. She's an advocate, a paper shows it's so. Her club provides....'

'Oh, this is cheap anarchism,' I say. 'The club? You don't even get to have sex there. Innocent or guilty – what's the point?'

'They didn't make you pay,' he says. 'Justice costs. Those waiters must be paid. Of course – *you* paid with your expectations: those, you lost. Delinda was the price. An evening out – you paid the forfeit. You may be odd – but came out evens....'

'You're right, but it's not what I mean,' I say.

'Sleep under the bridge,' he says. 'And what's the best thing – you get deported; or you get a house and family? The second – and the burglar shoots you both while you are having sex, and rapes your child....'

'That's why my project is all wrong,' I say. 'Your idea of the future – it's all you. And you are tiny. Why, you're the height of a drinks table in a bar....'

'You mock,' he says. 'Be aware! The end is visible! You'd say it's "just water", covering your island. You're wrong ... See – there's no water in your bottle, the fire's incinerating your pitcher.... Do you need a supreme court, a protocol, Delinda even – to adjudicate all that?'

'That's today,' I say. 'The quick part. Time moving fast. But then, there's evolution, teasingly slow. There are all kinds of speed, all kinds of hurry and procrastination. And – sleep: a country where you can't feel hope. Love – where there is only hope. A rocket: fast and loud. Making emeralds: slow and soft....'

'Well, well,' he says. 'Write it up. Or down. Nature's reduced me – but I can recover. You, Jimbo – you could have had a happy life, your first love: Delinda as a second consort, counsellor. But, you never take the last, decisive, step. You're a specialist in failure, whose hopes lie in a future that does not exist and breathe....

'If I were you, I'd concentrate on how we face catastrophe, and reconcile that with our hopes for a long life.'

'You said it all before, Mithat,' I say. 'People on a roundabout know they're going round and the trees and stuff are standing still.... It's obvious....'

'Go!' he says. 'Find Delinda, bring her home to me, tell her you will need a lawyer.'

*

'That's you settled,' Melissa says. 'I am wanted. That's good enough. Jimbo – you're good at wanting. Too bad – you're straight, women don't like you, you attract men: you're a living pit of the emotions.

'Me? I have my squad – we grow the food the Africans won't sell us.' She has a pitchfork, and she waves it – in threat or invocation.

'*Can't* sell us,' says Slick. 'They must eat. And – remember, Melissa, I have an African inside me.'

'When the day's work is done, and we three cuddle down together, me, you and Dromy – yes, I feel there's many more among us,' Melissa says. 'I'm glad we'll all survive, each with their market stall, and getting used to harvesting the different fruits.... Now, it can all come out of us – the peoples buried, the animals glimpsed, shot, milked – all that's within us. Poor Jimbo,' she punches me, quite lightly,

'You thought because we all went to those clubs and fell in love, or paid for sex ... had rooms with chairs, were saddened by the massacres of people, and of flying things – that we'd arrived: maturity – a plateau, satisfaction, beginning and an end. We're full – antiquities, beliefs and plans, and tribes and clans they say have disappeared – all will come out, be expressed, and then we'll take in everything extinct, worn out, hidden in cunabulae.... I'm there. It's me, my life. It isn't yours, you don't believe in any of it, and you don't believe me, don't believe *in* me.'

It may be so. It means – Melissa is a flux, I have no hope of blocking, harnessing her flood....

*

Then, there's Giselda and the opera – both long unopened, waiting in the drawer. Someone will find them, draw out their beauty, their need to be performed. Giselda still won't talk to

me. The opera is silent too; hard, alarming as a boil, hard, big as
a billiard ball, beneath the skin....

'You make me forget, Melissa, my name's not Jimbo,' I tell
her. I let my hand touch hers. There's no response. No hostility,
one can always try again, although – what's urgent, is dealing
with Mithat and having Delinda on my side. Before you act, it's
best to have your defence set up.

'This is better than it was for other generations,' Melissa
says. 'We are useful. They worked to make money for someone
they had never seen, enough that they could live to do the same
next day. Us – we make life continue every hour....'

*

'Dromy,' I say. 'The clubs – they meant a lot to you, if I
remember right....'

'Oh yes,' he says. 'Melissa is our love, Slick's and mine, we
are a team, a trio – but, yes: I've a life membership, a club
where I will live and serve my time. There is a room ... when
you are moribund, they lay you out, with all your goods, and
people come and take your eyes, your lungs, your teeth – all that
is useful; and your gold, your shoes in cryptonite, your guard-
dog and – your documents, your passport, certificate of
circumcision, all that can be used again ... and leave the little
pile of skin – and in come scribes, and on your pergamon they
write a history of how you lived, were known, and if they loved
you, or remembered you....'

'Those like you who work there,' I say, 'do the piano bar.
Slick and his group on Saturdays – when you're not dancing
with Melissa. How do you live? When you're alive – how's
life? There, in each club? How much does it cost, who owns it,
how do you pay....?'

'The hours?' asks Dromy, seemingly embarrassed. 'We don't
have set times. There's music, ceremonies. What else is there to
know? We work when there is custom, it's tiring, sometimes we
work for days – and then ... a nothing. We don't have children
now. We go to other clubs ... there's other guys, a plenitude....'

*

'He doesn't know,' says Slick. 'And he won't tell. Much of all that is illegal, naturally. Everybody knows – there's a notary on call, and lawyers too. What it's about? – I don't know, except we have to make sure that we don't close. There's lots who think we should record, it would be better, make our playing sparkle, a legacy on plastic. Definitive it would be, that's for sure.'

He laughs, Melissa pulls his ears: 'Enough of clubs!' she says. 'We fill the places, run them – but it's hard, uncomfortable. It's better here: the earth, the soil.'

I have nothing on her; no hold, no sympathy – so I can be bold. 'This richness, Malissa, that you have inside – how'd it get in? Is it microbes? Flora? I fear – it's metaphor – no better than anybody else's. You say the invisible is richness – suppose I say it's poverty?'

'You love being just a customer, Jimbo dear,' Melissa says. 'But – it's not that everything's for sale, or hire, or given out for free – it isn't always clear, how you turn from worker into customer, and yet, it always happens.

'You're into histories and futures too, your opera on all things past and present, your theories of what will come and how ... but, I wonder: is there a club for you? For me, life's making food and leading on the punters.... But for you?'

*

'Forget relationships, resign yourself,' says Mithat, lying like a tiger rug, flat, disembowelled, upon the floor. 'They're not for you. You don't know how the club and its inhabitants persist, instead – you fantasise. You float.

'I've set you up, my friend. Your task's to guarantee *my* future. See – my body's unreliable. It flickers, it deflates, spreads. A furry lichen A change of scene may give me strength. Now, my future's in your sights.... I have a mission for you which is my salvation – or my end. And yours, Delinda's too....'

He's a blob – maybe the best idea, the best prevision in the universe ... something completely novel, one of a kind.... A new organism, all body, all muscle, and all sense. Inert. It creeps. If

novelty is dead for us, mere obsolescence waiting to appear –
the unique still stands tall, effulgent.

Mithat suffers terribly ... a victim, or a Galahad ... a splash of
lymph upon the forest floor.

'Nurture me,' says Mithat. 'Feed me, tickle me. Stop me
falling through a crack, infesting the building, spreading like a
virus, an infernal web, a super-toadstool, through everywhere
like dry rot, without a voice, a language. I know what I can
bring: a future, rapid, a whirligig, for people who are in the dark
attacked with flaming javelins, innocent and guilty ... people
who have lived in slow time, the wrong time, believing the
wrong things and walking slow, slow, slow. Believe me:
understand me,' he pleads, and his eyes are glass. Stand behind
him, he won't see you, stand in front – it's just the same.
Unreflecting glass.

*

'Don't touch me,' says Delinda. 'I'm driving us – almost round
the world,'

We load Mithat on the roof, draped like an omelet. 'The new
air,' he gasps. 'Will revive me, give me a skeleton.'

He's soft to touch. Clammy. How does he fit a search for
justice? You can't touch opera, but it's vivid in my mind: touch
and smell, resin on the ballet shoes; sweat in the pit, conductor's
smelly *frac*.... In the interlude, have them do a can-can, a twist
of *fado* – put all the senses in, the tastes, the cannabis, even the
silver thruppence for the pudding.... Lots of cognac, wrap the
chorus up in blankets – old gold, maple red....

Mithat is yellow as an ostrich yolk.... But justice? Time? He's
an organism, Mithat; one-dimensional: fast times have flattened
him, like clay upon the wheel – the wrong speed makes a
pancake, or a pine.... He's a comment on fast speeds.... He said:
'We stand upon a pile of metal discs, all of us, mechanical
monkeys, we revolve, the big bottom disc moves very slow, but
the little ones up near the top – they're spinning so fast they're
blurred, whizzing to invisibility.... Your arms and legs splay out,
fly off' – and that's you finished: ready. All of us. A Mithat.
Can you be born anew? Do you desire it?

If you don't have Melissa to lust after, Delinda to drive the rented car ... there's little hope, I fear!

Yet – like him, you have your friends. All is ephemeral – but your friends – they're virtual, but friendly always, so you cling to them.

Those plums – were they in your street, on your tree? Or in Yangzhou? You've no idea, your friends look like my friends, and no one's friends at all....

*

Delinda – she drives very fast – against the wind., we've roped Mithat down, we see his edges flapping in our speed. We've taken pills to make the time pass fast....

The athracite-grey roads go white, then brown. We bump along: Mithat gains substance – he shrugs: shoulders ahoy! What wondrous things, there's even slots to fit on wings ... A skull – shut your bain in one, secure: it lets you forget about it maybe trickling out and down your chin. Your teeth – will last millennia, then they'll be ground down and burnt to see how old you were. Mithat grows knees – now, he can play kneesies with the best, and kneel before the pope if he is sainted, or before the block if he's to be decapitated.

'Oh Mithat,' laughs Delinda. 'What a scare! How flat you were! What disillusion too! Now, you're a hero once again, Lohengrin, King Ludwig even... why, you start to corruscate!'

He is made bone – a miracle. 'I wish we could bring freedom,' Mithat says, scrambling in and joining us. He embraces Delinda, who purrs, does not object. 'No one chooses justice first,' he says. 'It's reparation. You never put things right, Delinda – just put another turning in the road, make the story take another bend ... more misery to some ... and not for us.'

I feel the absence – the absence of Melissa, her flesh, my elixir.... 'That you will never have,' says Mithat. 'Another's flesh – no, it's forbidden, that sweet fruit; tabu! Not Delinda's, certainly. Paws off, monkey! Not anyone's to pick...!' He laughs, she laughs.

'I don't believe there is an end,' I say. 'Not to this road. I don't believe there are some people, harassed and cheated, and we've come to give redress ... it's all a trip to bring some calcium to Mithat, by crossing the magic mountains, the savannah with its lonely lion, gas stations with the single pump, deserted, 'leave cash in the empty bowl' it says ... this is a route 666 that brings to some their health and destiny ... to others, longing, jealousy....'

*

'Drive fast and far enough,' Delinda says, 'and you will meet people exactly like yourself, exactly like the ones you left.'

I ponder this, and Mithat says,

'Your trouble, Jimbo, is you make a thing, and load it with your pleasure and your suffering – you send it off, like an exploring ship, and, believe me, they mostly don't come back. Something, the sailors find. You won't know what. Your opera – is chugging up the Amazon, perhaps they'll play it in the opera house in Manaus. And you're not there, not in it: at the very most, you're sitting in the stalls, a spectator of yourself. Me – I live, instead.

'You've witnessed me: I suffer terribly, my body fades, and then I reconstitute. Rely on myself, not on Delinda.

'Delinda is the prize, you get that at the end. It *is* the end, until another story starts.'

'I thought the future interested you, Mithat,' I say. 'Not realising that you know it all already....'

'It interests us all,' says Mithat. 'But most people see it dark. I see the future clear. I'm in it – it's not like what I have now, it's quite quite different, with different people, different plots, and all my senses rise a notch, an octave even. I shall die before the end has been worked out and fastened to what's gone before....' And on he talks, Delinda filling in with words when he is out of breath ... he, like Pier Gynt; and nature witty as she always is ... Delinda the stream, the current, bearing up the swimmer between strokes and breaths, a word, a phrase from her, as if she's learned a script.

'If you have cash,' she says. 'We'll call a bedouin guide, who'll pitch a tent for us, and light a fire, make us *mansaf*,and we shall lie together and at dawn he'll point us and our camels where we've never been and never heard of....'

*

'We have arrived,' says Mithat, striding ahead, all bones in place.

It looks exactly like the place we left, 'This is the future, this wasn't here when we set out,' Delinda says.

'It seems a fraud....' I start.

'Oh, we're not responsible for fantasies,' says Mithat. 'Those are problems you invent to flit around inside your head.'

The future: full of people you don't know, don't know you, don't care about you unless there is a legacy. Every effort to show that though we don't have tails, we're just as good as apes. Better! We and our ancestors – we're bringing the globe to an end, and no one else had even thought of that.

'Oh dear,' Delinda says, over and over. 'At least Mithat now has feet and toes. We can't live underground and eat the soil – if we could only get back up the trees.... That is a pressing task, poor Jimbo. You, with your scheming about intercourse and freeing slaves and making more; springing from jails and building more of them – you have to concentrate! Change your pills – we have!'

'Peace, Delinda. I never use,' I say. 'Find me a job in some quiet club.Those places that we visited, so full of people too – the Kurdistans ... but then there's a Baluchistan, lands of Hazaras, Uighurs, Rohingya, Kashmiris, all the rest, some better not mentioned, packed out with settled fugitives who don't yet have a name for where they want to be, places already in disaster zones, more people not wanted on voyages or in settlements.... I place them, all, inside my head and heart....'

'That's very good,' she says. 'Travel exists for that. Or you could stay at home and read a book.'

'Things: and why they are as they are. You have arrived,' says Mithat. 'Well done. Escape the causal chain. So far, you haven't done so well. Not with Melissa anyway. Delinda is mine. Every club has rules, and rather than give satisfaction, it hopes you stay, at least come back for more, and want the sex it doesn't give, a discount on the booze at least....'

'At least – I want some immortality,' I say. 'While I work things out. If I'm immortal – surely everybody else must be too.... Can anything occur otherwise than what it does, it will? Can I do anything other than what I shall?'

'We pushed against that door,' Delinda says. 'We reached our edge. No answer. None is possible. We changed, change happened as we wanted it. Or not – however it happened, it couldn't have been changed. Believe that, forget Melissa, forget me – nothing will happen as you want, all will happen exactly as it will. Relax: it's so for everything as well. Resign yourself – what happens is a destiny, you want, and want – you don't have free will that changes things – things, as they are....'

'No, no,' I say. 'It's not resolved. Another trip? Another club, a different rule....?'

'You'll never know,' she says. 'Maybe you're right, and everything is what you say and do. You will not know,' and she caresses me, our tongues encounter and converse ... and 'There! You see!' she says, and backs away.

*

'Last year, Hervé,' I say. 'After the failure of the opera, I had two serious affairs – it was a torment. I had to work in my club, to meet expense, and tried some manual work – it didn't suit. I was at the end, and then my Kurdish friend – he took us to that place that won't exist, a secret mission.... A wonderland, that Kurdistan. Some plan that will not work, because they're too like us. Like you and me, at least. They arouse people – the fascists, specially, the Americans, the new Russians, the old Turks, the dictators, all of them. And of course, it didn't function.'

Mithat had soft bones – all psychological. Cured, by miracle. For now.

'I had the taste for politics,' I say. 'It's easier than music, and in it you have a longer reputation. But maybe ... it's a talent I don't have for either. You need a blind persistence in seeming stupid and obsessed. My idea of what will come and what might, somehow, be done politically, to engage with people, and their world – it seems precarious. It wavers, rests on improbables. Finicky considerations, too.'

'What is success in sex?' asks Hervé. 'Surviving it intact, or the experience itself? I have my doubts whether the experience is worth a spit – you get more with sunsets or a cat: or what's called "scuffing up the leaves".

'I distrust mankind – they've pushed us, everyone, the animals as well, down the slope, the scree, into the sand. We're suffocating, Jimbo. Politics? To save us, when it's brought us here? Science and gadgets – just the same. Maybe the music would have kept us occupied and satisfied – like those Venetian nuns – the orphan prostitutes, who did such lovely work.... Better even than growing things, and having them ferment.'

'It's too late for all that now,' I say. 'In music, you need make too many contacts with crooked guys who act rich and pay poor.'

*

'This club goes very quiet at five,' Hervé says. 'Let's go to the arcade – I love those swift lights on the ceiling, like swallows going home ... See if they still have that game, the March of Pennies. Now, they're just bronze discs, of course – not in circulation, just tokens. Old English pennies: pence. But I guess somehow they can be redeemed – you put coins in, the pile nudges forward, a file drops like the Imperial Guard – and you stand to win.'

'And you get tokens for the tokens?' I ask him.

'You use them to play more games,' he says. 'Like your women – when you win or fail, it's all a practise for the next. It's like the saxophone – you play and play, climb up the golden buddha, and there's no top, no ultimate. It's like a hill, it's there to climb, and then you must come down. Some people write a hundred symphonies so no one can ask which is the best – the ninety-ninth is maybe better than the one before.

'You never reach it, it never comes, then it recedes: the final test. People are like that too, and so is the history of anything.

'You could ignore it all, of course.'

*

They don't win at the game – the weight of all those coins must
be immense, it threatens, every throb and pulse, each millimetre
forward, to tumble down the slot and make you rich with other
tokens, other goes. It's never spewed, not while I've been
watching, anyway. But of course, it must, some time, even
though the game is old, obscure; the pennies have dates a
hundred years ago ... give a penny, for one of those years? Any
givers?

*

'Round here,' says Hervé, 'there used to be some useful trades –
makers of intimate small things, combs, screws and hats: trunks
and tunics. Fullers and nappers. And you paid tax to clean the
heaps that people left – the dust, the waste of all the makings, of
florists, tanners, slaughterers.... Then the place slipped down:
more money and ephemeral trades ... the prostitutes, the dealers,
thieves and lenders, extortioners, fixers, punishers, gun rentals
and gun sales. All hard grafting, Jimbo.

'Then we showed up – it's fun and games, crap food and
rooming houses, porno shops – the smell and not the substance.
All history carried forward on women's backs, but
unconfessable so....'

'I know all that. There's groups here too....' I say. 'Music, fits
every tolerance. My opera – a galaxy, a milk and whisky way,
with brand new constellations – elephants and polar bears,
Venus lamps that shine all night.... Lucent with exploding
stars....'

'And you, on eagles' wings, you bring in the opera,' says
Hervé, more drunk than I. 'Your mouse. Maybe, dear – we
could see its splendour without your prompting. But – perhaps it
died: before its birth.'

'You do nothing, Hervé,' I say. 'You're a critic, not a
creator.'

'I'm a nighthawk, I suck blood,' he says. 'A cockroach: while you sleep, I eat all you had. And you, Jimbo, you're a cicada: pleasure, beauty, and invisibility – that's you. Among the leaves you hide and hope you can beguile – a female! Lost causes, all of those, and more.'

We scuffle. It's not sensible, for either of us. We fall down. We know everything. We run like fools. We're expelled from our nice club. We're wise but evil.

*

'Decide what you are,' Hervé shouts, lurching off. 'If you're something. It's uncertain that you are! When you've an answer, we'll see if you have got it right. And ah! the suffering! The people, their present, and the future – think of that, just once.... You're a foetus, Jimbo, with two mothers, and a twin – your musical. They'll miss you – you're their something that never came to term .....'

*

Giselda says, 'I look at you, and think you're an exile who hasn't left his country. Maybe you never will. You're a busy animal – a squirrel who smells winter and buries and digs up the treasures.'

'You imagine big and little things,' I say. 'Like a fox does. But – I once imagined everything, and captured it. My drama ... the curtains ... haven't opened yet....'

'You put everything in,' she says. 'You're undiscriminating, and everything is what we always see. It's super-familiar, leaden, banal. Those white Russians, who might have made an exploit of their flight – they had all the culture, the refinement, the delicacy of spies playing their double games – and they spoiled it all by squabbling, being monarchists and pitiful. Are you like that?

'The landscape – no more frontiers, we all burrow down. In our clubs ... it's repetitious. And yet – vast populations suffocate ... drive each other off the cliffs, eat thin bones – their own, their fathers', mothers'... You know it, and you're blind, you saw it, now you're impotent, you'll need a guide to help you walk downstairs.'

'It's true,' I say. 'It's coming to us all as we waltz round. There's no escape, the red death's in our blood. Pretend, feel, languish – one thing's as good as any other thing. What do you suggest: we pray?'

She doesn't say.

'And, Giselda,' I remember, 'you helped fuck up my first night.'

We lie side by side on the grass – stems are thick as hyacinths'. 'There's your future, there's your past – up there, promiscuous in the stars,' she says. 'You can't tell which is exploding in the past, or what you might reach in a thousand years, swathed in kapok in your pod.'

'You'd age so slow,' I say. 'Followed on screen by generations increasingly indifferent. On, on you'd go, intrepid Castorp. When you're dead, you'd still send back a beep.'

'Suppose you find, when you arrive, that meanwhile it's exploded,' says Giselda. 'And they didn't tell you at control ... send a dead Bowie, maybe, travelling super-fast to catch you up, but he transmogrifies en route ...You'd see the glitter, think he was star king, come to save. And instead, you're just two stiffs, disembarking on a clinker....'

'Or in a hole,' I say. 'They are called that, but really they're as dense as a black snooker ball.'

*

'Well, Jimbo,' she says, shyly: she shouldn't call me that. I'm a composer, after all – funerals and matrimonies, marches – a speciality; discounted rates for coronations and investitures.

'Your clubs,' she asks. 'Did you learn anything? They're more concentrated than countries were. Friendly – but they cost. The people throng there....'

'Love,' I say. 'They sought love. My love – it flowed in waterfalls. Unavailing, it all was. They say love matters – but when it's not reciprocated, never: it's a fraud.'

'Melissa was chivvied,' says Giselda. 'By coarse types, but with a domestic urge. They wanted a threesome, then a special

hug, and even kids. It's what the aristocracy once had –
emotions, relatonships, laid out like an estate, an ornamental
garden, full of dusty flowers.'

'You got beat hard in there,' I say. 'Love conquers all, but
they used paddles. How I wanted to be the saviour: oh Melissa!
How she smelled of honey, but the goddam bees ... they stung!'

'The club: it was a magic place, a *maison close*, a
sanatorium,' she says. 'Then Delinda – she gave purification
through the law.... She was a gemstone, so they say....'

'She was Mithat's,' I recall. 'And he had history in his bones
– he waxed and waned, and crept and hardened – he was an
epic. He could become as large and populated as – his
imaginary country, his Kurdistan.... I'd no hope with Delinda.
Did Mithat have hopes? He never said – he loved the law, its
embodiment, Delinda; but he never found a court, a judge....'

'Well, Jimbo, what was it that you thought you'd win?' she
asks, amused. 'You had your passion. Wasn't that enough? It
made you sweat and squeak – what more could you do with it?
Make it a war of liberation? Have it weighed and analysed? It
was a fever – did you want to pass it on? What for?'

'Death, Giselda,' I say. 'That's why. There must be
something while we wait for it, our decline, senescence. More
love, hate: a mission. Or drop out into gardening. Harvesting the
onions, the lacrimose; "hypochondrias for seven instruments", a
stately dance and so to bed, blistered with the digging, and oh!
those sackbut parts ... singing the mass, blown up like a toad
with reverence unfelt.... Animals? – we humans don't have
much – only trickiness, fearful weapons – and our dominance is
sham. Most of us can't hunt, there's little gathering, the soil's
not yours so you can't plant, no one knows which leaves are
cures, sex is a guilty burden....

'That's why we save the people, Giselda: driven by our
humility; and to have the company. "I am an other" – saving
others, is how you save yourself....'

'Maybe it's so,' she says, 'but you did not. Not saved others,
or yourself. Lost everyone, fought with your critic, your
impresario....'

'He was a minor devil, didn't even have the key to hell,' I
say.

*

'Where I live,' Giselda says. 'We don't have keys. We occupied the stables, those half-doors – they don't have locks.'

'It all starts down in the straw,' I say. 'Civilisation.'

I think of Melissa. Entwined with third parties, partying. Slick, trying out his third position, always a little flat. Enthusiasm abundant. Dromy – wheedling, corrupt....

'Hay,' Giselda says, 'not straw.'

Delinda, paid in the club for advocacy: the cash going to refugees, or buying tanks – rehabilitation, punishment. It fits, it figures. It must....

'You should cohere some more,' Giselda says. 'Work harder. Glue pieces together, don't hoard. Make a big sound – use everything, the brass, the gongs and thunder – the prissy puff and scrape is not your job. Grandeur, Jimbo ... if you can't think of something else.'

'It's a horses' hostel here,' I say. 'So many horses ... first, for show and pulling carriages. Then, the easy life – races won, and adulation. Fortunes made and banked: and – out to stud. *À bas la monarchie!* If you're a horse, you just need to wait, it all comes up much better than your dreams.'

There is a pause.

'Horses can't count – not most of them at least,' I say. 'Can't take stock, how few of them are left! Donkeys do things better.'

'There's a much smaller gate, down near the ground,' I add. 'I'm rather between accommodations for a while....'

'That's for the goat,' she says. 'I expected that you'd ask. If you lay out your values and your loyalties, a mattress on the ground ... you might doss there, if you will promise to be quiet....'

*

Goat's dreams. I am a holy goat. Horns and hooves, a black coat, a yellow eye.

There is a fire, long spars that fall ablaze, the galleon with its slave decks – the shackled cargo waiting down below, galleys becalmed amidst the sea on fire; the dragon-boat, alight, a corpse....

I hammer on Giselda's stall.

'Go away,' she says, leaning her long white face over the door, blocking the way in: 'I know your sort. If I wanted, I couldn't save you from your dreams. Nor from the goat's. Mankind is a tide – it breaks and breaks upon the beach, retreats and tries again – frustrated, it will snatch a cliff, pull down a cow – but I am sitting, warming my buttocks on the sand, watching the waters ebb and flow. I can't save anyone, not a crab, an oyster, not a dolphin nor a whale.... I'm just a fish that's struggled up, from the blue-green to the sunlight, grown my long legs. Now I can walk, breathe air abundant, luxuriate. Who should I save? Can you breathe the air, Jimbo? It doesn't seem so. You're still a fish. Your imagination, you think it's powerful; it should explain the whole shooting match, and even pin a tin medal on to it.... Dream – how you get in your tank and blast bad guys. It's legend! You're the puppet-master....

'You're frightened, Jimbo? Sleeping in the devil's stall – you ought to be; not that it matters, not a bit. The philosopher said – the world can do without your imaginings, but can do still better if the lot of us aren't here. That's beautiful, that's symmetry.

'I know about your dreams, and old goats' tales. You don't want explanations, you want to inveigle into me, you want another body, a warm and caring one, you'd carry me, shoulder high, a fleece, spare suit of leather armour, you'd chivvy me to soothe and cosset you.... But – I'd be hot and clinging too. Where'd you dump me, Jimbo? Why should I let you, why fall for it?

'Go away. Sleep if you must. Dream, if you can't avoid. Get out of my plan, until I call you.... Maybe I never shall. What's it to you? Do another show: featuring what you call everything: money: crime, smokes and booze, old age, decay, disease. Death premature or long delayed ... the committee to prolong the world, the *rassemblement* to cut it short: pity and brotherhood, addiction, digging up a pot of gold....

'Do it, Jimbo! Show us just one of those, as if we didn't know about it – but get away, out of my niche, my body and my mind – they're both my territory, they're hand in hand. Sing! If you must. Sing songs of sixpence, of the hanging garden, of Yanks deserting from their fleet, knights nameless, knights in the Rhine, nights on bare mountain.... Examine your bad dream. It's yours. No one else comes in to it. You are a lowly goat: I am comely, and not yours. Do what you must do, Jimbo, like I shall....'

'I understand, Giselda. Help me,' I say. 'And I'll do exactly what you say.'

*

'You're a connoisseur of failure, Jimbo,' Giselda says.

'It's true,' I say. 'There was my opera – you played a part in that. Nothing. Well done. The future – I didn't get far in that. It was a ruse, I expect, to get me as a passenger, to go to Kurdistan. It did not exist....'

'Like the future you didn't get so far with,' Giselda says, laughing a lot. 'You didn't even win that march of English pennies ... all spent long long ago, and to be redeemed with something else that you can't spend.'

'The failure's immaterial,' I say. 'If I had won – so what? It's playing craps. Today you lose, tomorrow – you lose too. Don't blame the wall, don't blame the dice. Don't blame anything. It happens as it does....'

'Yes, yes,' she says. 'Some things don't happen that you wish they had. Me: imagine I'm out to stud.... Maybe – my body ... up for grabs. They say you'd like to have me, possess my body. But of course, it isn't so. If you had my body, you'd be me. No special fun. Now, if I was a brood-mare, they'd stick coca up my arse....'

'I think you're wrong, Giselda,' I begin. 'They don't want you frolicking – quite the reverse.'

'Well,' she says. 'That's what *I* want, and you're no help. Look – my breasts are smallish, but desirable – you'll never have them, unless you are Tiresias, but they're like Belgian chocolates – you want them, periodically, then you find you want the lot ... they disappear.... A man, for you – would be the same. It's bits and pieces ... love and lust ... episodes, a scene remembered, reconstructed – select a tit, a coffee cream....'

'I know all that, Giselda, and it's so,' I say. 'You are desirable. But you're right, what is the you that I desire? – maybe it's me! And it's bits of you, quite passive, unless you bring the chorus on – to sing along and liven up your grunts and groans, your willing hands and feet.... All that – is not the point. It's quite anonymous, it's butchery – a nice piece of haunch, or brisket, a heart a lung a tripe. Come, Giselda – what is the game, the aim?'

'Well,' she says, 'we're getting intimate at last. There's science. We know all about the bees and wildebeests, the cycles of the ice and snow, the trees, and all about the stars we'll never reach, how many people you can kill with rocket "a" and missile "b". It's brought us suicide or sacrifice. Knowledge – brings the end of life. Was that its goal?

'Is it about colonies? A new disposition of regimes, the exercise of power, of management? The ancient in brighter clothes.... The new – it disappoints. The old – it terrifies. Quite soon, the new becomes what the old was. Share out the resources – who'll cheat and who'll miss out? What colour will the losers be? Will a big rocket take them to settle distant stars, and croak en route?

'Disease? We'll live so long we'll all catch one of those, incurable: if we die young, we shan't have sicknesses, but we shall still be dead.

'And money ... it comes and goes. It comes, and we've a mass of it, and as we multiply – it fades, it disappears. A golden stone, like the black one: we circle round them both ... It's what we came for.... But – these are all symbols, metaphors. They will destroy us, each bears a warning, each is the devil.... Neither's what I wish....'

*

'Yes, Giselda, I see the point,' I say. 'What you're looking for is – what would have come next, if we'd survived. How would we think? What would come next, for those who might survive.... Not the future. The style. That's your interest. Not what they'd do, but what they wouldn't do: how would they think....'

'How will our modernism seem?' she says. 'Our fashions. What will it see – the cosmological inventive, contemplative – eye. Our I. Not theories, not material things. What will their imagination, their imaginary, be?'

'You want to write an opera?' I ask. 'I'll help you. More money's in a musical.'

I know it isn't what she means, but – what does she mean? It's not the future, it's an invention of how we, they, might be – after.... After the death of everyone bar – the observing one, the few, the primal heap that lives on after revelation's done.... The next novelty.

'I wouldn't think,' she says, 'of anything banal like you, your tinkabelling drama, ceramic dobbins round and round upon their roundabout.... I'm not a hack that publishes results. My knowledge is enough for me – isn't it for everyone? It's knowledge; left in your brain, it would be incommunicable, hermetic nonsense....'

'Yes, it would be. I grasp that,' I say. 'Not much else.'

'You're limited. You want the answer before the question comes. How will we think? – if there is anyone? I seek an aesthetic, Jimbo, not your rattly stuff.... Look at your life. It's pitiful, that's why you chose to be the goat,' she says.

'I'll go ahead,' I say. 'No science, no finance. They're useless. Science – is no help. It will decay just like philosophy. No colonies – not in the stars, not down here – and no exchange, nothing that can be shared, no values, no commodities. Nothing shared. Money – a sad obsession.

'Hay and oatcakes – that is all I need. No mare's milk, Giselda, no kumiss....'

The moment comes when she'll invite me in her stall, and comfort me ... chase away my dreadful dream!

It doesn't happen so. She ushers me back – into the goat-hole.

'Sweet dreams, Jimbo,' says Giselda.

*

'I have a problem, Giselda, and now you have it too,' I say. 'I don't live in a place. I don't follow words and customs, I don't know what the young and old get up to, what's in what's out. I don't see a street, a town being pulled down and built again, the trees that struggle, the grass that's full of *crottes:* I know, that if there are acacia seeds, giraffes have passed this way ... but I don't dissect the crap, don't call on famous people, don't chat, don't gossip. I follow lines, lines in silence, in the air. And sounds, not found in nature or in studios....

'I'm sceptical; about this new aesthetic, even if it is a route to intercourse with you, my dear – some moments unforgettable, by negotiation repeatable too, their meaning plain when you are having them, but ultimately obscure.... I confess, I don't do romancers ... worse, for your project, I don't care, I'm proud of my obtuseness, exile, isolation, it's the many-coloured coat I wove myself, under my barren fig trees. The chroniclers, the mapmakers of everyday, their traces don't attract; their evanescent everything – I am indifferent to it. It's the cell they put us in, I smuggle in exotic food and company; my cat.... But all that wouldn't interest you, and indeed – if I expounded how I live....'

'It takes me back two centuries,' Giselda says. 'The unread greats – brief lives perhaps in school – that taught you how to snort champagne and dope, and twirl a parasol, exploit a tart – it's dead! Don't be nostalgic for all that, poor Jimbo. Tell me what I want to hear, and that's enough – don't pretend you have a public face.... I want you to sneak around, and bring me things I've never seen before.... Forget your music – it will end reverberating in the void, bubble and squeak of electronics, forged notes incised on plastic sheets....'

'I told you, Giselda, save me from my dreams, and I'll obey and serve,' I say.

*

'"The dead offer themselves as food to the living," Giselda,' I say. 'Stendhal says. We could start with him on immortality. Then – there's Garfinkel, on how it's useless to bring in science to describe our everyday activities....'

'You haven't understood,' Giselda say. 'I don't want to write a book, or transmit anything. I thought you too had realised – an evening in the opera-house is trivial. Do you expect some gratification? If there is applause – it's not for you that you can cash! I don't want your spun air, or confirmations of my certainties. I want to know how people will begin to think, so I can do exactly what I want to do.'

'"The idea of love is my only happiness", Giselda. The most important of the arts of the imagination.....' I tell her.

'Oh yes,' she says. 'I see you're in love with me already – it takes so little ... in fact, the least is given, the more you sweat.'

'Remember, Giselda,' I say. 'It seems the idea of love is about other people – but no, they don't need feel a thing. It's all in you, it's your own intellect. If you believe in cash, live in the money world, the intellect is a collective nullity. Love means independence. Money and power – depends wholly on other people....'

'Then there's nowhere we can start from,' Giselda says. 'Find another starting place and start from there. Don't ask me where I want to end. I want to start. I don't care what makes you feel alive – you are a butterfly, you only like sweet stuff: it's bad for you.'

'It isn't possible,' I say, 'to be original, unique – and have a mass of people value you and comprehend. It's contradictory.'

'That's where you can begin, Jimbo. Well done! That's what I want for a beginning,' she says, and hugs me. 'It doesn't matter what you think, it's what I tell you that's the thing.

'Anyway, don't believe all that stuff about lovers – it's not my genre; it's fantasy, a bore, a sham. I have a lover, so I know.

'And there's another contradiction too – maybe that makes three.... This place, a continent, a country, however you may look at it – it isn't doing well. We're lucky here – in the stables we are creatives, we do what we want because we have prepared. We fix these stalls, we're left in peace, and we don't hassle anyone.'

All this – is not good news. It's been quite clear – Giselda's not dependable.... I feel existence shaking, as it always does, but tiles are falling off the roof, ceramics off the structure.... I could travel round with Slick and Dromy, write their tunes, I guess. They earn – from cash that circulates in clubs and gigs ... not the eternal art, perhaps, but they get by.

*

'Dromy,' I say, 'old friend....'

'No,' he says. 'We can't cut anyone in, no songster, no parasites. No new tunes....'

'I can carry stuff,' I say. 'And – you know the clubs.... There's always custom there....'

'Is that a tear I see?' he asks, and laughs. 'Cash? Love. That's the route you take. A lover. Several. Read Stendhal – it's all in there.'

'Giselda and me,' I begin, trying not to sob. 'We've rather let our futures drop. She has a prop – some whiskery old guy, a lover in intelligence – a uniform hung up somewhere.

'Our rich world – has left us poor. We've nothing left to sell. Some things cost too much to buy: take law. The jails are full. The judges, though...? The cops ... worse still, don't even try. The politics has emptied out, it's emptied into scams, above, below ... We have our art, it's true. And love – I've never made those two pay. But surely – you and Slick will need a guy to load the van....'

'You want the system to give cash. It won't. As for the loading – it used to be a normal job,' says Dromy. 'Don't cry. People went on loading – since horses were invented, and then gasoline. The problem is – there is no vacancy. We do all that ourselves.'

'Of course,' I say. 'We all try to be autonomous. As for Giselda – she didn't spoil my opera – it's still there, exactly as it was and is. She destroyed a performance. Now, I'll help her with her own – but she doesn't have an opera. She never will.'

'I guess it gives you satisfaction,' Dromy says. 'Knowing satisfaction exists. Not as much as you had in the club, I guess. If you hadn't gone clubbing all that time, you could have put on your show....

'Satisfaction? I don't know what's the word for that,' I say. 'I'm sure it's in the book somewhere. I can handle failure, but, Dromy – you'll have nothing you could call success.'

*

'I have to bring you with me,' Giselda says. 'To give a name to all the colours I seek out.'

She chalks her name on the stall door. 'No one will take it now. They're all old-school intellectuals – a word determines everything. You write "goat" on your small hole – and hope someone looking to move in's an animalist.'

I'm not provoked.

We go all round North Africa.

'This rain!' Giselda complains. 'No wonder everybody here is miserable and wants to leave.'

'Concentrate, Giselda,' I say. 'They want to go down to Europe, be anonymous. More poverty, but without the shame, the frustration, family, religion, the jagged parts of life....'

'Oh, what a philosopher,' Giselda says. 'I don't want that! I see there's the cult of money everywhere. It's the great transmission belt, uniting unequals and the diverse. You need it to extend the self. Culture, Jimbo – does it lie in material things – plants, pants, houses, wives and lovers? Or only in values, perceptions, refinement....?

'How people think ... it ought to be immaterial, and yet they think of objects.... The line, the skyline – remembering your city makes you weep. An out-line for an out-law....'

'Here, Giselda, they want to find a leaking boat, go to Marseille....' I say, 'Either we assist, or let them go in silence....'

'No, Jimbo,' Giselda shouts. 'Look! There's crowds. Values! Look at the signs – freedom. What does that mean?'

'Look out!' I shout as Giselda leaps about and shakes her fists at cops disguised and guys in Martian gear....

'Run!' I shout, doing just that.

She halts. Something has popped her eye.

The consequence is infinite, or so it seems. 'I'm halfway to being blind,' she says. 'Do you suppose they'll pay? And how'll I know if colours are just as they were before?'

'Maybe your wound's unique, Giselda. You alone think of the chromatic loss....' I say.

'Someone should pay,' she insists. 'Eye for an eye. It must have a price ... it's not a coin. Only those are equivalents.'

'Wear shades, Giselda, and we'll leave,' I say. 'Now you know how people think. Forget the fires and floods – this is the lesson. Avoid the crowds.'

'Oh, Jimbo, how I trust you,' says Giselda. 'Maybe it's the first step to true love.... Though I can only see halfway ... a future conditional, imperfect....'

'We've seen enough. Enough is clear and known,' I say, 'Wherever we go, we'll find people with very little who want to get away....'

We patch her up: a patch is what she wears.

We go back to where we were. 'This is heaven,' Giselda says: 'Being a horse has never seemed such a fulfilment....'

'The journey – beautiful,' I say. 'A revelation for you – and we didn't pay a trafficker, you'd kept the cash I'd given you to organise my opera. Wise thought! It's not a fraud, it's providence, earthy and real, without a golden halo.... Now, though, we're penniless....'

I think of the grand March, the pennies that would serve us now. 'I should try to borrow from Hervé,' I say.

'And I can try my lover,' Giselda says. 'Though he's so irritable.... But it's clear, love is the province you and I did not explore. Time was short – and did it concentrate our thought?'

'Not much,' I say.

'Someone, somewhere – should take notice,' says Giselda. 'Be taken to account....'

'You could go on wearing an eye-patch – gives you character. Try to make a career with it,' I say.

'It's all helpful, what you say,' she says. 'To make a drama out of it, my handicap, even a little cash – it's much more complicated than I'd thought....'

'I know I see the worst,' I say. 'Wait for the best to come?! When it happens, it's at enormous cost, and after suffering immense ... just like the worst....'

'I can't ask you to lend an eye,' she says. 'Still less give me one of yours – you're so clever, two's too much for you! My difficulty – is that I seem just a stupid victim, unlucky in the line of fire....'

'You have to make it seem you were strategic there, picked off by an intelligence,' I say.

'Oh yes!' she says. 'Intelligence and love – lover, at least – are my inseperables.'

'You were brave, Giselda,' I say. 'Brave, not courageous.'

'I could feel this was a beginning,' she says. '*The* beginning. The country of the blind.'

'What, Giselda?' I ask, sceptical. 'Martyrdom or sacrifice? In your case, both unforced, so rather negligeable....'

'You've done nothing, Jimbo,' she says sharply. 'Maybe exploit an innate talent. Music? Big deal! Who doesn't nurture an imponderable? Something distant.that sounds familiar, an ad for something – Delibes? Thaïs?

'I gave up half my vision ... no: the world has taken half my vision. Now, I can address it....'

'The guilty make a speech, Giselda,' I say. 'The innocent are bundled off and to the guillotine before the sun is up, in silence.'

'Then I'll be guilty,' says Giselda, 'if that gives me voice.'

'Be careful,' I say. 'When you pursue your vision. You've lost the feel for depth – and nearness too. In Chile, say, or Hong Kong – you won't see the ball coming for your other eye. You'll be the blind seer, but there are millions of them.... We see them, they don't see us, or anything at all ...'

'I could find a donor,' she says, needling, 'or a surgeon. A corpse, a forgivable loan – a bulb snipped out and – you're on the cusp again.'

'That's the desire and pursuit of the whole, but size and duration isn't specified,' I say. 'A whole could last five minutes or a year....'

'You see too much, Jimbo,' she says. 'I'm more specific.'

'Well, then,' I say. 'Think carefully. You've one eye left. Spend it well. In a hundred years, when they hear about your life and the suicide we all are contemplating. We live with death, it's written in each diary, The End – not in everyone's December, but in June. "In September, when the leaves turn to gold...." only here, they don't start turning till November now. It's still warm. When the leaves are gold, you can't encash.

'What difference could you have made, Giselda? If it's suicide – an insect professor will decipher you.... Then, it'll be his turn for suicide or homicide. When things recover, the plants grow. The insects go back underground among the roots and multiply in silence – and in revenge they prick and sting. Bigger animals grow up, eat the green, they put on weight. Marsh rats, Giselda: they can't yet read, but they will learn, they'll develop numerate skills and build the rockets that will leave them with the choice that is no choice – suicide or homicide....'

'It's eloquent, Jimbo, I admit,' she says. 'All was in your opera, that I fucked up, remember....'

*

'Light, not judgement,' says Giselda. 'In the beginning, obviously, even twinkles, they must exist or else there's nothing, no energy. And once it's made, light endures and travels for eternity.

'An installation. Light – is my story, Jimbo. It's your "everything".

'There's me, my horse, the opera that's empty sheets ... my lover, the soldier, the crowds, the bullets ... and my vision ... halved....'

'I'll let you use my music,' I say, amused, 'but there's much more you must include: the clubs, the Faustian gardening, the race against the droughts and floods, and music, penury.... You've left me out.'

'Oh,' she says, 'my music might be "Cosmic blues" – more consonant. I'll set up in a gulf, an abyss – project it on the cupola: the public floats below, like lilies, on inflatables, watches the images – as they might watch God, in the great mosque of Isfahan. It will be a great spectacle. A success.'

(It's so. It was, it is.)

Then she concludes, 'And – you and I – we're not a couple, what passes between us two – it passes on....'

'Homicide and suicide – that's your material, Giselda, start from that,' I say. 'Put that at the beginning, finish with the science, the mechanical failures, the useful that then suffocates.... Think organic, no hypotheses. People will feel good.'

'It could be interim,' she says, undecided.

'Sad!' I say. 'Don't step back! Hesitate, and you're not worth an eye. Not worth a whisker. You have no feel for life, for each ingredient that makes it taste and stick together. Quite worthless – try again. You've one more chance ... one more eye. You must find a place outside the world where you can see it spin. Maybe there's a club....'

'You're not trustworthy, Jimbo,' says Giselda. 'You're not a teacher. What drives you is resentment for what I did.'

'There,' I say, 'you can see your landscape: this is how they'll think. It's here already. It's us, you, and me.'

'That may well be so,' she says, 'but I'd suggest – forget about love. It isn't you, not part of what you call your everything. It's a metaphor for winning money, feeling grand.'

'It wasn't in the opera,' I say. 'It may have been a lack. Clubs – that's where people live these days. Here, we two – we live like people did in the 1820s....'

'We live like horses did in the 1820s, Jimbo,' she says.

'It's time to take to the road, again. Fortune is everywhere – it should be easy to seek mine,' I say.

'You don't adhere,' Giselda says. 'You've tried – you've no one now.'

*

Life runs on doglegs. People disappear, entreat, berate, settle, once again they disappear. Shadows: we lack them. They'd be our confirmation, the archival copy....

We're hares in the mown meadow – our tall ears a giveaway.

*

There's a world of people in the stables – some dossing here, others come to gawk, or occupy them, to stop them being torn down or sold.

Estelle.

It's my fantasy, that women are more fun than men ... she's tall – that seems to point to wealth ... I sniff at her – 'Hey,' she says, quite loud. 'It's clear your mistress, Giselda, keeps you hungry, thirsty too.'

'Oh we've an old old story – a contest between us two,' I say. 'Not sex. Not with me – she's with her lover, trying to get cash....'

'And you seem destitute,' she says. 'You realise – sex isn't about sex. I hear you're a creative – that won't trot. People don't want novelty – the new means ageing, brings the end into a focus, then you tremble – all is lost. People want depth, but it's the depth they didn't know about long long ago. Besides – the human condition. That won't pay. If you write music, the money lies in poppy tunes – think "balloons" – you need a singer that can float them up and keep them hovering on the hill ... over the ridge, there's maybe fruit trees, brought back a thousand years ago by legionaries coming home from Syria ... the town that left them with expensive habits, and then – looking for a house, a room, a hole, like you.... All in a balloon, Jimbo – that shows you that your solitude is shared by everybody else. It's Werther, Jimbo. But – I can help you. Don't trust that Giselda. You're a friend of peoples now abandoned. That way there lies adventure: for both of us – investment. Money follows armies – that's a maxim, that's why the maxim gun was made....'

'Oh no!' I say. 'We've done all that. Giselda's eye was popped in a manif. I lost Delinda looking for a place that didn't quite exist.... Maybe we could compromise – and do a club....'

'Patience!' Estelle says, and laughs, and shows expensive teeth.

'This hole!' I say. 'I must get out! Abandon Giselda, but, Estelle ... are you a saviour, or recruiting me?'

'There's warriors,' says Estelle. 'Then comes the baggage train: paymasters, the tarts, the kids, buglers, amputees, armourers – it's life, Jimbo. It's a long straggle, platoons of women, men, the bosses, contacts ephemeral, demanding – and it doesn't teach! You guess what are the lessons, what you've learnt ... no one else is interested ... once there were philosophers, going walkabout and singing songs, then into monasteries and brewing hooch, and then.... Well, Jimbo, here I am. I give you motivation – sometimes satisfaction too....'

'I'm for the clubs,' I say. 'Those shake the bag, they mark the cards, fix fortune's wheel....'

'That is my province,' says Estelle. 'Trust me! No more washing in the trough – I'll cosset you and cuddle you.... Not sex! That takes you years of chastity, and tolerance of anything I choose to do meanwhile....'

'Take me, Estelle. Change my circumstance....' I say.

'No roasting,' says Estelle. 'You're a pig, but not a long one. My plan for you is wearing suits – me too. You have a pull, a presence, Jimbo. You're a narcissist, you love a solitary pleasure, but you like others seeing you enjoy yourself. And you've a puffer, Hervé, a campaigner ... that Delinda, your defence ... and for the human touch – Melissa....'

'It's fantasy. We split an age ago, those guys – last century....' I say.

'No, no,' she says. 'You haven't understood. We here – we don't yet have catastrophe. Old flames – you blow on them, and up they rise to warm you.'

I switch my loyalty.

'I'm clean,' says Estelle. 'I have cash, and lovers too.'

*

Giselda returns: 'My lover – he's come up with money, Jimbo ... We can move out and into property....' And she kisses me – 'Oh, how I missed you....' And I pull away.

'Too late, Giselda. There is still resentment on my part,' I say. 'I'll take a pause....'

'I've found an eye,' she says, excited. 'Bionic. The cash is also for my sight ... I won't see what's going on, of course. It runs old movies. You could message me. And the opera....'

'That would be imaginary....' I say.

'Oh, that's the best,' she says. 'You must aspire ... our life has changed quite radically....' And on she talks....

*

'Tell me, Estelle,' I ask her. 'What's the plan for me? I'm without a lodging. Giselda – she couldn't see me straight....'

I feel some guilt – Giselda, I could swear – she doesn't feel regret. She has a trajectory for herelf – she's on the launching

pad, maybe in midair.... I'm in the hangar, waiting to be armed
and fuelled.... And here's Estelle....

'Remember Bartok,' says Estelle, 'when he collected songs,
there's one about the emperor, the silver racing plates he fitted
to his horse, and this old guy ... he found one, cast by the steed –
it changed his life. In those old days, a silver coin could buy the
Sacher joint, and still leave change.... This is a contract, this
paper – "Songs of War and Peace". We might connect it to the
book. You travel round, these warring groups, they sing and
sometimes dance. Record them, Jimbo. There's a public
ready....'

'It's not my thing, Estelle,' I say. 'I write songs; recording's
done by phonics....'

'You'll have to learn,' she says. 'That's just the start. Those
warring groups, militias – they take oil wells, and phosphate
fields, and animals whose fortunes turn some bucks.... Often
they have capital that awaits their victory – but sometimes not.
Find those where we can invest for cheap. There's building
work and minerals, and stolen artefacts – and ministries to staff,
prisoners to ransom, used tanks to be recycled.... Don't take a
risk. You're a composer, anthropologist: – remember. Don't get
killed, don't get too close to anyone, except, perhaps, to me....'

Oh, Estelle ... what promise, and such promises.... And wise!
A queen bee holding out a honeycomb....

'It sounds quite outlandish, Estelle,' I add. 'Just for some
discs, that if you play them you can end in jail....'

'That's true – I hadn't thought,' she says. 'We'll work that
out.'

'It sounds big cash,' I say. 'I don't much care.... I don't
expect.... You know, I have no country, I have moved around. I
take the bits of places where I've been, and that I like, and I'm
implacable against the rest that nauseate. There's no one culture
that I understand as a subscriber, in intimacy. But, I have put
together parts, the best, of every one I find.

'I make a country – my Rojava. It's inside. I put it into music.
So, this question of the cash you want to make ... I don't feel
much enthusiasm....'

'It isn't about you,' Estelle says, bridling, 'it's for everyone.
It's good you don't have nationality – that's why you're useful.

You understand the people who've lost theirs, or are trying to take on another one....'

'Yes, Estelle – and there's the flaw,' I say. 'I follow the mystique, but when they start the politics – I'm off.'

'That's fine,' she says. 'No one expects you'll stay around.'

*

In wars, most things don't stop ... the everyday – goes on until it can't. You have to live, buy stuff, hoards of it, sell most of what you have and cannot carry. Everything costs hugely, but there's bargains too – enormous bargains, but you can never ship them out. You almost never see the soldiers, if you do, you wish you'd not.

There's sand here – but no sea. There's music, very loud. Guys driving up and down – they all have contracts for their songs. They laugh at me – I pass it on, the laughter. The songs – if you can grasp the words, you'd not want to repeat them....

As for investment – who'd I ask?

It's not a failure, it is what is called a setback. I sidle up when I return, report my nothingness to Estelle. In some important way she is a boss. I watch her very closely –

'Estelle, it is a thing I absolutely mustn't ask. If I paid for sex with you – how much would it cost? Are there extras too? And options – maybe I could charge expenses – return matches, that sort of enterprise....'

She thinks it over, like a boss would do –

'Usually it costs you nothing, though it doesn't mean it's free,' she says. 'Or else it's half of what you have and ever will, or even more. Is it what you really want? The price – maybe it's too low, or else – excessive.... In any case, it's something you mustn't ask. Maybe one time, long long ago – the economics was germane. Not now, unless you are a pig, a dog. It's like antiques – if they are genuine, they cost what you can't afford, but anyway – if you can, you'll bid, and then you tire of them.... Remember, Jimbo – desire is inexhaustible, but sex ... is finite.'

I didn't ask. In the end, or the beginning, my enquiry seemed quite crass....

'Oh, I like a joust,' Estelle says. 'I like a contest of this kind....'

I didn't ask her. A daydream. Maybe a thought's transparent: she'll see my lust!

*

It's true, the songs and dances were all contracted when I had arrived. Guys think of what they'll spend if they survive. Most stuff is not destroyed, and if it is – there's many people find a way of sticking things together, houses, legs and brains.... Making a buck. They've thought of who'll provide the cash, carry the debt. Estelle had not thought of that – the debts....

'Estelle!' I say. 'Your excellent idea – except, there are no takers there....'

*

'The development of consciousness,' I begin, 'that is our task.The history of science as it undermines our rationality ... we must accept, and go beyond.... That's what Giselda had proposed....'

'*Our* rationality?' says Estelle. 'I recognise the idea – not Giselda's, but you find it in Lenin ... in the Notebooks ... and Kelvin spoke of Darwin's notion of the "absolute futility" of philosophy, if you recall.... That quest should determine everything we do.... There's Mach too – to think of Lenin, the parts, the whole – it became a mandala ... sand and monks, you start from nothing but know where it all ends, not where your comrades thought, that is for sure....'

'It should,' I say, 'but mostly what we do points away, massively, from that. Your mission, let's call it so – is simple. Your search is for backers, for making gold from *grès*. Your work, so-called, means making work for others to perform so you and yours can skim your style from their endeavours....'

'It's so,' she says. 'We are a long way off from thinking in new ways. But – before you judge, remember the useless search for laws – the gravity to be found everywhere and weighed: the quanta and the particles – pinning them down like butterflies....

In the end – after my end and yours – we'll find a way to use our thought as means – not to discover what there is, as if it's predisposed, laid out like an exam question or a test, a puzzle, animals that burrow or who fly, or when you're looking elsewhere – they do both.... That's naive, metaphysical, materialism, Jimbo. We – or those who're better primed – will go beyond, for sure ... meanwhile, when warrior movements clear a space, we will invest, and make a buck that we'll invest again, ready for when other movements clear a space....'

'It's opportunist, that's its name, Estelle,' I say.

'And by the way,' she says, 'when you were failing in your task – you must have seen the cameras, and sensed the cameras you couldn't see – bionic eyes, the eyes of God – recording, diffusing – your image recognised, identified, and finally archived....

'Your songster bandits. Jimbo, when you were with them, singing their tunes, burying them, cheering them on, trying to establish copyright in desolated zones ... did you by chance or impulse, conviction or constraint – pick up a gun? Fire it in some direction too?'

'You must imagine, Estelle ... there's the cause, and then there's causes, situations exciting or extreme....' I say, remembering. 'Driving fast ... the excitement, history, death....'

'If you were there, recorded, fighting and rejoicing – and came back with a tale of simple sing-along....' she says. 'It's unbelievable. You're in the dirt. Try to get out of it, while keeping quiet about our plan, or else we too will have ... to make references to Cassirer, citing Rankine too – to show you came to us with dodgy plans, were sent away, brought nothing back.... Big systems, laws, the quanta, Jimbo – you may stand by those, but we've moved on.'

'What can they do, Estelle?' I ask.

'Imprison you or shoot you, try you and investigate, dig out your voids, rifle through your ignorance and innocence. Mutilate your life. Their aim is justice and: intelligence – it's very far from what you were engaged in ... all the things you'll say you didn't see, did not suspect....'

'But if who you call the bandits should win, Estelle?' I ask.

'Someone will always wish you'd lost,' she says. 'You ran a tab, someone will add it up. If your side wins, everyone will march in their parade.... Then, you take it from the top again, with brio ... but very cautious too....'

'You know we're good, Estelle, because we sing.... It's volatile – we are a bloom of medusas in an estuary, the tide's our master.... Shoot in the air! You might bring down an aeroplane.... There's really bad, and then there's friends, and friends of friends and enemies of friends ... it all ends so-so, but most of us alive, at least.'

'Oh, I believe you,' Estelle says. 'Why not? There'll be a record somewhere, and then a history.'

*

'Nous sommes bien Mais l'auto bazar qu'on dit merveilleux ne vient pas jusqu'ici'

– Apollinaire

Most soldiers don't get killed. It's a warm thought, and sometimes – a van arrives with noodles and with tea.

I'm in the old world, with its punishments.

Giselda and Estelle are thinking – how to think the new. How to find a glue that sticks huge quantitites together – the countries, living in their disbeliefs and fantasies, Americas and Asias, Europes too, or Africas – that fall apart like badly mended chairs and leave guys on the floor, legs pointing upwards – to unreachable stars....

History, geography, the vegetation that Melissa grows, the prisoners that Delinda defends – force keeps them so. It's force that makes them cohere, for now, then force that breaks them up. War is not something exceptional and avoidable – it is the ground on which everything, all human societies stand.

Hunter-gatherers? Maybe they had a chance....

Estelle's economics rewards the old, prepares for the new to repeat the old.... New values, new hopes, a new asceticism, new cuddling round. Will that keep us close, suspicious of our neighbours, dissatisfied with ourselves?

'True, trite, poor Jimbo,' Estelle says. 'You're superficial. Self-serving – I shan't let you get away with that! Your opera! – nip, nip – how it bites, erodes your soul!

'Your side – was on no side – it wavered in the wind, took cash, took weapons, made dirty deals. The good thing was everyone thought it was strong and had positions, though it was just guys like you, juiced up and wanting to survive, your strings in someone's hand you couldn't see – and now you're on a list, and so are we, even if we dump you ... which we can....'

'You'd be dumped too, Estelle,' I say. 'Love me! Tell some lies. How'd we both manage without your job...?'

*

'Beware aphorisms,' says Hervé – 'There's a bull in that field. Commonplaces – another field, a brother bull. Don't say love requires indifference – everybody knows that. You – just stick to indifference, you're good at it.'

'I'm not like that at all,' I say....

'You fought unfair,' he goes on. 'Despite that, I won our fisticuffs. Then – you enrolled in a foreign army. You're arrogant, you don't want states or religions. You go along with people's vapid projects because you want a place, a person, to stick on to. You know it's emptiness, but your empty is other people's full. You must seem normal – despite the opera.... You bring it with you – the brand, the motto: *ni foi ni loi*. That was invented to fit you, it's on your escutcheon.'

'It's ethnography, Hervé,' I say, heading him off, away. 'Call it terrorism ... collecting songs. Then there is fear and exaltation ... getting orders, always wrong. Making alliances – always betrayed. It's serious, though: something you can laugh at, not like ordinary life where it happens just the same, but stays with you, months, years. Going with my soldier-mates – it transforms into an energy. *Insouciance,* irrelevance, benevolence. Pity – especially for the animals abandoned in the fields.'

'I see why you wanted excitement and to get away,' says Hervé. 'The error was coming back. Who do you have who'll say you're a good guy? Not me, for sure.'

'Everywhere is ruins, Hervé,' I say. 'How can anything new be built if there's no past, nothing we can see we might escape from?'

'Your mates,' says Hervé, pretending to know everything – 'They joined up from necessity. Without possessions, they still belonged somewhere. You – have only the universe of creativity. It looks like ruins, but maybe it's the bricks you stick together in deep space....'

'You're a critic, Hervé,' I say, hope abandoned. 'You set the context.'

'Oh no,' he says. 'I'm not in the building line. I don't do restorations, don't glue on tiles.... I blow. If you believe in gods, I'm only a demi-god, my gift – the breath of nymphs.

'You're on a list somewhere, Jimbo. Concentrate on that. Your friends did awful things, for sure, whether you were there, or saw.... You need a lawyer...'

'Oh, Delinda!...' I say.

'... a refuge ...'

'Melissa! Of course,' I say. 'I can live in clubs ... what joy, the company is fluid, there is sex and booze....'

'Someone to say you've no affiliations and no faith?... That you live in comfort, talking of philosophy....' he says.

'What luck!' I say. 'It's providence: I believe in her ... Giselda.'

'And someone beautiful to take the rap for you,' he says.

'I'd regret – poor Estelle,' I say. 'Thrown off my sled, into ... the jaws.... She'll be the atrocity I lay upon my conscience....'

'Of course,' says Hervé, 'there's chance. They may not catch up with you, and your opera might be performed....'

'Let's try the March of Pennies, Hervé,' I say. 'I feel ... well ... lucky. Even with you.'

*

I'm safe. Who else is saved? No one, probably. Where do I belong? Places I must deny, people who might help me, but who never gave me what I asked.... Where's my picture, with my place marked in, my X to mark my spot? The Whole – which is called love, but could as well be called rhubarb – Melissa knows all about that, and leeks. It's limited. Volcanic sand, and volcanic cinders – grow the food, make the cement that sticks ancient Romans to us all for ever....

I take out my opera.... Gropius took a fine step: before, there were the serfs of the Ostankino, the artists of Isfahan ... but where am I?

Music has structures but no frame – it disappears, needs a creation every time.... I can't proceed, can't think it through, my head's too small; my loves – a try-out, a try-on, a one on one, hit or miss, like a fox's pounce. A couple coupling? It's small arithmetic ... squares and cubes. Bricks. It isn't much at all. The clubs take you back to zero. Start again....

*

'Delinda,' I say. 'Remember, I was there to collect tunes and make money for someone – truth and justice don't come in till later. The body count? History is rather unconcerned about foot soldiers, who you are and how you die, and the accidentals in your skin and loot collected in your sack. History's the bird of wisdom – looking for fat mice. War aims? There's four of you in a white car, pumped up and everything is loaded – maybe the car will go back to someone, one day – most likely not ... like you, your mates....'

'That's not a good answer,' says Delinda. 'Forget it. Was there a design, a pattern, that you can express, that fits with your world view ... that you followed, that you abandoned – admitting your uncertainty regarding how all fits together?'

'Uncertainty seems rather bad,' I say. 'Rather stupid.'

'Yes and no,' she says. 'It's what we build on to get you off, if ever you are asked.'

'Suppose they ask about what I didn't see?' I ask.

'I'm not a real lawyer, Jimbo,' Delinda says. 'You know that. I josh people in clubs. I love the law. I'd never trust a client or a court.'

'How's Mithat?' I ask. 'He has a cause....'

'He's flat,' she says. 'He's my idea, like Kurdistan is his. He's a great man, a genius, a baby and a bore, my child I found abandoned in a ditch, I didn't want him, grow to want him less and less, he's stuck inside my head, my routine, like how a day starts when you wash your face. He has no personality – he's massive, like the stuffed bear made into a hat-rack at the door, he's dead, like an old potted plant that flowers each season, flowers smaller and smaller, brighter, more intense, and when he dies, he'll be a handful – of thorny twigs, can't be thrown out, or dusted, touched – you'd think of varnishing them, but they twist and turn and stoop....'

I remember him – as a series of metamorphoses – a bat, a white owl, a coughing badger, raven....

'The singing guys I went along with,' I tell Delinda, 'didn't believe in sacrifice, nor in justice. They played chess, not draughts. They wanted to rebuild what had been knocked down....'

'That isn't possible,' she says. 'There's authenticity. They believed in what they said they were. They sang and traded, that's irrelevant. Probably reactionaries, they mostly are, unless they've read a book. And everybody says they want the same, as if there isn't conflict, as if the killing one day ends hostility, cleanses, and that peace comes after war – and so ... often the conflict melts away, there's linking of arms instead of firing them....

'Mithat – he just suffers, nothing for him would last, not even skulls and bones ... he is his thought, never the same a minute after.... Give him his desire, he wants it to change, transform entirely. The first step never comnes, of course, he has no feet just now....'

'Forget authenticity,' I say. 'I never had any. Don't ask me what I do not know.... Any future that you quiz me on – it sounds a replica of what I wouldn't want: species being, the organic society, the scientific corpse.... The self-consciousness we do not have, the science we invent that tells us nothing of ourselves. Part of our world survives? – move the pawns, crown some of them, feed some poor, bury some rich ... Leave me to be sceptical, Delinda – all the answers I don't want have been mooted, others have done their their Totentanz on cobbled motorways of skulls. It's possible my own answer is what I wouldn't want ... if ever I could get that far, arrest it.... You step out the mirror, then step right back in again....'

'Let's hope there's so many bad guys on the lists they never get to you,' she says. 'Good guys – I don't trust them – it's better to apply a law than look for justice.... As for you, you are not good – that leaves you lots of space to be quite bad.... As your advocate, I'd add "or gullible, or curious". That's an uncertainty we mightn't raise....

'The people you were with – they weren't at all right for you. It's a confusion – you enjoyed them; if you'd thought, you'd see it's wrong, not what you wanted, but it's always more or less like that....'

I grope my way through all of that: I say, 'I'd say that singing, dancing, shooting indiscriminate, even at people I hadn't seen before, or never saw – that was me, the animal. Wondering if it was wrong – that shows I was an animal who'd eaten the big fruit. I knew that there was good and bad, but which was which? That takes a bigger guy than me....'

'I'm not sure you are honest, Jimbo,' says Delinda. 'There is no fruit for that.'

'Maybe the good and bad – it's better to forget that one,' I say. 'And fruit as well. You say – destroying everything was bad – and yet we've done it, without guilt ... if the wolves eat the last porcupine – is that so bad...?'

'I shan't use you as a witness, Jimbo,' Delinda says, decidedly. 'I think you would confuse the case. Your cause is just: your side is not. You didn't have a side, and so you jumped on the first truck that took you on.... It sounds ridiculous ... but if you're on a list....'

'Lists are something only humans keep,' I say. 'But good and bad don't enter in.'

'It's consequences, as you must know,' Delinda says. 'Having a country is no fun – but better have one than be persecuted.'

'Wise words,' I say. 'Free will comes in – but in my case – if it is will, it isn't free. It's will.'

'Enough,' Delinda says. 'You were not there or anywhere. You were not you. You didn't know. You have no view. But – that's will. You don't live with the rest of us so you and we can exercise our wills. We come together to use our reason ... that wobbling platform....'

*

I have a fear of people dressing up, acting as if they're human, but someone else. The theatre lives on travesty: I'm terrified of it, the zombies, suppose they ask you up with them; be dead, or take your clothes off.... In music, an opera, they sing, so they're not pretending, they are humans imitating animals, like birds in trees. Mine is a fear, awe, of shamans, their being intimate with non-existent others, knowing the dead, the damned, familiar with hell and all its provinces and counties.

Lawyers: they send you for the chop, the knife, the guillotine – 'go straight to hell!' – the rope, piano-wire, garotte, the chair, electric divan, limb-stretch – poisons, hemlock, bullets ... on and on, they show you off, the guilty client, your face, as if they are a dealer selling paintings; then they stand, in actors' wigs, dressed like crows and cawing as you're sent down....

Dear sweet Delinda – fortunately, you just act it out, play act, false advocacy. Minister to every change in Mithat ... invent his territory that flickers off and on, a filament....

'Maybe you save my neck,' I say, 'maybe my soul, my reason, you may even save my will....'

*

'Estelle,' I say, 'I must go back. There. Maybe the consequences I find will show what my intentions were –'

'It won't get you off anything,' she says, 'but go ahead ... it makes you suspect twice, or more ...'

'... my intentions,' I go on. 'Not apocalyptic, not dictated or paradisaic....'

'Curiosity,' she says, 'kills lots. It's the songs bit. That undermines your tale. Songs are vacuous. If you'd have written up your exploit, made a movie....'

'Better than that,' I say. 'My battling will go in everywhere, into everything I do....'

'No good,' she says. 'People forget, don't wait. Pissed off with remembrances and warning....'

*

It's easy going back. What I did, and what was done...? Who wanted what...? It was terrible, and good, for sure, we sang when all was falling down, and big voices decided who should have whose pile of dust: strategic dust.

There's no dust here – the street. See – here we played billiards – still the torn cloth, pockets burst, sometimes all reds ... then only whites. A place to buy your batteries, a place to eat if you'd no family or passing by.... Men and kids. All undisturbed. As it was: there is rubble too – not here, not in this street. It's low, the plain ignores the blackeyed houses, most lie flat – you see straight on, the horizon.... A row of shoes. 'Take!' says a guy, 'they're going free.'

*

'That's it, Estelle,' I say. 'Banality. I didn't ask about the politics. No one seemed keen. But don't mistake – we did enormous deeds. I know. I know too – it's not my thing.'

'Of course,' she says. 'It's like the currents in the air, the sea – beyond judgement and constraint. You'll wriggle out, Jimbo – most people do.... And – I'd not insist, but – your mates?'

'Oh Estelle, my distant star,' I say. 'You run a pirate ship. You'll see their raft, their skiff, their plank, their yacht. You don't run up your flag, you are anonymous: they'll do for crew, or – you could drop them off, on a rocky place, or a new continent....'

*

I knew I'd not make out with Estelle. She'd not regret me, she has control few others have. Control: not my indifference, nor fatalism.

Giselda too – I owe her explanations, she doesn't listen, but people slide off her, she always has a lover, more dependable than you, with no address, no timetable, satisfying, always there – a trainer never needed, never paid. Never alone and never accompanied.... Giselda.

'My goat!' she cries. 'Jimbo! My giddiness, pride of my regiment....'

'I'm still your goat,' I say. 'But, Giselda, you're less horse....'

'Oh, my lover set me up: a place,' she says. 'Sometimes a one-eyed horse jumps well – she can't see the others, but my bionic eye – it has all this info streaming in....'

'My fear was that our lines of thought would cross and snare,' I say. 'Both of us, we wanted to avoid the marsh-gas messages, "science the conjurer" ... all that. How we might come to think! It's brilliant.... But Giselda, I forgot – you're in luck, to have so many lovers who provide for you....'

'I know,' she says. 'It's a handicap, being lovable. It's my life policy, I suppose. In the drawer, forgotten.'

'I ought to have stayed around....' I begin.

'You're not lovable, Jimbo. My opinion's sought,' she says, 'by everyone – itself, a terrible sign. Alas, it means it's not worth anything. Yours – might be valuable – we'll never know. But we'll keep an eye out,' and she laughs.

'I'd accept torture to hear your laugh, Giselda,' I say.

'I could make a record of it,' she says, and laughs. 'I don't go to manifs any more. All the goodness – meaningless. Protests. Interests. Street battles – I'm always on show, but one day I'll make my views be weighed and count for something.... I'm too current, see? Too right; too convincing. I put into words what the rest intuit.

'You – you're always wrong, Jimbo, but it's always an exciting trip. To me, anyway.'

'I never knew, Giselda,' I say, with much regret. 'There was between us ... fire in a slow-match?'

'I was so fond, Jimbo. I'd have done anything....' she says.

'The goat-hole,' I say, 'it wasn't spacious. I adored you, your quest, your daring.... But you didn't give me a good run....'

'Things that don't happen, misunderstandings that open like a trap and up the devil jumps and steals your scene – things imagined and dismissed – these are the worlds, the boards, we walk upon and cultivate, our plants grow tall and bright, never need watering – they're very small, so it is always dawn or sunset.... Memories are stuck, they barely change, but what has never been – it grows; it is the province of our love, dear Jimbo, we are the government and opposition, we eat well, sleep well, the panorama's infinite.... We are a society, we legislate and regulate – nothing occurs that's not intended by us, we are benevolent – and, Jimbo, how we love each other....'

What can I say? I'm not prepared for that, I have no quote to back my amazement, probably we'd all feel that, but not exactly corresponding to Giselda's way, unique, ethereal....

'I have a date,' she says. 'My lover – he awaits.'

She stands quite still, and waits for me to walk away until she's out of sight.

*

I sit on the stoop outside the club. A tall man sits beside me. 'Ah, Melissa,' he says.

Silence.

Then, 'I know you can't know everything,' he says. For both of us. 'But you should have your space, ready to put the revelation in as it comes to you. Leonardo made us all and each – a Leonardo. To see the world, and commit to show it all in paint, to paint it all – you obviously can't reproduce everything there is in multitudes of paintings like a pangolin's scales, thousands, even more. So you select, put all reality in a handful of your crusts.... You see? I am a doctor, but I didn't want to see the skeleton, the blood run out, the brain a cake of soap – the patient as a life and death. I wanted to put the flesh back on, a person representative, undamaged. A statue. Magnificent.... It isn't done, they censure you. There's so many many people ... so many illnesses, but the copies, reproductions – they all die without a thought of – why? So much that can go wrong, badly installed, worn through....'

'I understand that,' I say. And he's a stranger, what do I care what I tell him? 'I put everything in what I do – an opera. Even – a war....' I say.

'All the young bloods are going out,' he says. 'It's terror that they seek. My best friend died – I didn't grieve, because I knew I'd never see him again, not evermore. It was finished, complete. *Genug.* Nothing left. No one understands, and yet – oddly enough, they can forget ... what they've not understood....'

Yes,' I say, 'that's "everything", what it entails. You can't do better than possess that in totality, not by studying little bits of it. Being a pundit! Knowing a fraction of it well ... just fancy!'

'Everything,' he says, 'goes into anything. Collecting rocks – you can use them in a garden to pick out a path. You don't need expertise.'

'I see the point,' I say, 'but it's so very small....'

'Tidiane!' Melissa says – 'and making friends with Jimbo, who's a genius, and what luck they never did his opera, it's all waiting somewhere, unheard, like a cuckoo in its shell, along with all the problems of him handling fame and acclamation still to come!'

She's capered up, she wears the costume – a sheath, open here and there, green hood curled right over, like a jack-in-the-pulpit, silver slippers neither of us heard approaching.

Melissa tells me, coming through the door, ignoring him. 'Tidiane,' she says, 'he never made, never uncovered, a complete human. He never found another one that wasn't eroded, self-destructive, just decaying in nature, by nature – it seemed an impossible task, patching up the obsolete. I took him on here – people have such a desire to punish and be punished – except they start off by not meaning it. Then it comes on naturally....'

'It was pleasure, Melissa,' I say. 'You were into pleasure and anticipation, then you changed: and it became utility. Food. That's all over everywhere, where there's money, plenty: everyone is full of it!' We laugh.

'Dromy and Slick – they garden still,' she says. 'Of course, if you don't have food, you don't want to see it all day on TV.'

'I know I made an easy compromise,' says Tidiane. 'I seek, but I don't cure. But this Jimbo guy – I'm sure there's something shady here....'

'You should see people as your instrument, Tidiane,' I say. 'Not as furniture you can restore, but ancient brasses, ready for you to play your own compositions on. That's beauty for a start – try for perfection in that way....'

'Still the opera, Jimbo!' Melissa says and laughs. 'You were saved. It didn't flop, and there it stands, inert, potentially, a flower upright in its little field. It's your eternal future.'

'They all say that,' I say.

I could cry.

'I bought into here,' she says. 'Hervé comes most nights. We have a thing between us – but it hasn't stuck....'

'I had such passion for you, Melissa – I could scarcely breathe....' I say.

'There was always something not quite there about you, Jimbo,' she says, looking at me as a clinician would. 'Complicity. Intemperance. Not violence exactly: – rather – abundance. Is vainglory the word? Full, and spilling over. That's the thought.'

'Dromy was a manipulator,' I say. 'Though there was nothing in anything for him. A big part in an opera that wasn't staged? Saturday nights as an *apache*, Sundays tending to the marrows....'

'He had the hots for Slick,' Melissa says. 'It didn't work. He was the opposite of you – he was gay, women went crazy for him....'

'Dromy or Slick?' I ask, losing the tack. She doesn't say.

'We never had our time together, Melissa. I forget why,' I say. 'I'm so sad, so very sad there is no past between us.... Hervé lives always in the present. Is that time? – I don't know where thought and speculation stand – not the present, not particularly, a river isn't only present, even a stream, a ditch, a sewer – is in and out of time, and in all times.... A critic's a sea-anemone – it swallows whatever comes along....'

'You're right,' she says, 'Tidiane can open up. We could go together ... we could go clubbing.'

Not to Delinda's club, I hope – there are so many others. 'You're more down to earth than I remember, Melissa,' I say. 'Though you don't dig so much.' We laugh.

'I never knew you properly,' Melissa says. 'You've been down so many wormholes since that time. You'll have a sense of humour now.'

'No,' I say. 'I don't think that at all.'

'Tidiane can run the show,' she says, ignoring me. 'He hits them hard. It's disappointment. People treat themselves so bad.... He hates being shown he's right, he hits out, people hurting themselves ... it makes a circle ... he's vindicated, all are beaten worse....'

'Are there deaths?' I ask.

'Oh, those there always are: life is quite dull unless you take the risks like you have done.... And then there's failure too, it grinds you down. But – let's try the place where the philosophers go. There's many clubs, and some are secret, but in the end – there is a club of clubs. That's where they are –' And so we go.

*

There's club armchairs in grey and brown, deep as a badger's lair. 'Those are the skins of grizzlies and of elephants,' Melissa says. 'Philosophers don't give a toss about the animals, of course, but that's where where they sit and argument – they twist around, even those tough skins are wearing out....'

'It's quiet,' I say. 'The bar is dry – no flights of fancy here, I guess....'

'Oh Jimbo, I have thought of that,' she says. 'Eat this....' It's a large pill. 'And down the rabbit-hole you'll go.'

It makes me feel drunk, at once. 'And do we do philosophy?' I ask.

'If you've some trouble on your mind,' she says. 'It's like pub games. You choose a partner, and you say – "I have a brain, but do I have a mind?" and someone answers yes or no. It's a laugh! Why don't chimps speak Mandarin? That kind of thing – "what's a just war?", "how do you measure punishment?" – the kind of thing the other clubs avoid, or else they give you answers quick as light, and light as quick....'

It's exactly as it was, with Hervé, Dromy recommending that first club. Melissa's sheath is halfway off, her body goes fast forward, presses against me, she peeks up at me, though she has to bend ... she says:

'I love tall men, and, Jimbo – you are small and bent. But – this is now your evening come at last. Ask your question here, then we'll go back to my room. And if Dromy isn't there, playing electric solitaire – we'll consumate what we began those years ago....'

I ought to ask, 'what's my complicity?' This club is made to answer me. I engaged: in ignorance. To change the world, they say.... That's a big deal, especially if everybody tries at once. If I had stayed at home, I'd have given consent to anything, my side, their side, none, abstain – but knowing how awful things are done by every side – am I then liable for anything?.... Even for inaction? Is that the best choice or the worst?

'The cops don't come in here,' a guy tells me. 'Anything you say and advocate – is privileged. But you, my friend, you're jittering and sweating.... What did you do? What did you know?'

'Well,' I say, 'I think we know it all: the past and future – where our actions and inactions have led, will lead. The doing this or that: it falls on to a line, a spectrum, though I don't know who it is that draws it up.... Isn't it you?' I ask.

'Fortunately, no,' he says. 'We're just like you. We ask the questions, but the right answer has no power.... We live quite poor. This bar is dry, you need ID to get a ginger ale.'

'That's rather good,' Melissa says, dragging me away. 'Being dry as dust. There'd be hemlock chasers all around if they go wet....'

We laugh, we two. 'You're here,' she tells me, holding me up vertical, as I sag. 'To enjoy yourself. There are sights quite outré, remarkable, unseen elsewhere, and there's no hurt, confusion's good for mind and brain, and in the end you leave unscathed, still mystified and ready for another throw – those dice are round, not square, Jimbo, you always win, but there's no stake.... The stake is in you from the start, your telltale heart.... Trust me, my dear – I'm your white rabbit, I'll help you find love, and your way out of it....'

There is a press, it's difficult to reach the door.

The guys throng round, approving of her intellect, her jigs and jogs and slides, the references....

'Enjoy yourself, dear Jimbo,' says Melissa. 'You never know if this is your last time, you have no cash, you can't buy in, and Hervé never wrote his piece of puff about what you'd not done and didn't have performed....'

I hear 'cash'. 'Maybe they can help me with economics here,' I say, but she laughs –

'You think there'd be an annex? No, there's another club ... it's fierce! If you want a workout, bare-knuckle – try that – not today...! Here, they don't do rich and poor, it oughtn't to interfere with anything....'

'It's fun here,' I say. 'Melissa – I could stay, if I had a sample of those pills....'

'No, no,' Melissa says. 'A club of clubs is a logical necessity, but that doesn't mean it's always open, or that I'm usually supplied with stuff. Most people aren't interested in a dry philosophy club, the bar, that is, although philosophy is theirs, should be, about them, as they're people.... It seems contradictory – say, it contains contradictions: not the same thing; but it's complicated. And anyway, it's not my thing....

'Take me: I'm a real person, I make society, I supply a need. You, Jimbo, you create for no takers: you aren't part of anything. Where will you end up? With the fascists, or down at the economics club, looking for a handout? People we are, separate; how many philosophies might we need?'

'This is old stuff, Melissa,' I say. 'In a few moments we'll be lovers: we'll be something else – a couple coupling, multiplying, being one. Society and politics – they're there, Melissa, already. We don't make them, none of us does that. It takes millions to make them fall, still more to have them change. They're mountains, and there's no guarantee a transformation would be right for you.... What I create – it is irrelevant. If it goes, it goes, if not – you try to trot it round, do something else ... the same ... a variant. Nothing, zero: a result that can't be counted, so it doesn't count....

'There's no dilemma – as beings, we're the same, Melissa, but we've spent our time separately.... We were two, now we'll be one, and yet ... there's something odd about my maths....'

'Collect your coat,' Melissa says. 'If you didn't leave one, they'll give you another skin – the museum is de-acquisitioning.... They have thousands, animal and not.'

*

We go back to her club. I'm rubbery. There's a spiral stair outside I hadn't seen – tubular, like a fire escape. Melissa pushes me up, it makes you giddy, round and round, a rabbit-burrow in the sky – it's very high, the wind is powerful, the skin they gave me at the club of clubs flaps in the storm – it's of no particular colour, transparent, it would seem – that's how it ought to be, fits all.... I'm giggling, and I say, I shout! – '*je est un autre* – I am Jedermann – the phantom of the opera! the perfect sacrifice in Tenochtitlan, the flayed man, the victim dead that brings another year of life ... the monkey on my back ... hurrah! – I have a tail!'

Don't look down, never....

Up and up until I'm in a room....

Round and round it goes – the furniture – there's an unmade double bed, Hervé asleep across it, mottled, naked; in an alcove; pictures of vegetables, mostly leeks, not hung, standing against the walls.

'I feel,' Melissa says, 'that what you want, to be one, then maybe two again – the act you have prescribed, anticipated, so you say, for years, until it's stale, you're stale – it palls, the sex; we're bored before it starts....

'We can't wake Hervé, he doesn't eat or snore.... Forget him, forget why he is here.

'Sex. Love. In the real, the act comes up against one better or even worse than you imagined; or maybe the disaster: just the same in the reality as you had fantasised.... You always say – distrust the real. But what if your imaginary should coincide with what is real – you've killed imagination, Jimbo! Consider what you've done!'

There's laughter, but I don't see anyone except Hervé, who sleeps and sleeps, mute, no wall to bounce off, dice or balls.... I ask 'Tidiane?' It seems he's shut the club below, not found perfection, taken out his rage – disposed of clients, quick and dead ... then, his room somewhere, full of irritation....

'Your plot, your fantasy,' Melissa says, hugging my arm, 'it seems, well – medieval. At the most – enlightenment: the great debate. Is each of us the judge? Fumbling to uncertainty? Or melding into everyone, consensus, union... Where do we come in, Jimbo, between the crooked timbers and the mystic union?

'I had another thought ....'

What might that be?

'The opera!' Melissa says, 'Dromy and Slick fell out. There was a duel with spades – Slick protected his embouchure, his knees were unprotected – he fell ... a trench....'

'I don't want Dromy in my opera,' I say. 'I don't want my opera in travesty, tiny, three people....'

'The spirit always lives,' says Melissa. 'Dromy does the voices, all of them. You see time pass, the voices change, go up and ultimately down, they crack, they're composted and as the stage comes round – it starts again....'

'What would this be,' I start. 'Is it always that you, Melissa, can't distinguish the punishment from the prize?'

Melissa laughs, and mimics me: '"... can't distinguish the punishment from the prize?" Punished for what? What you've done and it is finished, gone? Rewarded? Or what you hope will come but don't know when? Maybe prize, or maybe punishment? It's my job, Jimbo. If you want certainty – put nets on your strawberries, like we did; don't risk falling out, like Slick, or you might fall in – where you don't want, a black hole for the leeks, a trench, the loam you'll never sprout from....'

'Dromy's a seducer,' I say. 'Who of us has he seduced?'

'Because he does the voices?' Melissa asks, amused. 'He's just a boy. He didn't send poor Hervé off, into his sleep....'

'I could believe you gave him pills, like you did me,' I say.

'Pleasure and utility,' she says. 'What does either need of pills?'

'With your rules,' I say. 'If we were immortal, one day we could make something happen. Since we're mortal – everything is postponed, death intervenes, and – then you can't continue....'

'But what a splendid life you've had!' she says. 'Listen, we could resurrect Hervé. He would be a useless lover, if he were awake – criticising after the fact, or the non fact.... No one listens to him now – who needs another critic? You do it all yourself!

'Your opera. Even in miniature – it would have the essence – the turning world of work, accomplishment, through time – the everything, the voices changing but continuous.... A little dull....'

'There'd be no public,' I object.

'There's you,' she says. 'The rest – what would they add? Would they grasp more than you do?'

'It isn't what I wanted,' I say. 'I know – nothing is, nothing can be, what you wanted, and it's good that way....'

'No, no,' Melissa says. 'Not good. It's terrible – like, maybe your opera's no good, but anyway, it is your chance of life. A tiny opera is all you get, down in the rabbit-hole.

'Dromy – the soloist, the chorus, the supporting cast – it sounds eccentric, second-rate – but really it is the most original thing there is. It could be yours, all yours! It's the world, when Valhallah's burned. Who survives?'

'I don't remember, but there was a sequel planned, there always is,' I say.

'Well, this time, our world, there will be no after-thought, no one to after-think. You should have written the last scene, not blamed lacunae on poor Giselda. You held it all, in that small throbbing head,' she says, squeezing my temples.

'No,' I say, 'the last scene – it couldn't go on for ever, so everybody must decide where to make it end ... of course, the end's unknowable until it happens and then it is too late. You must realise that; compromise, applaud. That's a fine ending. My idea was – it was to be intuited, carried home, like the steak you couldn't finish, took home to your dog.'

'There,' she says, 'you're reasoning like me! Don't gobble food, think of the rest – give Dromy his big break.'

'... not what I wanted,' I say.

'If I want something else, what you wanted either isn't what you want or what you can't have,' she says. 'Be reasonable. Take what comes – even in miniature. Besides – I hear you are wanted too – a bandit, terrorist. In many parts they string up dissidents – religion, politics, colour, even use of language or of dress.... Each place on earth – it has a reason and a case for shutting you away, or shooting you at dawn – or, quite by hazard, driving past. If somewhere you'd mistook the line you mustn't cross, the rules, the orders, your disorders and your rules – no one will be surprised. Or shocked. An excess of spirit on your part? It seems unlikely, marginal, that you are dangerous – but it'll take your life and more to straighten it all out....

'Let's do your opera, and have done with it.'

*

The house rocks like a tree – the room's a twiggy nest – it seems those never fall. I'm still high, under the spell. 'Where's Slick?' I ask, as Dromy enters.

'He's a bogman,' Dromy says. 'I spaded him, buried him in the black soil. He'll root and in the spring, we'll eat him.'

'There!' says Melissa. 'The club has taught you something! See, Jimbo, that's where sex can take you. Spring onions.'

Dromy's voice – is quite remarkable. Five octaves, sonorous in each.

'I've done a medley,' Dromy says. 'Your stuff goes round and round, Jimbo: it ends quite arbitrarily – so, follow the logic; I'll do it in short order – "swallow me" it seems to say! Let it go down your throat, like an elixir ... blow out your pipes and blow your brain....'

'Cool it, Dromy,' I tell him. 'I know my work by heart, Hervé's asleep, Melissa can't hold a tune.... You've buried Slick.... We reach an end. What more can my creation bear? Don't rouse the fiery beast, the dragon. In this room, we are an everything, it's all contained within our skins.... What's not included here? Do you glimpse some other profound effect I can bring off....? I can't imagine more....'

*

How we all dug!

Those gardens – I see down through their undergrounds, there's catacombs; silent Hervés, Slicks greasing slides and polishing their bells, Melissa with a taper, her black sheath flapping shut and open as she inspects the cubicles, the living dead, the boneless skins – a pinch here, a punch there – encouragement and homespun sense.... Sleepers. No sleeper wakes....

Maybe ... the monkey skin. Does it suit? Do I keep it on, what is its end, should Dromy bury it like he says he's done for Slick?

'The monkeys have a catacomb,' Melissa says. 'Just skins: once, they were all the rage, as talismans ... we can lay you down right there, Jimbo, you naughty boy, you monkey! – always thinking of your sex and showing off....'

*

'Hold it, Melissa,' I shout. 'Let me come down, or up, into the night, out of my hole, into the whole.... I'd need set up the opera, Dromy must have his note.... But – I'm disoriented, now's not the time for food of love.... That pill – so powerful, my love, Melissa....'

'It wasn't a hallucigen,' Melissa says. 'You looked hungry, that is all. I gave no pill: a biscuit, though ... even a madaleine, to help bring on the grand, the grandest opera...!'

'It needs more work,' I say, 'to bring it down – to chamber size, even for soloists, song-cycle.... Dromy, of course – if he's available....'

'There!' says Melissa. 'All settled. I'm exhausted – tomorrow I have early shift, down at the club.'

Hervé grunts, he doesn't wake when Melissa pushes him to make herself a space.

'Tomorrow, Jimbo, we'll discuss your plan,' she says.

*

I wait till all is quiet – Dromy, now fugitive, makes off.

The spiral staircase; in the wind, it yaws and pitches, but I make it down. I check – no, I left nothing behind, nothing at all.

I set off in the dark.

2

ROUND THE WORLD

THE TARPOT fell from the top of our mast into a grey-green wall of wave.

'We won't capsize,' she says. 'Perk up! There's two kinds of sea-sick – storm and saunter. You should eat so you can throw up.... It's quite rough. We have lost our smudge....'

Lateen, feluca, norfolk rig: going-about, the yard-arm ... *à fleur d'eau* ... all hands, the plank, the deep.... I remember the words, none is as wild or heaped so high as these seas now.... Don't panic: think motion, control, and calm. This – hers, Sabrine – is an adventure; you're supposed to seek those out. It must need me, the chronicler Miro, come for the story, to find a space between the stays, the anchor, capstan, porthole ... to devise the news I hope will not be me ... my fate. Full fathom five. All these names, the stuff tied on, just to ride the sea....

We see wobbly rubber boats, trying to put an awful land behind them. The people waved, we waved. We're all mariners. We made smoke to show we're here, but probably they knew. We can't do anything, interrupt their crossing – it's not a river, there's no boatman: they've spent their obols on their craft.

They must have some hope.

'You must love risk, Sabrine ... those guys, they didn't have much chance,' I say.

'I understand them: it's a test, you come through and your life is wholly different,' she says. 'You can rest, do nothing, nothing for ever ... or face the rite, the extreme: you've been tried, you overcome. That's it. There's enormous danger – you face up to it, and I'll come through, then it will all be safe and different.

'When I make land, I get the cash. It makes the past worthwhile, the future profitable.'

She's busy, busy, hauling on some ropes.

'I need some colour ... my readers don't want battleship grey,' I say. 'Meeting mermen, flying fish? – our friends the whales. Solitude, desolation and despair.'

She's dry as oatcake. Imaginative as plaster board. She's dry and clipped, I'm soaked.

'I picked you up to give you just a sense,' she says. 'A run across this enormous bay – a sketch, a cross-hatch of my experience, to give life to the interview. It's the wind – it drove us off – it's pneuma, breath. You need it, must submit and bend.

'You do the tribute to me, not you, remember.'

*

A great mistake: sailing alone around the world – the world is land, not faceless sea. Lands full of people speaking what you cannot understand.

There's a group of welcome on the quay. As I try standing still, the asphalt rocks and chassays like Jonah's tuna, trying to spew out prophecy.

*

There's snappers – the fish, and guys with cameras: that's whimsy, can't put it in my piece, but can't get rid of it. I laugh.

'Fear's good for you,' she says. 'Then you feel light.'

'The fear is with me always,' I say. 'This was extra dread.'

'Why does the paper send you, then, if you're a cowardy?' she asks.

'Like you,' I say, 'the cash. I do what the others wouldn't want. The dangerous parts of life.'

'I've had the danger, you were simply tossed about,' she says. 'Nothing. Anyway, if there's trouble, they come and fish you up. And if it's worse – you drown. A common grave – all sorts ... sea-boots and cement shoes, a last gasp, and you're fish dinner.'

'Of course,' I say. 'I intuited the mechanism, not the point of what it is you do. Or hope you won't....'

'What other stories have you done?' she asks.

'Oh, bio-engineering. Pointless scientific stuff,' I say. 'They take a bit of flesh – or gloopy substance from your brain, and see how far you'll go, and if you'll have a happy life. They think they're on to something wonderful....'

'What's your take on my exploit?' she asks. 'My adventure?'

'A pointless peaceful show,' I say, offguard and nauseous. 'Some guys with knife and bomb can shake a people: you show you are the opposite: a person facing down the tempest, entirely for themselves, for a fleeting wonder....'

'That can't be all,' she says, irritated. 'Maybe you're post-catholic?'

'Or,' I say. 'When whole populations are persecuted, expelled, imprisoned, terrorised – you show an individual can take the stage and show they're powerful, disinterested – heroine without a cause, a warrior without an enemy....'

'You're wrong,' she says. 'I have an enemy. This godless sea, its uncommunicating shapeless beasts, its violent moods, the longing – drag you down and suffocate, the swashing contrary of peaceful grass and cows....'

'I suggest – the world spins – instead of beating it, try standing still. Not round the world, but "the world round you...." Though, with your muscles you could haul a barge, and be of use....' I say. She doesn't listen –

'My agent should be here. He has the cash....' she says, searching the departing bunch of puffers, snappers, and the brassy band.

They have transport, gas – it seems that we do not, must not....

'It's all too late, too bad,' I say. 'You thanked your team. That is your signing off. Your contract's done.'

'Then, for the moment, I am destitute,' she says.

*

This, then, is my story. Not Zola, Dickens, not a Tragedy. No apparent Crime. No Swann's retreat – not yet a swan-song. My little article, falling, dropping like the philosopher's tortoise from clear skies, bang to my small profit. More and more, always the same. The life, more life, then the death, again evaded by a canvas ... of the super-nova, Sabrine. Remember the name, or you'll forget it.

*

'I have a room,' I say. 'You could come, briefly, there. Don't tie up your boat – they'll make you pay. Just let it make its history – drift, if it must.

'I have one preoccupation – all of us who're fearful know that suicide is our last bet, our last throw. You must have often thought of that, when you planned your escapade, and every day, with cool death just beyond your gunwales, you were just a step away ... maybe you thought survival was a shaman's attestation, that you'd been down to hell, aand therefore suicide was a pleonasm, a second death – it might be called your *scaramanzia*, a means of conjuring away bad luck....

'I don't want this, your death, to happen in my place: I am precarious. An unknown athlete in my bed, self-murdered after some great test – it will not hold.... It won't compute with cops....'

'I hadn't thought,' she says. 'It's true, I had death close to me, my berth held death, we slept together every night and every day – there's nothing else.... I'm finely-tuned, dedicated to a muscular life, my emissions negligeable, and yet ... maybe you're right. I made myself so strong that suicide, not sickness or an accident, was my only hope....'

'It's so banal,' I say, 'and yet you do not know you're blind, although you cannot see. You proclaim life and struggle, but seek death, surrender. Is your lesson this – tread the line between death and life, if the result is death, it's fate, or chance, bad luck or clumsiness.... The sea is that, fatal and unpredictable....'

She hugs me. 'It must be so. Don't write it, though. I'll tell you what to say....'

And so she does.

*

'Who would grieve for you?' I ask, as we eat our separate food.

'Oh, I've no one,' she says, 'I'm insupportable, I live quite alone.'

It's a lie, quite evidently. Everybody lies, so it's the motivation counts.... I know all about her, she's been researched. We, staff, write our own biographies. We're fired if we conceal... As a writer, the truth's my occupation – it's very hard. You have to cheat, all the time. People are brazen, do anything, clean themselves, tell more lies all round. I remember the *Maison de rendez-vous:* 'there is nothing in her eyes'.

'You don't show your cards,' she says. 'You have nothing in your eyes.'

'I'm sorry,' I say, although I'm not. 'Communication depends on repetition, it doesn't matter if it's true or not – we communicate because we've heard it all before, over and over. Lies keep the troop together, it's what water is for elephants; they walk, nomads, vast distances, to quench their thirst. We live by first and last words of tales – beginnings and ends: "hallo" and "I wish I'd known them better." Sometimes, for a change, "in the middle of life's journey", then – "my ship of genius catches the wind for better waters...."'

'Which of us is the genius? You've given up your ship, it's become a metaphor....'

'Hallo is quite neutral,' she says. '"Hallo".'

'You're not going to understand me,' I say, 'I can see that. It's going to be a dull few hours.'

'If you only quote,' she says. 'It will be purgatory. Remember, though – "the moribund have two fingers only – but they keep them crossed". I could be your lucky day.'

'It's true,' I say. 'Though I can't live on fortune – covering the stories the others wouldn't do. If you want a publicist....'

She laughs, 'O no! I've been through that. I'm not looking for an elephant to ride – that slow motion trudge, the little eager ones, dying under thorn trees ... breaking those heavy mothering hearts.'

Hers is a story of fame, summits and abyss ... not to be trusted.

'The solitude can kill,' she says. 'But those big overloaded rusting ships – a desolation.'

*

'Either I'm me,' says Sabrine. 'Or I have a team to help me challenge. I'm the same, still me. The cash from the last adventure funds the next. Or else it is the void. Nothing. Down among people like you, Miro.'

'Your image, Sabrine – I see it clear. A handmade pic. A wicker throne, two small elephants to water you, a lotus in your hand ...' I say, 'Lakshmi!'

'Exactly so,' she says. 'Immortality is excluded, but worship and divinity persist. I'll take what I can. But – it must be feats. Not stunts.'

'I'll ask around,' I say. 'There's boxing. And there's teams.'

'Sticks and balls?' she asks. 'I don't see too well. Besides – there's too much touch and kiss. Boxing – much the same, except the kiss is one of death.... I've had all that, the normalcy. Living with a beast, a species unpredictable, with habits indeterminate – promiscuous; deserts the kids ... in nature, you'd say "solitaries", all behaviour there's the same. Like – we humankind: you're born into a family – there's people round you, watch you eat ... strangers, then strangers in your bunk, all claws and suckers ... oh! the sea, the sea! Endless solitude. And you, Miro – you feel a bit the same ... the vodka, and every evening on the street ... you swim alone.... On your own, you've escaped. You're not in nature....'

'It's to pick up stuff,' I say. 'The gossip. It's our trade. We mix with different crowds....'

'Crowds:' says Sabrine. 'On you, like a hydra. Like mating toads. I know – sex is a species thing, unavoidable It's indiscriminate, like where you work, always a bunch of guys unknown. I understand; and it's not me. People club around. Poor things. My boat – asked nothing: on its own, it floats. That's good.'

'We're supposed to be the individualists,' I say. 'Do you see Chinese sailing round?'

'Lots,' she says. 'They're not reported: they must be there for something else ... They have cheap boats. Those never sink – but they aren't comfortable.'

She discards assistants. They're young – they scatter. Older – there's nothing. The very old ... a host.

'You've no loyalty to your friends,' I say. 'No mentors. But there's the ancients: why, Sabrine?'

'They're a bore,' she says. 'They want to hold your hand and cuddle up. But they don't move. You can decide exactly when to leave and when to come.... What they try to say – is all in books. But – they're on a threshold – like sailing off the world....'

'I can understand you,' I say. 'You want to know all about death, but not a word on ageing. I can't believe you're interested in their wills. Death is more determinate than sex – neither gives you satisfaction, but when you die, you can't try it all again.'

*

Deadlines. When you write, you don't have evenings free, so beginning sex – it can't start.

Besides – Sabrine chatters while you concentrate.

'The time between one thing and another,' says Sabrine. 'Is awful. Awfully long. When you're on the sea, there is no time: just lots the same, and when there's change, there's death in every breath of wind....'

'Anyway, you've done all that,' I say. 'What next?'

'What you just said – is right. It's wrong, but catches part of me: if I had children, I'd love them so much more than whoever I had had them with – and they'd be cold to me, think I was a mere performer,' Sabrine says. 'They'd neglect themselves, and die, die before me, leave me on my own; and all the cash I meant for them – it would be wasted. On the ocean, I thought all this through.'

'It's easy,' I say. 'You won't need money, so forget it. Don't do anything you are afraid of.'

'You don't listen,' she says, and laughs.

'Hurry!' I say. 'They've forgotten you already.'

'I can't believe you're right about sex, and all that follows,' Sabrine says.

'Is it an adventure?' I ask. 'It seems so, perhaps, but – nothing follows. Sex is an adventure lots of people have – it's hard to feel it's special: so, it could be war, or spying: pretty much routine. Look – I've a five-litre can of vodka here – sometimes, if you drink all that – you die. Peter Pan might have considered that....'

'Drink's so impersonal,' she says. 'Like you. You're probably a modernist, walking to Antarctica.'

'Being impersonal's the point,' I say. 'If you're doing something. Otherwise you wouldn't. Wouldn't take the risk. Wouldn't do anything at all.'

*

'I've spoken to the people, Sabrine,' I say. 'People who can fix you, everything. Do something that we didn't talk about – doing something useful. Scientifically, at least....'

'I'm not sure I believe you, Miro,' Sabrine says. 'It's too easy.'

'We put you in a pod,' I say. 'Wired up, we send you round and round the earth. We'll monitor your ageing, then your death. Measure it all. You won't have kids. Not much sex. You can't have cash – you're extra-territorial, they'll jail you if you try to use your card up there: export of capital. You know it all, exactly, how it goes on, and so – there is no fear. You're better off than those they send up further – to find a place to colonise. Better than being bombarded.'

'Yes,' she says. 'Choice is like that, like you say. My options? There's walking. Saving animals, or archaeology. It's all a dream.... Like those Americans, got left up on the moon; their ship, it broke ... they had the cyanide....'

'Yes,' I say. 'The guy who writes these stories – irresponsible, but I envy his imagination ... the Russians wanted to send them up some dogs for company, but the Central Committee put a stop to that....'

We laugh. We're not amused.

'You didn't sail all round the world, Sabrine,' I say. 'I wrote the story, so I know the truth.'

'There's always something not quite so, a little extra, or a little less, that you don't emphasise,' she says. 'Nothing that is written down is real. It's real, that is, as writing down.'

'You need a challenge, and we'll find you one,' I say. 'And write it down.'

*

'Julietta – she's my friend – she doesn't live here. We touch antennas,' I tell Sabrine. 'We're a mismatch, we don't want to separate. We've both read similar books – we're the only ones who have, round here. She has ideas....'

'That isn't new,' Sabrine says. 'Having an idea. It makes no difference....'

'The truth,' says Julietta, 'I despise it. The false – it comes in many colours, it attracts, it jazzes up – it leads you to the slough, creates despond and mirth and boredom....'

I explain to Sabrine. 'Julietta's in electronics. Instant news. This true and false thing people are disturbed about. She runs all over that.... I expect she'll think of something you'll do next, Sabrine.'

There's lots of silence. Probably suspicion too. My room – gives nothing away – me and Julietta, never eat there, watching the jaws move, like big ants'. I work nights, or sleep, she goes deep in town with me; we separate.

'You two aren't like all the people that I know. Of course, my people are alive right now,' says Sabrine. 'I don't know if you're dead or coming round a long long bend in future time.'

'How are we different, Sabrine?' asks Julietta.

'You're like two eggs,' says Sabrine. 'Quite big, quite white. The people I know are multicoloured, messy. They have sex with people who're too old, or very very young, their relatives ... they're scared of jail, but not enough ... if they're being rooked, they shout, don't pay. They have a point of view and tell you, loud, so you can't avoid. They don't know quotes, they know who all the famous people are. They go to places you've not heard of.'

'That's ordinary,' I say. 'Heroic times are gone. You join an army for the pay, and to get vendetta done and pardoned. People risk their lives to get in here, this country – just down the beach, they lose their lives for trying, even before they've seen the sea.

'Live hugger-mugger, sometimes make a splash – it's not for us. We live like somebody.'

'Off-white eggs,' says Julietta. 'We do exactly what we want, what we can. We're not sloppy, that is all. This way you can go anywhere, not leave a trace.'

'And there's a single rule,' I say. 'Don't steal from friends.'

'If I believe you,' Sabrine says, 'then I'm a friend.'

'That's news to me,' says Julietta. 'You've got rich and want to give it all away. I'll help you forget all that, and make you thrill yourself.'

'I'm not used to talking,' says Sabrine. 'You're quite demanding – I'll stay quiet, just lie down here.'

*

We go out, like we usually do, Julietta, me. I ask Julietta, 'The surveillance. How far have they got?'

'You're confusing,' Julietta says. 'Controls and order: controls go on, of course – that's science and its march, it doesn't heed your questions or your fears. The big chiefs think more control means more order. It isn't so. Reality, with gas and gun; that grows; hovers overhead.

'You stagger on, poor Miro! And now your sailor with her yarn, fate's knitting.... Distraction!

'In the next country down the shore – there is a coup. We must pin it down! Write and snap!

'Here we're needled, bleed and suffer – but we vote. What do we know? Provocation makes the whole scene totter, we're a pile of stones without cement, built high and shaking.... Wake up, Miro! We must be on hand, report the news to save our souls, stand in the front line, and then prepare to flee....'

*

No doubt she's right. People will call the soldiers in, they fear the poor and foreign so – we're mostly both of those. Or else they find the guys they vote for are crooks who steal their cash....

I know all that, I can't be bothered with it.... I'm in a paradox.... My interest in Sabrine has turned to sex. You'd call it attraction, love; but no one does. Gender – that comes in as well.... I have no interest in finding new adventure trails for her....

*

But Julietta's right. Danger has come ashore, like a tide-wave.

The street where we hang out each night changes its colour like a blob, a jelly in the sea that blushes on the pink, turns indigo or flame.... We have no refuge – we are chroniclers: as precarious as happenstance.

*

There is no resolution. Sex with Sabrine – sombre, evanescent: impossible, as well. She is a pilgrim, trekking to invisible shrines. I'm the tempter – but not tempting....

Julietta – ready to analyse the scene, not ready to escape the danger to our lives....

*

'Ask your Sinbad,' Julietta says. 'What "round the world" means to her. Maybe we've both done the trip already many times. We should go to the big manif – wear your armour, Miro, don't bring your horse. Bring Sabrine, though.'

I ask Sabrine, 'Round the world – one go? Or is it distances? A lot of trips, all adding up...?'

'It's sophistry,' says Sabrine. 'What difference does it make? Round is a long dull lumpy distance. "In one go" – ridiculous.'

'The cash?' I press her –

'It goes to charity,' she says. 'It goes to me, and I decide which one. And when.'

'To me, it doesn't matter – I'm not a literalist,' I say. 'I record, I don't investigate. But....'

'I sail,' Sabrine says, 'upon the sea. You don't. To circumnavigate, to do it all at once, would be a blind obsession. Monstrous. Compile the distances you have covered, in months, in years – it's professionality. Persistence, discipline, and loyalty.'

'In the end,' I say, 'it's you who sees if there's anomaly in what you say, how seriously you take it....'

'No,' she says, 'the problem's you – you make assumptions, then blame me....'

'Explorers, pirates – it does happen so,' I say. 'You say you went to Canton, but it's Boston; Bahia, not Mumbai. In general – I'm for it. People, places – should move around, shuffle the charts, manipulate the maps – it's rather good. Then there's the Polo trip – tales from the Persian markets – in the end, someone went somewhere else, brought back the tale, a sack of noodles.... All's for the best. It's bringing the human down to human size: – modesty, containment. Like being lovers – all there is, is love, and nothing more; you have many lovers, but never drop your pants....'

'I never heard that anywhere before,' she says. 'It sounds perverse.'

'You're interesting, Sabrine,' I say, peeking at her salty clothes, to see how they settle and unsettle, pitch and toss. 'You have so many registers, and voices too – street, naive, unique.... The most alluring things is – you do big useless tasks, like Hercules – but have no vision....'

'I forget,' she says, 'he must have had a point, a goal. Someone to screw, some insult to avenge....'

'I have a vision, Sabrine,' I say, and slide my arm around her. 'To me, the world is juke-box. It plays every melody you've ever heard of, from the top; but when it reaches the disc marked "tragedy", it stutters, goes back to the beginning....'

'Yes, it's sad,' she says, pulling away. 'But you have Julietta. She's a tragedy....'

Tragedy means having the exits sealed. Not disorder, not regret – just having no way on. It doesn't fit Julietta, not at all.

*

'Julietta struggled to be impersonal,' I say. 'It means being
treated as what you are. Then, the flat, the factual becomes our
work. We report, but we don't judge: can't give money or
bandage someone up, comfort a child. We are gods. Don't
intervene. If you have readers, they suffer lightly, like sparrows
feeling the sun's heat, then fluttering on....'

'Do they care?' Sabrine asks. 'You could criticise me, but it
wouldn't matter. Do I exaggerate? Someone would say the
opposite. And – you must have crew: they'll have pills for the
moribund, a caramel for orphans....'

'They resent working for us gods,' I say, 'while they are
mortals. For everything, they blame the boss, not life. With us,
they risk, with no reward. We too have no reward. Truth and
falsehood – neither weighs, has worth. Do I mention truth? The
truth, Sabrine – it's huge,' I say. 'I see the feet, a toe. It is a cliff
– you can't climb up, besides, there's fierce birds and mists,
parrots in their holes that nip your fingers. I can describe those
feet....'

'Cliffs don't have feet,' she says.

'Then, it's something else, a mountain or a sculpture, human-
made – Babylon, or Mount Rushmore; Masada, the Assassins'
fortress.... My exaggeration? Don't be a silly, Sabrine. Question
the metaphors, be a sceptic. Disbelieve me. Follow lies, live
them, make them ... I've found you out. What do I care? I know
you're human: you've made your body look like one. Today it
might just be true. Shortly – just brittle boney twigs: or suet ...
all truths are fleeting, end up false.

'Maybe you're right about Julietta too – a tragedy. Waiting
down the road....'

*

'Monkeys do rough justice,' Julietta says, 'But, as I observed in
our back yard – the animals who ingratiate themselves – it does
no good. They end up massacred. Humans don't do justice –
they do food.

'I decided not to end like animals. Do not ingratiate. Don't fight them, the humans – you will lose. Watch yourself, don't watch the animals, or anybody else at all. Choose hard things. You gave yourself a tough life, Sabrine, so no one else would give you one. Where next?'

'Here and back again?' Sabrine asks, rhetorically. 'Back round the world, unwind my wake? I'm adrift. Enough, the sea. It's ready to swallow all of us: it has no gut, no throat. It's amniotic death, amidst those bladdery shapes....'

'Miro,' Julietta goes on, not listening, 'thinks the truth is on us, imminent. You can find it – just a look, a gesture. There, he thinks, it is: awaits discovery. It isn't so: truth must be made, like lies. The manufacture's similar.

'He would have been a Tupamaro – not in the street, but up there, safe in his brain. Keeping the secret truth, "the world is as it is, but we can make it different".... Then onward.... The path appears. You follow it.

'I know his argument. I'm on his side, but steady, on my sidelines. The people oppressed – they'll have their days of liberty, manifest, demonstrate – get killed, get pumped up with their victories: then all reopens; the flag has changed, the stores resume ... cops, the soldiers, commerce, treaties once again ... and the people wait, until the next false dawn....

'The country next to us – is like that. We'll go, record – but it will end the same.

'I'm tired of militants. I want to find long-sighted folk.The question now is this: Suicide? Or Survival – in some radical way. What would those people look like, who are preparing for that choice?'

'When they decide, we join them?' Sabrine asks, 'or maybe not?'

'No, no,' says Julietta, 'we tell the story, we don't join. Those second comings, floods, the plagues, over and over – this time it isn't God who threatens us, it's guys in white coats with slide rules, who advise, and warn. Science, Sabrine.

'Science says the end is nigh, unless.... Miro says that science only tells you why what is is as it is. It can't ask: why? Why are we here, why did we struggle so to reach a top, a knowledge of the mechanism; how while doing so, we broke the grand design, and off we're swept ... the earth becomes a whirling ember ... forward, after times incalculable, strides another sour fruit of evolution. Maybe it won't eat pomegranates, enjoy incest, write villanelles: but it will climb the ladder, up to the stars, and when it falls – it knocks the light, breaks it, there's darkness for some million years – and then up rears another creature – a millipede, perhaps, a tapir ... roots around for centuries, then sees the ladder, up it climbs....

'Miro – is partly right. Science can't ask why we and future creatures, and those past too, magnificent! the flying lizards! – why we're spun round, acting out this epic ... the monsters are defeated, but the sun goes out.... We tame the waves – and finish buried in the sand....'

'I'd no idea!' says Sabrine. 'So, journalism is a job that deals with ultimates.... I never bought a paper. Maybe now....'

'Oh, we're not freaks,' says Julietta. 'We see things as they are. We're scientists of course – we know why there are storms.... But we don't know why you and I are here, what will become of us; nor why I am convinced that choosing right will bring me immortality, and choosing wrong – the furnace, where the broken things end up, smelted down, losing my shape and bubbling as a molten nothing-in-particular, being re-formed. Maybe a kettle. Or a pan.'

'Yes, that's terrible, I worked to hard to forge a hard-edge to my shape,' says Sabrine. 'These people you describe – will they welcome us?'

'Don't bet on it,' says Julietta, tying guard-pads round her knees, a mask with impregnated gauze around her face. 'People get desperate, and lose respect for neutrals who're observing them....'

'We're not there yet, Julietta,' Sabrine says. 'When we're at the frontier, I expect we'll have to walk, they'll steal the motor, and yet – you're dolled up, a warrior already....'

'Miro gets things wrong,' says Julietta. 'Not as wrong as you, Sabrine – but he thinks it's enough to be afraid, to cling on, sweat, and ride out storms. That's truly wrong. I'm every way prepared: I don't trust the sun, shining up there, and promising tomorrow....'

'Miro says he's attached to you,' Sabrine says, 'but you're so smooth – there's nothing to hold on to. There's a contradiction there, I'd say....

'For a chronicler, Miro's an anomaly. He can't read other people, what they intend, how serious they are, if they'll attack him, love him.... Life is a mystery for him, not beneath the surface, but specially the surface.'

'Well, where we go,' says Julietta, 'people run to and fro, and throw things. What's there to understand? Miro brings the cash to bribe us in, and get us out again if that is necessary. That is clear. It doesn't matter what spin you might put on it.'

*

'It sounds strange, like you put it, Julietta – as if you live in a hallucination, and come out of it by going to another one,' says Sabrine: 'These places, here and there – how involved are you?'

'Where are you from, Sabrine?' asks Julietta.

'Everywhere, I've been round the world,' Sabrine says, 'and nowhere; it was water. You know all that. But you – taking the risk, looking for what's underneath – you two live by not belonging, just calling back like storm-cocks to the other animals in the wood, who think all day of dinner, consuming neighbours; all night of breakfast – just the same....'

'It's not a joke, don't be naive, Sabrine,' says Julietta. 'You're a publicist's armchair. If you're not on TV you don't believe you've left your bed.

'We aren't from here, we aren't from there. Of course, we are not humanists, we don't believe in species being and a destiny. We love the animals, the humans too – not all, of course. We live for truth, it comes in at our eyes and out our fingers on to keys that don't unlock a goddam thing.... Miro and I – we're people exactly like you are – we don't need an other person living with us, cuddling us, impregnating us when we don't want, helping us go round the world....'

Sabrine gets irritable, sees Julietta's provoking her.

'That "go around the world" – you know it's crap, Julietta, to sentimentalise, to make it sound a quest – everybody does it....

They buy tickets.' Sabrine says, 'You make it sound a special thing....'

'No more sugar, thank you, Sabrine,' Julietta says, annoyed. 'And no more vinegar. It's time to concentrate.'

*

'Your sporty girl,' Julietta tells me, while Sabrine listens carefully, aside, 'is unspeakable. She plays the ingénue, and when you humour her, she laughs and says you are ingenuous. She's an anchor, Miro – drop her, quick!'

'With me,' I say, 'it's sex....'

'You know how to do that,' Julietta says. 'Be done. Get over it. Spin the wheel, Win, Lose – look big. You know how it's done. Then you and I.....'

'We have to take her with us, Julietta. We're going to a wedding, remember, not a manif – the tale convinces if we're three, not two....' I say.

*

The cops, the guards – they've all gone into town.

'You guys,' Sabrine says to us, 'if you know how things turn out – the days of contestation, concessions, victories and not – and then ... the militants in power, get whittled down, and so, and so ... why not stay home and write your piece...?'

'Oh no,' I say, 'you have to watch. You see the mechanism, how it operates, how it might not. And after all, it is our side, and even yours, Sabrine, in action.... Although – you try to set yourself in quite a different role: an oracle, a disappearing goddess, sleeping princess ... fiddling on some hidden imaginary that gets a bunch of guys to celebrate your trek, without a clear idea from you or them.... And even though you fake, those heroes you invoke, recall, they impersonate the only history we know....'

*

We stash the jeep. We lumber on, Julietta and I. We're armoured, Sabrine is a spirit free and sleek.

'Your pioneers could start up here,' she says. 'If the world – or civilisation – ends, Suicide may be attractive. Survival – my! it's difficult. But you need a spot where you can start to dig....'

It's true. Plant trees that live on sand, drill down, all land floats, there's water under, somewhere you will never see. There are no habitations, no roads or tracks. There is the frontier you can cross, a line invisible.... Millions die for it....

*

Sabrine – maybe she sees herself planting, tending here ... doing husbandry, renouncing husbands.... Sabrine – central in the winking eye, waiting for Survival. One of the very few.... Or Suicide – passing the poisoned chalice round, sweetening the sour, promising the unknowable, skipping into the improbable....

*

'How she loves pain,' says Julietta, as Sabrine runs ahead. 'You conquer it just once – and there it is again, lying in the road, a flattened dragon – up it jumps, you wrestle it, proceed, and there, across your path squashed, a fiery toad.... You turn your fear into a suffering. It never ends.

'We live on nature, flee from it; deny our nature, fantasise it – then, briefly, give natures another try. Heroism – .against nature.... It's not an expiation – Sabrine has no fault. It's pain, starting as fear, and then becomes a pleasure....'

We trot, we're breathless. Julietta shouts to me –

'Put her where she wants, Miro. The forefront of the battle. Avenging angel .....'

'I don't agree,' I say.

I do nothing. Let her take our pain, and see if it will cure my itch.

The front line.... They can't miss, even if they'd wanted to.

Sabrine's death – she's won the challenge.

She doesn't suffer – not much, if anything at all. A martyr. For some cause. A virgin too? Who knows. Not in my sphere....

*

'Well,' says Julietta, 'we put her where she would be killed. Death is the opposite of suffering, and so – we must do our best to give her immortality....'

It doesn't follow, but in our trade, it's what they say. It doesn't signify.

'The line, Julietta,' I say. 'You over-stepped. You gave her monkey justice. Punishment of Sabrine's fear, a martyrdom , unconscious, for some trivial ends of yours, a speculation....'

'No, no,' says Julietta. 'Martyrs are needed, always useful, if not to themselves – better Sabrine, who set herself to make a prominent end ... than some exalted guy with kids and skills.... Better the innocent than somebody with useful passions.... All heroes make their trip so as to learn – and Sabrine learned. She can't tell what: that is the way! It happens so – she was our Robespierre in her air-blue robe. She'd managed to enchant you ... there was common ignorance all round....'

'No, Julietta,' I say. 'Sex. For me – the primal urge. Only myself involved....'

'That's the way with ignorance,' she says. 'The heroes drop it round, unheeded, like a magic dust.'

*

'It didn't happen so,' says Julietta. 'The news is often upside-down, exactly opposite. It's rather a sad enlightening tale of altruistic suicide.... We turned about, we fled – Sabrine ran out, tried argument, delay, to protect the fleeting crowd. She was the last of us escaping, she had turned, dissuading – and she fell, trampled, clubbed, shot, even suffocated – a victim, maybe innocent, the ignorance for sure was there....'

I didn't see it so – but it is plausible. Sabrine – after all, she isn't here.

*

There's a side alley, a bar is open. That is odd. We drink, and watch the armoured vehicles drive past, and then the outriders on their khaki scooters, their passenger shooting birdshot in all directions, indiscriminate. The gas, as it weakens – gets in everywhere.

There's youngish people at the bar – Julietta chats to them. I say, 'Julietta – you know these guys...?'

'Oh yes,' she says. 'These are the ones who bear the future – theirs the choice expectant, pregnant.... Continue? or strike out .... Suicide? Survive? A new way of life.... Define its terms....'

'They don't seem people of another type,' I say. 'Rich kids who've found their pedestal. You socialise with them? Join in their play?'

There's guys who look like lawyers, ordering champagne. 'Oh yes,' says Julietta. 'You must hunker down with them, to read their thoughts. They're clean, and fragrant. They don't pinch or sting.'

'And sleep with them?' I ask – the loss of Sabrine, scarcely registered so far, erodes me ... sainthood for her must wait. A heroine? – it's hard to say when that gets certified. In any case – for me, my story's gone, one of my futures, hypothetical, rubbed out....

'Oh,' says Julietta, filling a long glass with gin, 'the guys here don't think like that – the tacky bed and breakfast scene, embarrassment, false intimacy. They have some special tricks – we are all friends, and so we pass ourselves around, no jealousy, possessing, all is trust, it's all on all....'

'It's not what I had thought,' I start to say.

*

And why's this bar still open when those guys are shooting everywhere?

'Oh they don't shoot at us,' Julietta says. 'These here are the experts, people who keep things driving on, or – at a certain point, they may say "no" – "enough". Did you imagine that the manifs determine what should come?

'These guys decide. They give their views, and so, and so – there are concessions, maybe not, coopting, contacts – all that stuff.... They decide.

'You write about it every day – you ought to know, but here is where the wind may change ... blowing from the throats of managerial types....'

'And Sabrine?' I ask, quite desperate. And Julietta laughs.

'She lacked the gravity, the being known for something definite. She had her name made doing something else. It's difficult to recognise a person who starts in one frame, and steps over to another one, quite unconnected, coloured differently, drawn by another hand.... These guys here – they'll do the sum, weigh up her death.... When the old ways can't go on – they'll be the ones to start off living in the different way ... telling us what it's to be....'

I say, 'I can't believe it, Julietta. These guys are doing well.... They can't imagine the catastrophe, new crews of rough guys with inspiration, the world turned upside-up....'

'Oh, these sophisticates? They'll be rebels, revolutionaries too, when times decide....' she says.

'I shall prefer,' I say, 'to search out more gritty, independent guys.'

'Maybe some Bolsheviks,' says Julietta, 'they were like that. But – they didn't drop from stars. The Jacobins ... they were produced by the machinery, guys who looked like these –' and she waves over at the jolly crowd – which waves right back.

'It's easy here,' I say. 'There are the People, who'll be shot and beat. And on the other side – the shooters and the beaters. It's so different from other riven lands, where it's all complex and you can sympathise with those who stand in indecision.

'Here, Julietta, there's people on the run; and there's these cosmologists ... silky guys, ready to hide, tough out world's end; killing themselves if all goes wrong. Or winning through, becoming our own grandfathers, and us their puzzled offspring. All spilling out from the burrow, into a world where all the other animals are miniscule, fresh water lies a kilometre underground, huge salty seas rage on the shore....'

The bar is getting loud, 'Miro!' Julietta shouts. 'Where do you excavate this rubbish? You write the stuff for cash, of course, but spare us these trite fumblings. You know nothing about anything, so each day you'll shock us all – saying the opposite of yesterday, not conveying any sense, except that you're confused....'

*

Oh Sabrine. We'll see you in the news, and in the pics. I'll write about you....

*

'You're simple, Miro,' Julietta says, taking my arm and running us, bent, beside the umber houses, out of the city, back.... She goes on,

'I'll protect you, but I can't protect your innocence.... The times – there's no use now for mourning. Heroism's out. Here there's a manif. Elsewhere we'll submit: or take to arms. Sometimes the drought decides our strategy, sometimes some guy's redrawing borders, closing them. Sometimes we're with the people – yes! ... and sometimes not....

'You're so old century, Miro, my friend. Sabrine ran after being a big heroine – a *feu follet!* Gone! Our ancestors fought for individuality: she's just the echo, the last bird in the forest – it's all gone, gone, gone! The world is filled with tiny heroes, chronicling on their screens and turning terror into games.... Be more aware, Miro....'

We reach the jeep. We didn't think of Sabrine's corpse – what good's a corpse? Here, all's been vandalised, the tires, the battery, and yes, the seats....

'See!' Julietta says. 'We can set records now, tramping home, through the sand....'

She has her spot prepared – a witness of the future; the determined guys who will decide.

*

They're not ready for anything here – or else they'd take the jeep, drive it away – not steal parts to patch the old.

I can't wait to leave.

*

I tell the interviewer, the editor. 'If you want, I'll change my "look". To work better with your squad: for me, surgery is nothing!

'Of course – I have experience. Past and future, humans, other animals....' She doesn't smile. 'I have experience, flying time-machines.'

There's a pause. 'In a new country, maybe I should change my face, religion. Politics, of course,' I say.

'It won't be necessary,' she says. 'You're so full of yourself, we could pour off another candidate just from you.'

'It's true,' I say. 'I know most things. But – I'm also desperate. I just lost my lover – a militant: rights and such – killed on mission. I have another friend – a lover, almost. She informs me ... on whole world crisis, politology....'

'That's interesting,' says the editor. 'Boasting is dull, but every human is the same. It's what you do in intimacy – your private, that is critical. Lovers. That gives the taste, the smell, consistency.'

We all talk as if we're satirising. 'You have no depth,' she says. 'That isn't bad. If we lose you – we get over it.'

'It's mutual,' I say. 'Truth. Is indifferent to everyone, all humans. Animals as well. Truth is neither hot nor cold. Not deep or shallow.'

Another pause.

'Where do you think it leads,' she asks. 'All your enquiries? We pay you something – but no logic says you shouldn't pay *us* ... to spread the light, the word. God used to pay the good, his friends, but, you can't rely....'

'It's like the song says,' I say, "my problem is my problem". I'm not just interested in truth, you realise: truth and lies. Deflowering ignorance.'

'You don't believe in anything except yourself,' she says. 'But that's gone, departed. You love yourself now, not your individuality. Don't think you are unique.... That would be unconfessable. You create personalities, you don't need one yourself. I don't believe in you and me. We are endless strings. All of us – parents, us, children: – the colour of the strings, the threads, will change. They're different shades of white. They're like worms, tape-worms: cut them, they join up again, and there *you* are, woven in the past, like in a mummy's shroud.... Woven into cloth: on the loom of history....'

'Cristel,' I say – her name's on her breast. 'We'll be fine. Load me on board. Trust me.'

It's my best speech, ever.

'In this place,' says Cristel, 'this country, sport and politics – they intertwine, become the same. Manufacturing and sport – the notables: all the same. The people? In the stadia ... all fascists or too ignorant to know they are ....Outside – hundreds-and-thousands ... a poke, cake decorations, every combination you can conceive....

'Tell me who the people are, worldwide. Ask why they're different but all react the same. Tell me – why the end is nigh, but people don't think that their end may be involved....'

'It's a revelation, Cristel,' I say. 'I was always on the people's side, against the rest...'

'Well,' she says. 'You've had your sleep, decades, it seems. Now, this new reality is your terrain, your work.'

'I was moved as much as I could be, by Sabrine's death – anomalous, unnecessary....' I say.

'Yes,' Cristel says. 'I've seen your sample piece. It doesn't say you lusted after her....'

'I didn't write this, Cristel,' I take the papers from her, as she hopes....

'Of course not, Miro,' Cristel says. 'It is never so. You don't come up to scratch, you never will, none of you do.... The story flares up – it's a match. The light. And you remember how it was, sat in your gloom, your dark. It's sad and sooty. So, in house, we have the brighteners. If you've emotion – we remove the patina and make it glow a bit....'

'My friend, Julietta,' I tell her, although I ought not to – it's my story, after all. 'In our little land, we lived anonymous. We travelled everywhere, went around the world. There's places cool, and places hot, congealed and liquid. In some there's silence, and in others jails, or maybe you just disappear. We knew a liquid place ... quite close.... A past obscure and difficult, now sailing on towards the storm ... a pirate ship, a daring crew.... There's those who read the charts and where they're blank – they scribble in their fantasies....

'She knows these guys.... They plan for after the catastrophe. For them, the future's yet to come. It's not like "more today". Some places have populations who are now surveilled, in permanent constraint.... They are congealed. Where we were – all flows....

'Julietta's guys see – there's movement. People run, throw stuff ... poor Sabrine...!

'People there are volatile, not cowed.... The question is –

'What do you do afterwards – after the big collapse? You can't live in the old way, this time, the bosses cannot either. These guys, they think it out ... "You've some resources ... how to expand, to colonise and move around ...In the beginning, live like the Inuit once did – a diet horrible, climate unspeakable.... Not many of you, scavenge for your food, get sick, starve – all that. So, you live without conflict, never rock the sled. Semi-nomads, nomads too. A barren desolation you can roam around." That's what survival may be like.

'If you've avoided suicide – be aware, beware – these guys – want to be boss.

'There's no custom, no tradition, to keep everybody quiet and self-controlled – it's all to be invented. This crew – must work out how to direct the new world, bear it up ... to where it falls again....'

She's not impressed.

'You added in the last bit, Miro,' Cristel says. 'I'm sure we'll never know if what they do is as you say, and where it leads.... But – surely you agree: bosses are dull, and mostly pigs.'

She leaps up, both forefingers pointing to the sky.

'The manifs! Around the world. Those interest me. Your task would be a tribute to Sabrine.... To travel round, visit where the movement is, write a brisk piece.... and on, and on....'

She hasn't understood ... the fascination of improbability.... Finding a human who matters, matters to me too. Company. Locate an intimate. To seek out someone, some personality, a stimulus....What Sabrine might have been for me.

'Cristel, there's demos everywhere – "no power, no cash, no water, too much rain",' I say.

Then there was Sabrine – landed, stranded....

'I'd hardly see you, Cristel....' I say. 'If I'm around the world, collecting likenesses....'

*

'See! These are former cosmopolitans, they travelled, and they faltered. Now, look at them, enchained....' she says, opening a shutter.

There's guys sat at desks, their screens have images of dogs and cats – cute, doing cute things too.

'And these were all your lovers, Cristel,' I ask, taken aback.

'Well,' she says, 'these were all people who passed the interview, and said they loved me. They represented every sex, and every point of view. They went off, followed the movements ... back they came. Burnt out, bored, disilllusioned. So, yes, they are my lovers. But....'

'I understand,' I say. 'Now, I'm the nameless knight, or off to seek the grail....'

'Send back those pieces regular,' she says. 'And then we'll see.'

*

'Another of Cristel's lovers,' Florian says. 'We're sixteen – in a bed, we'd make a novel, a triple-decker, or a movie series. It starts and ends the same ... for us, not her.'

'I saw you in your zoo, Florian,' I say. 'Maybe we should work together – Cristel inspired me to do exactly what I didn't want. The demos....'

'What you would prefer,' says Florian. 'Is sterile too. What she proposes is your test of loyalty. In the short term, life is difficult, for everyone. Beside the rest, there's dealing with the people you don't like, the guys who keep you down. In the short term, life is always, very, difficult: – it's the fault of false gods, outsiders. In the long term – there's is no long term.

'If there's nothing, no eternal days to come – what can anybody do? Of course –

'There won't be nothing – life will be very difficult. Extremely. No one now does what's to be done. Not ever, Miro. You do something else, or somebody takes all you have and leaves you in the snow. There are no trees. And so you freeze.

'Telling this – it's sterile. So is your big project ... what we might do when civilisation ends? You know, Miro – it's already been preserved. It can go on and on, just call it up, on to your screen. Even if there's four of us remain – we have it all.... Sites real, and yet to be dug up. Thoughts for today, celebrity: all ready for the call. Your pics.... We'll die – but civilisation will be there, encysted in our tools....

'Cristel does this with everyone – turns you from big subjects on to mobile ones, the fire and splutter, bright colours, eerie squawks. Then, you end up in our room, and wait for someone else who will arrive....

'There's other things you might have done. A movie on the anti-drug brigade. Civil wars in the peripheries – poor against poor, the gangs, the vigilantes. Poems about yourself. Start with the very small and see how it is everywhere. The struggle for existence.... Or – prison zones, the Sahel, Xinjiang ... desertification, tree loss, and salination....'

'I know all that,' I say. 'I lost a friend, down there, in a manifestation....'

'I know all that as well,' says Florian. 'But you're emotionally dead. You have no passions, you're a fly that roams from carrion to moribund, you're gullible as well.... Those pioneers, who're planning how to rule what's left after the catastrophe – why waste your time....? Your partner, Julietta – she goes along with that, the young aspirants, their rhetoric. She's bored. Governance of future times – that's feeback, acoustic dross....

'Or do – entirely something else ... feather ornaments, smoked fish, the Volga water system....'

'I understand,' I say. 'It's to get rid of Cristel?'

'Her and her bosses too,' says Florian. 'And are you with us, Miro, old friend?'

'I'm only at the start,' I say. 'I'm free. That is our weapon, and our flag. Freedom – we're already there....'

'Yes, yes,' says Florian. 'We're the only ones who care. No one bet a soldier on our fate. Our freedom's in our fingertips – and there it stops. We are not loved nor valued, my friend: if we were really free, our message unsullied and our consciences sparkling bright – there'd be invidia instead of scepticism, anathema.... Freedom and truth – they're different things ... small eels with tiny heads....'

'I know,' I say. 'Writing. Like cleaning out your ears.... Most people do it, no value, no reverberation. But –'

'There is a price,' says Florian. 'We go out often, clubbing – discussing how to throw out Cristel, and her mates. For new comrades – there's a fee, the pot. Five hundred....'

'Oh no,' I say. 'I've not been paid, and starting so, with plotting and conspiracy.... no way!'

*

Later, I tell Florian about the honorary lovers, spendthrift and unscrupulous, clogging the corridors, until the workers conduct the massacre, 'sweeping away the corpses of these useless giants'.... What is to come? – perhaps, they said a century ago, all is in vain, and our glimmering spiral only lights up for the amusement of the shadows.

'No,' he says. 'That's vanity, sheer vanity. You can't foretell the end from the middle.'

'Can I trust you, Florian,' I ask. 'Despite our differences?'

He looks surprised, then, 'Of course!' he cries. 'Because of them, perhaps. Trust. The sense is not secure, of course – there is a root of rust, of time obliterating everything, especially the word.... If you're not with us – it is evident to everyone.'

'But –' I say. 'There's more, it's nuanced.'

He shakes his head – to him, everything's nuanced, I suppose.

'The question is – how do we think,' I say, a breath of inspiration fills my sail, '... like animals – in our case: apes and jackals. Our brothers: hunters, gatherers, gossip parties....

'But the philosopher says – "Thinking scientifically". The latest mode of thinking, being here. It's a way, that follows after other ways, it's like a subject that you learn in school. There's animal thought, that comes most naturally, and that endures: though, we're a strange scintillating, shimmery beast. Changing our mind and double-guessing everyone.

'But, thinking, Florian. When we settled in our smelly towns, and had all day to chatter in the alleyways and do our deals and sell our stuff, take breakages and rubbish to the tip ... wear uniforms and sit at desks – we start with magic thought. Then, we systematise: there's religion, bigotry, theology and metaphysics.... It's evanescent stuff. Then – the enlightenment. The god of reason. Empire and colonies, the ever-lasting war. After, there is humanism, experimenting and scepticism, the early science – putting things in drawers and stuffing birds and hammering on rocks, tormenting frogs, splitting the rainbow, sniffing all kinds of glue, and taking pills ... all swept away by massacres unique, long-distance wars more powerful than before, whole populations into the mill, the hopper, ground into dust, to nevermore....

'Then – there's the universe laid open: its strings that tie, and lights that vanish, corners lurking round the corners.... On, on we go –

'Abandonment of earth, up to the stars and start again....'

'I'm not following,' says Florian. 'You think, Miro, in very odd modalities!'

'It's an example, Florian,' I say. 'You think of angels, god and paradise. It shapes your day, your world, you pray to keep your place each day, and hope the picture firms upon the screen. And then – if you think scientifically – all that is swept away. You lose it, lose the poetry it makes, you look inside, write up your world yourself, make the toccatas, passacaglias – the *dies irae* ... do that yourself in public with your gun and gas.

'Science. You peek and poke, and do experiments – immense the scale, digging, felling, melting melts – bigger than the flood, arks dwarfed by carriers of this and that, messages that flit and flow like moon-tides, aimless migrations of stunted geese....

'Come in, Florian!' I shout. 'You're here! With me, with us! You see it – guns and gas and plug things in, and save this bird and kill that bug, use lasers that will kill that guy and give that other one his sight....'

'You're off piste, Miro,' Florian says, wired up and laughing.
'What do you think now? How?'

'I think "round-the-world" – much seems much the same, and
I am curious about what's not. I think ... like Sabrine. I try to
make my life add up, the parts to make a whole. Like her – I
don't know what it's for ... she gave her cash away, what others
hadn't stolen first.... I'm quite like that. The easy con. A fish. A
chicken – depending where you are, they call me stupid....'

'Oh, Miro,' Florian says. 'They flatter you, they think you're
selfless: holy fool. It isn't so at all. Stupid is stupid. Holy fool is
holy fool.

'You're a newsman, Miro,' he goes on. 'You collect the
scraps, and sauté them. Anything that's curious, some habit,
song or instrument, experience – anything you'd find in ships or
shops, netting birds in Cathay or in Malaga, a grass in Ghana,
horse in Haskovo, a cat in Kičevo.... You're into chronicles, the
curiosity box, the nineteenth century – the house of grist, the
mill of rumour , inexplicable objections, objects unclassifiable,
beliefs incredible, the commonplace – displaced.... Cosmology,
disastrology.... You're not a humanist, Miro: you'd do quite
well without the species ... but you're curious, curious about its
end, its beginning, it's doing everything all over ... the same? Or
different?'

'I think a little bit like Cristel, Florian, that is true,' I say.
'More than mere magic, more than curiosity. The wood-beetle
isn't curious when it wants to build in ebony ... and –
everywhere is the same because everywhere is different.

'Ennui, Florian. Like Sabrine – the sea is boring, yet she went
all over it, its ups and downs ... a horror. Always something
needing doing, always the same shuffle and dodge, the
spinnaker on and off, the boom bangs on your head, the mooing
in the fog, the tarpot, smoke of distress ... it's all in stories,
Florian.

'In the end, the sea ends in slavery – first: yourself. Then –
your Friday. Then your cargo – a million tons of gasoline, for
driving up and down.... The landlocked sea – is what we're all
afloat on .... Sabrine – drowned by forces, forces of order, the
waves, repetitive and lethal.... She knew them well....'

'Why are you telling me all this?' Florian asks. 'It's magic. Jumble. Or you think you are a shaman? Selling snakes and snake-oil? Probably the people who read your stuff ... they think the same. That they're original, unique. Or that only you can sing the song, trill every trill, do every curlicue, juggle a hundred nails....'

'I'm not interested,' I say. 'I want to know these different ways of thinking about reality, and what's behind what we call real. The maths and physics – they are there, it seems, invisible, you can avoid them as you run like wolves through unseen birch-trees. All your life – you never think of them, they are no branches on your head – you're busy dodging projectiles, apologies for massacres – your hunger drives you on.... Those philosophical puzzles that obsessed our grannies – unsolvable, like God and god, and nature, slipping from beneath us like a wayward horse....

'But I don't want especially to think in one of those ways, not any one ... like, say, the venerable one – magic, taboos and miracles. How we saw everything, when we formed troops and packs, animals among the animals. Stories. Every stick and opal had one, every curve of sand. Nor "true or false", believable evidence.... We straightened up – other guys thought we were deluded ...so we accepted the game of true and false. How often we've been wrong or fatally half-right with "true". If you do our history, the species: you look in those big mirrors. You raise a hand, and yes! – it's you! always and for always. These are all just human things; who did what and when. People want to know that, but it's a tiny part of what goes on.... Like sailing – no one is responsible for anything at all, but if it all goes wrong, they sometimes rescue you. If it goes well – you only see them at the end, when they make landfall where you are.... Then right and wrong come in – another scatter-shot. More birdshot.'

I think of Sabrine, the brass band, the few not-notables, their motors in the spume, rusting out the bodies. The human enterprise, the factories, made everything for her – the boat, her clothes, the challenge, but she was mostly quite untouched by anything, unimpressed by herself and them, her cinderella courtiers....

'Original thought, you see,' I say. 'That's the distant light I've always followed – surely, it can illuminate us all, there'd be no shadow you can hide in, not you, not Cristel, and not me.'

'It's not original at all. It's your stew, your salad, omelette, pizza – what you feel like throwing in.There is no plot, no recipe – just an unrepeatable taste: rancid or a luxury. Anyway, there's no point telling me:' says Florian. 'Until you pay your whack, you're out....'

*

'You know,' says Cristel, 'there's a fronde against me? Me and mine. You.'

'It's a secession,' I say. 'They have autonomy. They have nothing to do with it, I imagine, as you still pay them for being a disappointment. Now, they want independence. Where do you take them, Cristel? Just a company among the others? Sending us out, like ravens from the ark – to feed a prophet somewhere, bring back seeds, fruits of knowledge and of indulgence....'

She laughs. 'Oh, how you're moralistic, Miro! I have a vision, and resource. They – only their ambitions and personal projects ... based on seniority, but so what. Alas, they're here, under contract, I can't expel them nor win their loyalty – but I shan't let them decide my destiny.'

'They're my colleagues,' I say. 'But I don't need them. Maybe I do, but I need you too, Cristel.... Stuck here with them, that stuffy room, the family pics....'

'You don't know what you want, even when you have it, you won't know if it's what you want tomorrow. Are you loyal, Miro?'

'No,' I say, 'I don't think I've ever been that. You'd think I'm superficial....'

'Yes,' she says. 'You are, though you think you're not. You don't do the thinking part. You veer about, change tack....'

'It's the wind, Cristel,' I say. 'It isn't me, It's how it hits the sails. Who decides that? Not you, not me....not anyone.'

'That's what the sailors say who don't want to reach land,' she says. 'You're scared of ports and land, Miro, you can't steer, that's why I want to send you round the world.... A random trip must bring you back to starting-place, but, how you love wandering....'

'I thank you, Cristel,' I say, hoping this interview is finishing. 'That's what I want. The world. That's where I belong. Though – the fear is everywhere.'

'Companies proceed,' says Cristel. 'You don't need be a boss to grasp how capitalism works. It seems that's all there is. No alternative: the default setting for us all is a structure like the one I've set up here – for profit or for loss – there's nothing else imaginable. People come in, are fired, promoted, everybody tries to find a role ... those guys, your colleagues, my lovers – they understand they're discards, that another lot of discards will come after, with fresh memories and projects, and stick new pictures on the cork, and reminisce and not do anything at all except complain, write memoranda, spill their magic bean to anyone who drops on by ... maybe that stranger will plant it in a little pot, but it will only grow in that small stuffy room....'

'Maybe,' I say. 'When I am dead, I'll come and lie there in a drawer for ever....

'And you won't understand a word that they are saying, or how angry sometimes they become ... not doing what they could do, the lengths they'll go to try....

'I'm with you, Cristel. Give me the tickets and the cash, and I'll be off,' I say.

*

In the package for my mission, there's an old world map. It's mostly empires. If you pencil in the new ones, it should be simpler, but the lines, the borders, are more confused and scribbled over. The sea is countries now. There is no cash – just a currency converter, flickering, and not much use. No ticket and no cash.

'Cristel!' I shout. 'Is this your trick? An invitation?'

'To do at least the first stage?' she asks. 'Begin the trip with you?'

'You know, Cristel,' I say, 'you pack a heavy sexual charge, you're deadly, a real cannon. Mantis – that's you? That's maybe in your mind? Are you frank with me? You have a lover ...

almost everybody does, it doesn't mean a thing, I know, but on a trip, that is encumbrance....'

'You know I have sixteen!' she says and laughs. 'They're in the shuttered room, at play.'

'I had a passion, Cristel, for Sabrine,' I say. 'Another one for Julietta – I never got a step inside their dark....'

'For sure,' says Cristel, sitting close, 'they were spirits locked in slender trees. You should have knocked, and maybe rubbed against the bark – you, a bear, more likely a boar, a gesture intimate, unthreatening.... Instead, you were a woodsman, with your chopper raised to cut them down....'

'Coming with me, Cristel, disturbs me. It is not a good idea,' I say. 'Nothing is permanent, or stable. On the move, you waver even more.... Sex....'

'How right you are,' says Cristel, touching my left hand lightly with her right. 'I want the sex I had when I was just fifteen. Can you? Can anyone? My return – eternal, trapped inside my head.... No – it's my dream and tragedy, my fantasy, my story that I spin to knights like you....'

'The task's impossible,' I say, drawing away. 'Though I've no other plan, except to roam, circle the world, come back to where I start. The journey's self-indulgent, signifying nothing but time passed. I've no resource. To save a soul, you need the cash – the story is the same, the rich must want to save the poor. The question's one of quantity – a lot of cash to save a legion of the poor. What you propose instead – is travellers' tales, Cristel. That's what you want me to bring back....'

'Oh Miro,' Cristel says, buttoning up her shirt. 'You were once a Kantian, I'm sure – work out the rules in rough, and how the world goes round, and hope the others follow you on paths identical. And then – you just gave up.... A task unrealistic, unfulfilled.

'My lovers? I'm for Rousseau: we argue and we vote, reach the solution so, so, and so – in centuries perhaps....'

'I know,' I say. 'The voting could mean peace or war; damming the stream and let the others downstream croak.... Beside, your lovers in the shuttered room – they hate you! They vote to string you up.'

'Well,' she says, 'I might lapse too. Theory's like disco – dead. You're right. I lie. That is permissable – we are not straight; nor well informed....'

There's not anything left to say.

She says, 'There! You know I'm a cheat and a liar. I'll make you suffer terribly, and you'll end up with nothing but bad memories. Do you still want me to start out with you? My taking part – it isn't in any story line, you know....'

'Oh yes, Cristel,' I say, fired up. 'Yes, yes! Come, come with me...! Fuck fate! Shoot the black birds. Fear everything, expect the worst, revel in it when it comes.'

'What luck!' she says, waving something. 'I bought two tickets, just in case...!'

*

'This *pension* could fall, at any minute,' Cristel says. 'The two buildings holding it up, if they just shrug – down we shall go.'

'I stayed here, Cristel, once before,' I say. 'They think Morisot did the decoration on this wall. It's characteristic....'

'I see you're wondering why I took one room for two,' she says.

'No, not really,' I say.

'Well, you should,' she says. 'Everything – bears many interpretations. Usually – not the exciting ones.'

She's wispy, flexible – a whippet. I don't remember much.

'These guys are smart,' says Cristel. 'They have four soldiers, maybe five, but they dress them well – the tops. They have an empire too – it doesn't cost, or profit them: it's language – there's an enormous tongue that spreads around the world. There's millions speak it – some not too well, but it's a dominion – a realm, like medieval times when you were king but local bosses did the work.'

'What's there for us?' I ask. 'Now everybody in the world uses a language no one speaks. They all communicate, but no one reads or writes a book, or converses face to face, and yet these guys....'

'That's trite,' she says, 'and isn't true. But – you're a writer, so you say. Find another one like you. Let's find the secrets of this place....'

'I know a couple, writers. They write each other's stuff, use every medium – dance, movies, street – and graphic books and spoofs ...' I say. 'They're what I might have been – respected, rich, a dangerous life promoting causes and themselves – they are a team....'

'Well, Miro,' Cristel says, 'we aren't. This is the end – I have to leave, a date back in the hub....'

'It all seems programmatic, Cristel. One night, and off to someone else....' I say.

'You took money from my bag, you jerk,' she says.

It's just a joke –

'To pay the bill,' I say. 'We shared the room at least ... and is this really all? It seems quite slim....'

'Joubert and Marcelline,' she says. 'I'm sure they're ready for you. He's just done another one – "Saint Paul to the Americans – a fresh discovery...."

'You had from me what was on offer – now you complain. You want a repetition – sex more and more; you know each time it's just the same. Then, it becomes a ritual, a boredom, frustration ... resentment too. Is that your goal, your aim – as if you're learning prayers, as though I were a Book you had to learn by heart, forgetting or ignoring all the rest? No, my dear – I'm not a book. I've start and finish – but no development, no middle section, no reprise. I am a movable type, I can be composed in infinite ways.

'If you can't remember what I'm like, obsessed as you are to want another joust – try with someone else and use the memory tricks the Jesuits had, divide youtr lady or the lad in cubes, mental, of course, laid out like a garden, into flowerbeds. Like you would do to me....'

'You're more the promontory type, Cristel,' I say, with deep regret. 'Your final cliff is reached – then there's the endless sea. You're right, of course. Experience dilute is wasted, it thins out, becomes a shadow show; you know they're clever puppets, but behind the cut-out actors on their strings and sticks – there's other actors, doing the lines, the voices.... Behind the screen, the screen, the curtain – curtain....'

She grows impatient.

'Emotions are good for you,' she says. 'Bad or exalting – makes no odds. They pep you up, no matter what, you shouldn't be judgemental about what's good or bad. All feeling turns back into sand and limestone: – accept, don't analyse; remember, tears clear out your eyes, they let you see the fluffy birdlings through the shells, the rose while still in bud....'

And off she goes, just like she said she would.

*

Joubert is playing tric-trac with the haughty Marcelline.

'The epistle? It must be, the saint arrived just as the Americans walked over from Siberia. He took one of those enormous Chinese ships....' he says. He talks on, I seem sceptical. 'Your literalism,' Joubert says. 'Must be a pain. You sex-life must be barren – a Rockall, in a frozen sea.'

'You know, Joubert,' I say, '"each epoch dreams of its successor" – you're up to the minute, with what comes next. And after that?'

'That's easy,' Joubert says. 'What comes after next is – what comes next. Theory – it holds you up. It's dead: the old.'

'What interests me,' I say, 'is your obsessive war against the Touareg. I walked the desert: soldiers are there, but not your enemy.'

'The enemy, no doubt your friends,' says Marcelline. 'We made a desert – now we'll dig it up... Don't stick your finger in the termite heap....'

'It's not exactly as you think,' says Joubert. 'Marcelline goes back, far back, before the modern stuff I specialise in now. All the world's already here. You want next steps? Just take my train....'

He has a train! It might be steam. It's not – the track is straight, the engine is a rocket shape. A wonderful design.

'Of course,' says Joubert, 'we can only push – if we light it up – we'll end in Mars. This is the future, Miro, and perhaps it works.'

I say 'It's like they say – we run without a care over the precipice, after we have put something in the way so's we don't see it. That is wise. That's where we are.'

'It never happens,' says Joubert. 'A continent is waiting for the fall – it's happened, a hundred times, there's always someone left.'

'You've written about Africa,' I say. 'You must have *mal d'Afrique*.'

'Africa is here,' he says, 'and *I'm* the *mal d'Afrique*.'

'It's not really what I want to hear,' I say to Marcelline. 'Rebellion, revolution, godless crusades, the Empire, the mess that's left.... I need a thought to set beside my own....'

'I share nothing of all that,' she says. 'Joubert's a genius, of course – Hugo and Zola into one, but we never talk, don't share. It's the best way. As for your question – it's too big. Not put right. Too big to answer. It's better there aren't Touaregs, believe me, better for everyone.'

They've nothing left to show me. The big questions – walk around, they're there, like garden dwarves.

'I'd offer you a smoke,' she says, 'But Joubert's working on a film – the anti-drug brigade. It's very very violent, but the music's great.'

'I don't want anything,' I say. 'All I want's someone to tell me lies. So long as I'm convinced it is the truth.'

'That's usable,' says Marcelline. 'You could stay, help us both.... But we have long careers. That usually inspires us quite enough.'

'All's best observed by the camera, rather than by the naked eye,' Joubert adds. 'Obsolescence. Me, my work, the scene, going gone. Be aware: time passes, leaves a mould. Puff yourself up – then you must concentrate, reduce your everything to gemstone size, a tiny jewel. Marcelline's already there, she's made her microcosm. I'll get where I am going to. People change throughout their lives – my subject is the change, not life.'

'It seems inconclusive,' I say. 'What's not true, is not just to be thrown out....'

'I'd like to help your friends,' says Joubert. 'But you must bring them here.'

'Go away!' shouts Marcelline. 'What do you expect from us? We're bourgeois. We make ruins. New ones. The old ones are made by people we don't know.'

'It isn't so,' says Joubert, with a pale smile.

*

Cristel didn't leave a plan. I wander. This place, the city, capital of everywhere, is circular. It's still my world: there's almost everybody here – except for Touaregs. Go to the desert – it's the same. The world is there as well, with soldiers too: you'll never find a Touareg.

Joubert and Marcelline – I feel they know it all; they've left a crack – anybody can squeeze in, and trade their line. I'd find it hard to settle here – my fault, for sure. Where next?

I take the bus to Sjenica, then think of moving further on....

*

'This is not a place for you,' says Jozo, sat beside me. 'If you were here before – it was waiting for modernity. No sweat. Instead, they got the war. Thirty years it ought to take, burying the dead, and then the living. It's not been so – who's not escaped stays here, is poor, without a chance. The periphery has started at the frontier – after Graz: the fat – where there was country, prickly and stark – it's all periphery. Keep going, going East. There's war, then sand, then poverty, and then there's China. Nothing anywhere for you, Miro. You'd like to move on from the Balzac. Those are all still living: cousin Berthe, grandad Gaston, the misers and the cutthroats, the bankers and the landlords, all a bit reduced, some fiercer than they were. No place for you, Miro, my friend.'

'I remember long ago,' I say. 'Horsemen herding, knitting long stockings as they rode....'

'That's your picture,' Jozo says. 'You should have had it framed. War, Miro, accelerates – then, when those have gone into the smelter, their children are fallen in the next war, the one you fight with cash ... they were enforcers, tarts, or maybe walking up and down and waiting angry. You said it would take

a generation – and they were stupid, hopeful too – they made
more kids...!

'The landscape stays the same – no digging, no big fields
with poison strewn – it looks the same but now, it's acid. It has
eaten them. When they die, there's just a shell: you can put
dozens down the same hole....'

'All these tourists, Jozo,' I say. 'What do they come to see?'

'See if it's different, that is what,' he says. 'To spend a little
cash: do cheap, what their parents never could, unless they were
the soldiers. That was free, the soldiering – but not for me; you
wouldn't want – and I'm like you, not the killing or the caring
type. More the sort that knows it all and wrings its hands,' he
says, dismissing me, pretends to sleep.

Well? Next? Old friends in Moscow, transformed –
scrabbling poor or teetering rich, still sharing what they have.
Perhaps. India in the fog? China – those empty cities, waiting
for the millions to arrive...?

'You're too demanding, Miro,' Jozo says, turning, face
against the glass. 'Reading "Nothingness" in bed, I bet.'

'You must engage with me,' I say. 'Or else we can't be
friends. Lamentations – everybody's a virtuoso in singing
those.'

'That's no good,' he says. 'You must learn, Miro, friends
made casual so, on the bus: it's old. Watch the scene instead:
take it all in, think and pretend how good it was, will be; how
bad – the same. It's not my world, it's no one's.'

I can't go round and round if they are all like this, I think.
Joubert – you can't hook on to him. Marcelline would brush you
off, you're just a stripy bug ... I must place myself, somehow,
somewhere: not as storm-tossed, not a *feuille morte*. I must
stand on some ground, or no one will listen to me. Shouts at sea
mean only 'help'. That's the thing I do not want.

*

'These are all relatives,' says Jozo: there are no animals, silent
people sitting round. 'Beasts cost,' he says. 'There's so few you
can afford, you get attached – at the end, it's like you're killing
them with hand-grenades.'

'Nothing's been happening here,' his granny says, tells him all night, all that there is. The threats from young, the debts.

'You're not really old,' he tells her. 'Here, yes, I am,' she says. 'We all went like this once: like beasts, we lie down in the field, and then – we do not know what's next. I do not care. I do know – that afterwards they make a fuss, and put on suits, and pick some flowers. And wreaths – like huge glass paperweights hung fading on the stone, another sacrifice, another trial, and justice done....'

We eat dried things, hard white bread and curly squares of cheese, all metered out. You don't enjoy, but all you need is show you do.... The reek of kerosene sticks to your clothes.

'Just a thought,' says Jozo. 'But if you have some change to spare.... For the kids, you realise.'

*

The night is very quiet, you see the stars, their depth. Perhaps the last time you will see each one.

*

The bus is late. Jozo says, 'Why bother? Moving on? The world's still full of people just like us. We are the sea – some of us float, some of us – are shoals beneath the surface, we defend ourselves, then come the seagulls – far from land, they dive on us, we go compact....'

'Is it enough there's lots of you, defenceless, Jozo?' I ask him, looking away, hoping the bus will come. 'Everyone is desperate – the seagulls too.... What then?'

'Cross a frontier here,' he says. 'There's news there is a gold mine opening up – riches immeasurable and unforeseen.... There's disadvantages as well – it's there, not here; the big advantage is – it's there, not here.... Go, find out. The wealth – it's all unclaimed, just take a spade and out it comes; before they put a fence around....'

'Crossing?' I say. 'People do it so nonchalantly – it's the air. You see nothing. But on land – you go from Joe Blow to being miscreant, even much worse, or a suspect, assassin ... just a step.

On sea – it's worse – you can't see the line, but as you all deflate – it matters, more than divinity.... Even when they fish you out, the hole you go in....'

'The bus won't come,' says Jozo. 'It's a holiday – ours or theirs. Suss out the mine. Maybe they will have a sale. Bring back a bucketful of gold....'

He pulls me up a path that disappears in trees ... a sign says 'mines' – 'That's not the sort you want,' he says and laughs. There's a thin girl in a blue dress – maybe it started white, or pink. Maybe I shouldn't guess. 'This is Sveta,' says Jozo. 'Svetlana. One of us. She'll lead you further on.'

She has a ratty face and ratty hair – maybe it's the rain. We all came out of Africa – she has lost the sheen, patina, colour – but the features are still sharp and fine. She's one of us, whoever that may be.

'Who's he?' she asks Jozo.

'Oh,' he says, 'he's the angel with the bucket for ingots. Lead him up the hill, where he can watch them digging out the mountain and the pool where they clean off the earth and stuff.'

'She's reliable?' I ask him. 'I don't want being handed in, or taken, in the woods ... bad things.'

'She'll do what you want,' says Jozo. 'Write your stories, interpret. Carry your bucket. Trust her – if she asks, pay in advance....'

'Svetlana?' I start. 'Like my Moscow friend ... Sveta?'

'You don't look the sort with friends,' she says. We scramble on.

Another Sabrine – supple, mute ... Julietta – in control, indifferent.... Cristel – a fleeting sentence, full of vowels.

'You're not up to much,' she says. 'I'll be frank – you don't speak languages, you're out of shape. You have a yellow eye, full of deceit and lust.... It's my fate, I know – my mother's fault, but you're my bed and board, my food, my entertainment....'

'The mist here,' I say, uncertain. 'It's thick as bread.'

'I'm hungry too,' she says. 'And this is rain. These clouds come from the sea – salty and incessant.'

'Jozo will know where we are....' I begin.

'Oh, we're all family, of course,' she says. 'We must lose him, or he'll trade us.... I'm lucky – I'm too thin to dance.'

I don't ask. It may be evident.

'You don't seem the predatory type,' she says, looking at me very closely. 'You have the eye, but you all have that. You seem the sentimental kind. I suppose everybody has a psychology, with its little folds and pockets – you can deceive yourself. But – not me. That's good.'

'You're very smart, Svetlana,' I tell her. 'You want money, I want love. There's the basis for a deal there.'

'Until the fog clears,' she says. 'We'll have to bunk down here, in this old hut. We can't see the mine until there's light.'

Of course, I know there is no mine. No love either, naturally.

'You know the languages, Sveta,' I say. 'Probably each one. You could do a piece on where we were. I slept, I saw the stars. I don't know anything, and what I do – I can't communicate. The local colour – put that in, some dirty deeds as well....'

*

Je me brulay à la chandelle
Ainsi que fait le papillon.
                                    – Charles d'Orléans

She works on my piece. No questions, no pauses.

'Send this to your wife,' she says. 'Or whatever she seems to you.'

'Editor,' I say. 'Nothing. The mechanic. But, Sveta – a comment – allow me. This piece – I haven't been here, where you say I am. It's misspelt and dangles – I don't know even where this is. The flags. The conspirators, the odd geology. Those characters – you go into their persons, their fears, resentments, castration, Oedipus, their fiddles with their brothers, sisters too – the nurse who isn't – then the ambitions, the ideologies – Lenin, the Qur'an.... And now the streets, the guys on scooters shooting at the windows, birdshot, the tanks up sidestreets – it is not me, not what we were in last night....'

'I put the colour in,' she says, 'just like you said. But I've been through all this – most people have. There wasn't time for rape or misapproapriation – I could go on. I promise you, the people love these ordinary things. They couldn't give a fuck about the stars, the cheese ... still less about the bus.... Probably you ramble in your sleep.'

'You remember everything,' I say. 'It does no good. My friend in Russia, Svetlana – she remembered nothing, she was born too late. It does no good.'

'And you, Miro, your head is full of other people – what they said, people with the same name, different cities, history, catastrophe, dclarations of respect, affection – all bundled up, like in a foresaken trunk. It's because you're nothing much yourself. That's not depth, it's scatter, Miro,' Sveta says.

'I'm sure you're right,' I say. 'It makes no difference. I don't want depth. It does no good to me, or anyone – I'm here to pick up sparkly things. If you ever have a nest – you'll hang them on it. Much good will that do.'

'The kids used to come up here to do their drugs,' says Sveta. 'Now they don't bother.'

'To climb up? Or do them?' I ask, irritated.

'Often it's both,' she says. 'There's more joy in selling than there is in using. You need a thin body to go with thin legs to get up here,' and she looks critically at me. 'On a man, thin legs are rubbish, especially if the body's suetty. You must be one of a piece, Miro.'

'I try,' I say. 'But ... we're stuck here in the edge of the edge, staring down into a pot of cold steam. The world – it's changed ... goodbye socialism, hallo China, suicide and depletion of our riches.... They say suicide is eating gold – well, here we are, mouths agape, a-dribble for it....'

'You're snide,' Sveta says. 'This is the world. To make a kilo of gold, you have to junk a mountain. This is the mountain. This is the world. The people here, if they can, go all over – they make it all spin ... they're the *plongeurs*, footballers, bankers, generals, bombers and security ... they'll never speak the language, give their real name. They feed you, defend and threaten you, make your clock tick and your blood turn sour....'

'The books don't say this,' I say.

'That's why they're books,' she says. 'What I tell you is what is.'

This rouses in me – a great curiosity. About her. About her body. I've seen her soul....

She goes on, 'People may be crap, but the world without people is a squashed rock.'

'We can sleep here,' I say. 'The mine will open up. I'll keep you warm.'

She grins.

The night is very dark. Animals wander round – bumping into trees. No one howls. Sveta sleeps curled like an open ear on a bed she invents. She's nothing to say: for sure, she doesn't give invites.

*

'This is not the centre of the world, Sveta: you can stay, I must go,' I say.

'You have to go round,' she says. 'Not find a spot. Besides – when you look out through your eyes – who shares the view?'

'No one,' I say. 'Listen, Svetlana, I've heard all this. Each is the centre of their world. "I see, therefore it's there". Something is. It's false, all that. An elementary mistake. In any case "your world" doesn't belong to you, however much you move around. See – down there, there's no mine, no movement, no security.'

'Gold – you can't see it, naturally,' she says. 'It lies invisible, beneath the soil.'

'I'm hungry,' I tell her. 'Don't hit me with these feeble fantasies and metaphors. What we came to see – it isn't there. Enough.'

'Well,' she says. 'What next? You are so finicky – if it doesn't fit a philosophy, to you, it can't exist. Stout Cortès would have stayed in bed, if he'd been you.'

'I can't travel with you, Sveta,' I say. 'You're so small, a waif – they'll think I'm a paedophile, or trafficking you....'

'Maybe you are, maybe I am,' she says. 'Make a fire and cook these peppers that I found.'

I do. The peppers are the best.

'I don't want this,' I say. 'It's the wrong kind; a story not for me – the intimacy, the cuteness, my stock role, the anomalies, the conclusions piddling and discordant.'

'It's you, put the lust in,' she says. 'And then you cut it out.'

*

'There is gold here,' says Sveta: 'It's not in the ground, though. It's words. Not yours. To leave here, guys need lots of cash. You're here to help.'

'I can't speak the language, though,' I say.

'Don't worry,' Sveta says, 'It's a small affair. We need someone to protect, someone from outside. It's just the way it's done – take care of me, and I'll do the same or more for you.'

'I haven't understood,' I say.

'That's the best way: you are a guarantee,' she says. 'It's best if you don't know.'

I don't understand a word they say, the three of them: the two from down below, and Sveta. Two big grown-up youths from the town beneath, who don't look directly at me. They don't ask why I'm here. They know, I don't.

It wasn't like this the last time I was in this place, which to most people – doesn't exist.

*

'There, it's done,' says Sveta. 'The prospectors have gone, staked claims, struck the lode, paydirt, panned out, robbed the earth – all that! None of us, we didn't feel a thing, and you, my dear, were ideal. Pig in the middle – the people here oughtn't eat pork, so you are safe. You can stay or go. Jozo loves you I am sure, but he won't be waiting up for you.'

'I'm happy not to grasp....' I say. 'There's nothing for me here.'

She doesn't react to that. Nor to anything I say.

I complain, 'I'd have asked you to be a guide, inform me about something – you're not much fun, and now even that has gone. You're compromised, indifferent.'

'Oh, even you can understand, I'm not welcome here to swan around,' she says. 'But I don't profit from the deal. I'm as I was before....' She looks downcast.

'I have to go on round....' I say.

Neither wants to cut things short, and neither has a different idea of where to go. We leave it there, for now. Together.

'Meeting Jozo didn't bring you luck,' she says. 'You won't get anywhere with him – I'd say he was ... the hole in the canvas, a person scissoring themselves out. With no foe, no friend.'

'Like you,' I say, hoping she'd react.

'Like me,' she says.

*

Early on Sunday mornings, the black limousines take the narrow mountain roads, out of the province, that to most people does not exist, cross some frontiers, load up somewhere with food and drink for commissaries, bring back another load of diplomats and fixers, promises of reinforcements, military. There's soldiers everywhere, looking for trouble. It should be what they don't want to find. Their trouble would be on them heavy, if there's trouble here.... If only they were ingots, like Jozo said, everyone would be content.

'I could take you on to Moscow, Sveta,' I say. 'But I'd leave you there. That would be no good for you.'

'I'm not sure the world turns there any more,' she says. 'If once it did.'

'Oh, once it did, or else people would not have put up with it,' I say.

*

We go roundabout. In Poland, we find my sad friend Jiri, still sad – happy last before he had been born. 'There's nothing new,' he says. 'Though it all is.'

I tell Sveta – this world we're in must be a minor purgatory for those in life who failed to do their good, or bad. The punishment is going round and round, all their promises not fulfilled....

'You shouldn't make promises, Miro, I don't,' she says.

'You don't believe there'll be a future, that is why,' I say.

'What difference would that make?' she asks.

*

In the Moscow Metro, I start to tell her all the history; who built this marvel, a spread of riches not seen above ... the people foaming down the escalators like a black-brown spate, a waterfalling – and do those ladies still stand below, to stop the mechanism if they see there's a collapse...?

'Wait here,' I say. '"Komsomolskaya" – I'll be back.' She is impassive. I go right out, beyond the end of the extended line, to the periphery.... There's the low blue house where Nina lived – windows empty, where she stacked her jars, the bottled specimens all gone, the plot abandoned reedy, yellow... Poor Nina, lucky Nina. Dead, moved on. Good destiny or bad? Promoted or exploited; both?

Strangers with stuff in plastic bags push in and out the low blue door – do they have the right? Did she? What right have I? I pass on by – don't recognise the neighbours....

I wonder if Sveta waited there, where I abandoned her. I don't go back, don't stop to look. Leave her.

She never expected much.

Where next?

*

Out East – the first snow. The animals – if they have seen a winter, grim; they know what they have to face, the others, the new litters – catch a flake. Yes, it's wonderful, but watch out!

I should avoid Xinjiang, my crooked friend in Urumchi – my visit, improbable, no help. The nightmare of the Ush revolt and massacre – still hanging on....

Watch out! ... Everybody!

Too late!

*

I send a message for Cristel, the ice queen. 'The project will be to reduce the population. There'll be a global movement. Self-denial, species massacre, suicide? Those who will be left – how will they be chosen? As a sample? Or eugenics – a test to select the resilient?

'An education with a single culture and curriculum: order. Prettiness and nostalgia on the side. Organised by corporations. Science shackled to the boss....

'The remainders, survivors, the saved, the chosen – herded into what is left as living space. That will be stormy, dry and smelly, except when it is hot and cold and foggy. They – we – will be orderly, all in the same way – though some of us will march against, and sneer. There'll be resistance – cults and sects, chiliasts and Muggletonians, nationalists and true fachos, the unshorn, exalted, the tattooed all over, and the spotless.... False victories all round. No inheritances, low incomes, low taxes. Paternalism, internment, toleration and intolerance.

'Not many beasts – signs: "do not eat the animals". No cats and dogs – can't walk the pooches in the fog, cats' fur blocks our lungs.

'I see it put together, Cristel; now. The future still wears old clothes, executioners bear the ancestral axe. But – the worse is being prepared as well.

'What was our defence against our nature, that has gone. Something more ordered, decisive, arbitrary and stifling, takes its place. An ideology of constraint....'

Cristel replies at once –

'No!' she tells me. 'Move around, you bug, you slow worm! No speculation, repetitive and ephemeral. Instead – colour! Difference. Movement! Don't try divination, futurology: nothing will be done – we follow forces without grasping them, we'll huddle on a rock, the last above the waves, a trillion of us....'

'They'll watch movies of the whales like we watch movies of the dinosaurs,' I tell her. 'Or there will come the next big bang. Time's wasted: then its hands are blown away.'

*

Cristel tells me: 'Do not despair. It's not allowed. Be wicked. Do not look down the telescope. That is for real mariners. It makes no difference to them or you, seeing things big or small.

Don't do it, don't spy out the future, don't try to write it down; you don't do it well. Everything exists, except the future. Look at your clothes – blood, brains, lymph and bones – not yours.... Mourn and rejoice. Did you forget the wars already gone, the massacres and deportations, the wrong guerillas, terror, horror and despair?'

*

'How many of the passers-by,' I ask myself. 'Are narks? How many, addicted? How many ready for a trip, over to the other shore? Dissent? The cops here are very big.

'I missed the war, back in the forest, with Sveta. She missed it too, though every day it's with her, heavy and invisible. You miss things, but there they are, in you for ever, twisted like coloured glass in paperweights: that doesn't gyre, but everything else gyres on a spiral.... Step into it, the twister, the maelstrom: easy to say, if it's playing on a screen, a loop.

'I'm my own actor. I'm already all my consciousness. I think, think on and on, every day – "stop this, start that, run, fight, parley". You can get closer, view, participate in a famine, in a revolution, a demo – but you can't be all of it. You're in a little part, clutching your wobbling existence.... The whole, you see it later; when it's a frieze, a tapestry. Sabrine jumped fully in, and ignorant – and now ... she's nothing. A martyr. For other people to interpret, or forget.'

No one answers, thoughts don't ever count.

*

Over there – the Ostankino serf museum and estate.

'The serfs – had to be freed,' says a seedy-looking man, sitting down beside me on the cold cold bench. 'Not kindness. To modernise the agriculture, and send off labour to the industries.'

'Yes,' I say. 'Not enough left the land. They stayed; then there were kulaks, grain requisitioned, famine....'

'Those musical serfs, the artisans the gophers, they would have been happy and fulfilled,' he says, not paying heed to me.

'Even working as the *servitù* for the nobility. Food, warmth. Your mates, some sex....'

I turn away: it's getting reactionary. I'm afraid of nets, of being caught in something – real, or mental. Cops. He is on me, like a fog ... a fisherman.

'I'm Yuri, here's my hand,' he says. And there it is – quite muscular, he holds too long, and squeezes rhythmically. He's shaved – not well. Probably he lives alone, and doesn't give a shit about too much....

'The other shore,' he says. 'It's been appropriated: like the wild side was. The other shore: it now means "gay".'

He looks at me, a question.... 'I'm afraid I'm straight,' I say.

'It's not just that,' he says. 'The populists ... invented it. The alternative, the shore, the people....'

'I know,' I say. 'They're not like populists around us now. Those social distances then were just too great to make them signify....'

'The other shore! – we know what happened then. Instead of landfall in a revolution – reforms arriving from up top,' he says, rolling his eyes. 'Now, everything arrives from there. Or doesn't come at all. It's always what you are – a pig, or a dissatisfied: conformist or a revolutionary. Dead in bed or on the steppe. Of course – there's empire too – no one can shake those off. They cling on like a conjurer's cloak. Big magic pockets full of doves ... and magic rabbits too. The dragomen in osprey plumes, with hangers; the colonised in rags.... Always an anomaly, empire: quiet emptiness annexed, a tragedy at first, then – it drags on ... and on.'

'It's cold,' I say. 'I should be gone.'

'You should,' he says. 'Your blood is thin. To pump it up, to where you think ... the brain. Yours – starves! You need a Russian *dusha,* soul. A heart, that is.'

'I'll take the underground....' I say, backing off.

We travel round and round. He takes my arm, we talk the nineteenth century. It's warm down here. I've made a friend – a friend I didn't want. We end up far away, in the periphery.

*

'I'll warm you up,' he says. His house is low, a greeny-blue, garden forlorn, the onions gone to seed – they threaten, they rear up like knobkerries... the garden trips you, all rusts into earth, here's a bath, a scythe. Inside the shabby hut, it's very cold.

'Going round the world, eh?' he asks, pouring a cloudy shot of vodka in a cloudy glass, and waiting silent while I get it down. 'You'll have to take part in many cultures and their rites. They'll suck you in. Here, we have an autocrat, again, more potent ... shoving in, after the revolution! That's perverse.... Perversity is regular, of course. It's history. Like everywhere, we are at war, inside and out – you saw the big guys, the soldiers and the cops ... not just here, but spread all over.... War used to be the last resort, the exception – now, it's a sign of health. A good economy means – the prisons are full up and spilling over every day. A gathering of nations: there's photos and a kiss ... behind the scene – you'll bet a people's being singled out, put into the camps....'

'I'm not a part of that,' I say, stumbling towards the door, 'I don't join in....'

It's dark outside. 'It's late,' says Yuri. 'You won't find your way.'

It's true. I've nowhere I can go.

'So,' he says, lighting a kerosene lamp. 'You have no choice: for you, it means the other shore!'

'That isn't here,' I say, playing the game. 'It used to mean the chance for transformation. It's changed its sense – now, it must be a metaphor....

'Here, there's the biggest stock of land you'll ever find, until it starts to melt.... I go around the world, and so – there is no other shore. I know! It's round!' I'm shouting now.

'Maybe the shore is coming here,' he says. 'That makes it easier for you.'

'Oh,' I say. 'I'm with you. The shore – it's where I didn't think to go. The East, the East! Once red – now, who can describe it? A cinnamon? An imported sherry tint – of straw or reed ...Is that the very best? Sip sip, luxuriate: good taste's insipid! Better – hooch! Vodka, genuine – home-made.

'The future's beige....'

I take another shot of alabaster booze.

I say, 'Now: China. They were the pioneers – their plan was "control the population". They were the first. Now it's imperative: survival ... It means a smaller market too, alas. We're in the soup, hot and steamy, but we must economise, or it means we'll have to eat each other ... we spicy dumplings ... yumyum, I just love that steam-boat...!'

'Whoa!' says Yuri. 'Don't gallop so, my little horse! Of course – we have this empty land: and they have made a dustbowl. China will be rebuilt. In Siberia. It's begun already. What Russians couldn't populate, the empty empire – others will, for sure....'

'I thought the other shore was what is happening here, the secret opposition....' I insist: 'Come on! Now you tell me it's a charitable act – land in exchange for people....'

'Yes,' says Yuri. 'But people not like us! Once, we created the new man, the Soviet hero. Then, he wobbled, staggered just like you ... the drink, my friend! These people coming have the qualities we lacked ... they make kitsch, a mountain of it, with not a hesitation, not a blench – they have no resources, so they make tat! And sell it. Genius....'

'It seems to me,' I say. 'You sow confusion. These previsions – they're delusionary....'

'Maybe so,' he says. 'Once, the world was set on moving left to right, then left again; peace to war, and back. Now – it all comes on together. We have peace and war, left and right, order ... forced labour and consuming stuff you do not want....'

'I'm tired,' I say. 'Tomorrow, no more rhetoric. I'll leave. Just let me lie down here.... I don't know if you're an opponent, a dissident, a provocateur, just an eccentric....'

What can he see in me? A revolutionary? A pig?

*

I can't believe Yuri had sexual interest in anyone beyond himself. He used the terms, he used my body like a lecturer would use a lectern – but there was nothing sensual; not at all. He had no depth, no psychology, only the worldview he's elaborated. He wants to grasp the whole, the reality he's turning out ... baking quintals of reality baguettes each day.

He's not alone –

Our Presidents, all – they have no depth. They want to win at what they want, money no object, even if the wanting costs themselves ... a bomb, an army: use what is required ... create a famine, a desert; make everybody walk, live in bakelite long-houses; torture, bribe – it's of no consequence. A consequence can always be deferred, discounted: cheated by a suicide, assassination – death and transfiguration of the golem – of the Prince, Princess....

*

I'm convinced – no one has depth. Some have silence, seem mysterious. Complexity is never depth, it's a mix: of motives, interests.

*

Yuri is close to China. He shows me catalogues and documents. Hides things secret that I see, can't read. His business? Trade? Or change ... grubbing out the roots of life, tamping in the new...? Maybe sex comes in: the earliest form of traffic. Smokes and pills too – those temple virgins and their priests ... the pioneers.

'Well,' says Yuri. 'You've been wavering all night, you've tried to analyse. Your "round the world"! – you've found the world's not round, you can't return to where you started out, your tales are memories of mirages, inventions....'

'Forms of thought,' I say. 'You've brought me back to that. You are my subject, Yuri. You're a fascination. Modes of thinking – that's where I began. The scientific, the magic and the metaphysical.... The mind – it dances to so many tunes – more and more: rejects them all in turn.... Maybe there's new rhythms, melodies, yet to be felt....'

*

Behind the cold cold dacha – a big industrial shed. Inside, a clicking – 'Soldiers?' I ask –

'No,' Yuri says, 'they're dressed like them, but they are not. They're doing goods.'

'Good?' I ask.

'I think so,' says Yuri. 'Not everybody does. There's people here, want the monopoly of everything.'

'I understand,' I say. 'This is The Other Shore: I see the sign outside. You import stuff, corner the market ... you must be someone's bridgehead. All you talked about – cosmology, the world: it's tinsel. It's what you are distributing, deceptive things that first define, then they *become* us.... When we're all dead –'

'Coffins too,' he says. 'And spades. You are quite wrong, though. The crap – is to cover up the platinum, the ambition underneath....'

'It may well be,' I say. 'But – I do something else.... I report! I cannot stay....'

*

'Cristel!' I shout, 'how did you find me....'

'I know where everybody is,' she says. 'That was my job. And now – they've fired us both. Your pieces? – nonsense! And now – this dump! At least, use the scythe to cut the flowers...!'

It's not a good idea – not to come here, not to be fired, not to bring criticism.

She takes a shot of vodka –

'It tastes quite strange,' I say. 'They make it taste like this – they put it in to mask the taste it starts with.'

'I'm sad,' says Cristel, pouring more. 'But it's a wonderful day – "such as only cities conjure forth". Forget the rain and sleet....'

'Cristel,' I ask. 'Did you fire me first? Then they got rid of you?'

She doesn't say. I tell her, 'They're stupid, Cristel. The story here's the biggest, biggest ever – it needs a fine mind that can unravel it.'

*

Cristel asks Yuri, 'Why him, why Miro? What is he to you? A writer – swift as a sharpened sabre? Eroticist? A mystic warrior?

'You're import–export, Yuri. It's me who has the contacts. I am useful. Miro – a remarkable adventurer, a genius who'll lead you through the marsh, no doubt ... but – an aimless wanderer....'

'None of that,' says Yuri. 'He is not the first I've importuned. I pick them out – they're sat, solitary, and contemplate dead souls. Serfdom.'

'You're not at all like that, Yuri,' Cristel says. 'You hustle, organise. You plot. You have no model: you make pacts, and you betray. You settle continents – then see the people swept away. And do you weep, or suffer...?'

'I'd not thought,' says Yuri. 'I don't have answers to all that. It's you who has the questions, Cristel ... you have drawn your map.... One thing: we all betray: the three of us, we do....'

'It sounds profound,' says Cristel, 'but no one's bothered by this prissy talk. Everybody wants to know when they will die, who's loved us, did we make love with them? Did we try fixing something ... or happily do nothing much.... I just tell you like it is.'

'I never met anyone who did just that,' Yuri says. 'Truth and honesty – I don't know how I'd handle it. I can deal with liars. Fakers. Miro too. He has the lust, it claws his scalp, a heavy vulture.

'But – I've never heard of honest people getting anywhere....'

'People here, rich people, people on the make – they live in splendid palaces,' says Cristel.... 'But you...?'

'Well, I live basic,' Yuri says. 'Primitive. The people! Yes!'

'Miro and me – we were never lovers,' Cristel says, sizing Yuri up. 'Shan't try it out again.'

'It's very cold in here,' says Yuri. 'You'll get used to it. It isn't even winter yet.'

*

'Yuri may have a potent plan,' Cristel says to me, 'but he looks dirty. I'd say he smells too.'

'We all do,' I say. 'It's very cold. There's rainwater – but it doesn't rain in winter. One day I expect it will. We'll probably be dirtier then.... The soldiers – they manage well – look like they just came out the carwash....'

'They're not real soldiers,' Cristel says. 'They just dress like that.'

'Yuri wants me to write about his case, the enterprise: The Other Shore,' I tell her. 'Say what he wants; defending him, if he is caught. But – you got me fired.'

'Oh,' she says. 'I'll get you an accreditation, that's no prob.'

'Where will you go?' I ask her. 'To be anonymous. North Africa? Europe is shot, Africa – it shakes....'

'I'll be a Rimbaud,' Cristel says. 'Going where there's lime-trees. Trading in anything. Tusks and muskets. Now everywhere is hot, so choice of country doesn't matter.... You'll moulder here, Miro. You can't do proper journalism, and you don't grasp what Yuri wants. Another Collateral Campaign? Cracking the codes? Moving the planet further from the sun?

'Or something radical – start civilisation off again, left-foot first this time: you have the scythe outside for agriculture. Grow grain: they say that starts the state, and makes addiction too – ferment, distil, you'll need the vodka ... that old bath – washing is civilisation, *luxe et volupté*. The soldiers – your security, your army.... Remember, if you can, poor Sabrine ... there'll be room for martyrs too.'

'You're snide,' I say. 'You and I, Cristel, we should be allies. We're not in a good, transparent place.'

'This is no good, Miro,' she says. 'This place. Movement of populations, shifting balances. Out of step. Who wants "civilisation – a replay"? There's no responsibilities now – everything that's begun is too ambitious or it fails before it starts. Hand the initiative back. The people, Miro! Let them take the rap....'

'You've glimpsed a trail, Cristel,' I say. 'Yuri's plan is – go back, do serfdom properly, then abolish it. Renewal – comes from the East – but it's been done bad. The Mongols, Cristel: they left a scattering of peoples driven on, scuddering before a wind that slept on ponyback.'

'That isn't his idea, Miro,' she says. 'It's yours. It doesn't
sail. They'll spot his cash, and he, and all of us – we'll go to
jail.... It doesn't end with something new, Miro – it's the old
duels, madness, Lermontov and turning up the ace....'

She could be right.

'Well, it means I'll have gone round –' I say '– not the world,
that's past our efforts, can't be saved.... Round the history.
Nothing to be done. It's circular. We're trapped, doomed.
Nothing ever can be undone, done better, not done at all.'

'You don't want civilisation, Miro,' Cristel says. 'In Yuri's
version, it's serfs who settle, buy, and then stay on for ever. If
that's the end, you don't want that.

'You want another kind of life: totally different, and
unthinkable. You have accidie, my dear.'

'No one can think out of their life,' I say. 'We don't even
want the duel, where often one survives. We don't want suicide.
We want nothing, and nothing's on the way! Of course –
"nothing" ever quite arrives! It's an optional, but there's no
agent, no subject – so it turns out, it isn't optional. That's what
you get: the wait. I see it all – and you're right, there's nothing I
can do....'

'Magic realism has taken over,' says Cristel. 'Look in your
pocket! It's an ocean – above, there's fearful tars, singing their
work songs, riding the waves. Below – there is the deep, the
dark. Every shape and every appetite: the magic. The deep.
Cries of lost mariners: the realism. Forms of thought – don't
enter in....'

The loss, the fear of disembodiment, is strong.... I put out my
hand to Cristel, her thin pliable arm.... She pulls away. 'I can't
journey with you, Miro. You're all knees and paws.'

'I'm afraid, Cristel,' I say. 'Aren't you? I'm afraid of going to
jail. Of never touching another human. Of falling into Yuri's
design, of falling through the hole in my telephone, of falling
not through air or water but through stories, senseless,
intimidating: you can't start or finish them ... like the first day at
school when you knew you knew nothing, and never would; that
other people sized you up, wondered how to wrestle you, make
you smaller than you were, kiss and betray you, punch, deceive
you....'

'No, Miro, none of that,' she says. 'I have other fears. Of returning to my origins, where I began. Better the cataclysms than that!'

'Why did you follow me?' I ask.

'I have a plan,' she says, 'and you are in it with the rest. But – the plan is me. I make the rules, everywhere I go – but – I always move. There's never settling.... You'll find one day what I can't invent.'

*

'I need a publicist,' says Yuri. 'Someone to make me out quite different from what I am – make me an innocent, fixated on my profits and my good.'

'People don't believe,' I say. 'They can't trust evidence, don't know what it is. I can puff you, Yuri, or can tell the truth. It comes out empty either way. Besides, schemes like yours – they're everywhere.'

*

'You're finished here,' says Yuri. 'I understand – you don't trust the rich to save the world. My view – restore the serfdom, this time – it's inevitable, and this time, permanent. Desired, accepted. The old illusions – each person, a world unto themselves ... those have gone....'

'I can't move on,' I say. 'I'm blocked...'

He waves a hand – the nails are long and sharp – 'Look!' he says.

There's a slender craft outside – a ship? a plane? 'For you,' he says. 'Cristel can walk – she is substantial – Paris is near, besides....'

Here's Cristel, with a pair of carpet bags – one, she hands to me. 'If you go down the corkscrew stair,' she whispers. 'There's pallets, full of bales of cash ... quick, take yours, I'll be off with mine.... The last favour I shall do for you....'

Yuri's not curious: the very rich can act that way. They don't have an immunity – but, they think they are the rocket fuel of change....

'Don't stop to fantasticate, Miro,' Cristel says. 'Go! Go East....'

I've no regrets. The craft I've boarded quivers with desire – off, away; we rise!

I ask the captain, pilot – 'Do you know where....'

'Oh, Yuri often sends the failures further on,' he says. 'We Han, we always went around the world – settled Siberia, then the Americas.... It was all known, so then the ships were junked. The maps were in the archives, no one ever bothered with them. We sailed and flew by instinct, or by intelligence. The world was empty then, except for animals. Now, the animals are gone, it's emptying out of humans, but they cluster, throng where things are desperate....'

Now – I feel profound regret.

'I should have trusted him,' I say. 'Yuri had a plan – I feared him, and feared his failure even more....'

'Oh, Yuri,' laughs the pilot, as we see below, the grids of unbuilt cities, new rivers and canals dug out, the ground raised up on stilts, trucks full of guys with spades.... 'He has a plan. So do they all: don't trust him. All the truth you need to know: people welcome serfdom, if it saves their lives.... You have a task. Be a brave soldier – you must go on and circumnavigate, my friend....'

'But – I've nowhere to report my news,' I say.

'Remember Sabrine,' the guy says, swooping us over borders, sacred rivers, over yellow reedy empty towns, the great walls tumbled down in arid fields, grey combs when all the bees have fallen sick, termite palaces forsaken, crumbling down.... 'Sabrine went round, and no one cared – not even you. You, Miro? Writers don't write about what is, but what they think they were themselves, and who they think they may have known....'

*

The sea – grey, quilted: a flat chest. At last, the land's forgotten.

A spot, a dot upon the lens. Could be the start – of penicillin.... A new species? There rides an island, tucked in

among the waves. Moving blotches, grey and brown, as in we
float – borzois and chow-chows.

'People are stupid,' the captain says, as we wheel in under a
canopy. 'They live in a future, that they've been foretold. They
think that anything unfamiliar must be the past. Yet here we are:
it's now.'

'The people, though,' I say. 'However stupid – they're not
here.'

'It was a base – when the Chinese left their continent,' he
says. 'The Americans had no need to stay and frighten us. It was
a nuisance to pack up – so, they left it all, the PX, the "hershey
gold" – pretzes and peanuts, what a treat! – the Doctor Pepper....
The dogs eat the caramels but can't work the machines ... they
don't have the coins. We find it hard to hold round things: – we
Han are smarter than the rest, we put our cash on strings, but
monkeys are more handy, as though they had invented
everything. Even time – it seems that's round, it rolls; clocks
stand still, their wheels revolve, hands circle round for always....
Watching them – oh what *tristesse*.... We should have a
timepiece that is linear ... that creeps along the ground, goes
somewhere like a path, a hose, moves on – or is vertical, reaches
a height, and disappears so's you can aspire.'

'What now?' I ask. 'I know Yuri well. He pictured me, sat
here on a bench, waiting for the serfs – paddling their log,
coming ashore. Maybe he didn't mean "serfs". People move
around now, the land deserts them – perhaps he meant slaves,
but who owns them? Serfs perhaps we are – in bondage to the
soil, our harvests and our mines. Our time: comes with its "up".

'There's slave-owners, they mostly don't recognise their
slaves. We feel it, though – the yoke, the whip, dependency. It's
what you're born, like if you are a Dalit, and you feel you are,
resent, struggle all your life.... Anyway, Yuri has a theory of the
round, the shape of time. Beginning feudalism, herding the dogs
for wool, then digging down – here in the unforgiving sun, start
it off again, expound free trade, hypothesise that peoples are
born free, too bad there's no guys here to colonise and liberate
... build cities on the ruined cities, invent religions where the
magic doesn't work, you can't speak with the dead, or roam

round in hell. There's industry and oligarchs ... and then, and then....'

'Yes,' says the captain, 'Yuri dreamed that up for you. You failed him. He had a chapter waiting that you didn't read. It all goes different. It leaves you out, him – he's the great mover.... You are a reject, Miro,' and he laughs.

'You read the chapter, then?' I ask.

'No no,' the captain says, putting on his wings – the pilot once again. 'I don't do futurology! Besides, I'm happy as I am, a serf tied to the air,' he laughs again.... 'I don't believe he'll ever finish it, the chapter of the now, besides....' And off he goes.

*

Cythera? The banal Eldorado? I wander round – the dogs are tranquil, there's macaques and bonobos ... the grass is tall, pampas denser, higher than a human ... the red blue yellow buzzing waspy things ... birds tiny: birds gargantuan....

A pleasant profusion and neglect, a struggle for display, scenes, colours that invoke a Klein.... I feel the need for someone ... not selected, as I've clung to them by instinct or by desperation, but for the compatibility I've never found. One day....

My friend, invisible and delicate – she leads me in a hangar, down the steps. Americans! Gone home....

It's where they kept the armaments, the rockets, bombs. They left them primed, in case they need come back. What care, it's quite pernickety! – each bomb and rocket labelled with a name, a city and its population. Some are fizzing. Harmless of course, I think, and there's a coat of foam on some.... There is a sign – 'China first' it says. Some names chalked on I recognise – Guiyang, Zigong, Jixi, and many that I don't ... then rows of stranger ones – Palu and Syktyvkar, Blysk ... there's more and more, Paris, Saqqaq ... the Americas, Japan, Arabia ... Mopti, Noranda ... an atlas of the future, every friend, rival, competitor, ally gone sour and out of love, potential, actual foe or mere indifferent. And chalked on most – a message blunt: – 'enough!' 'touch-down!', 'dust, dust, dust!' 'goodbye commies' ...

'croak!' '... bankers' '... surfers' '... miners' '... minors'. Obscenities on most. Girls' names, boys' names – ah yes, the family. Lovers.

A global malediction, or – for sure, a joke.... In any case, the spoof farewells become illegible when they explode – there must be thousands, millions here, all wired together, in relays, for every continent – a gazeteer....

It's clear, this is Aphrodite's isle, the island which will survive, ensure, and cause obliteration of the rest, whichever way the geo or the cosmos veers, whatever the diplomacy and not. The answer here is comprehensive.... Even, it reassures, the personal, the human touch, last rites: a *marameo* – derision and contempt ... to each – a farewell gesture: the umbrella.

How all I've met have wanted me to find the final answers, clear at last. These silos answer every hypothesis and doubt, make light of all apostasies.

Forget all that. It's speculation.

I wander down the ranks, inspecting; almost all are well turned out, their fins erect, their nose-cones bulled, shiny-wet like labradors'.

There's so many! – how to launch them, even hundreds at a time? The island – the surface must be just a lid, that raises up: exposes ranks, files, of hostile tubes, a buried army, each warrior handmade, each tailored to its target, a state assassin, huge, medium, and small. And what will happen here, to us, on the land? We all – me, dogs and monkeys now, and once the soldiers too – do we slide off, go down down in the sea? Or, surely, the squaddies would have left, waited in boats...?

Though – sacrifice has been a winning theme in human epics....

.

*

THE CATCH

The lid, that lifts when the weapons have been primed and raised – is there a catch that's held it down? For curiosity – what keeps it shut, the lid? – and could the gadget slip and fail one night and throw us helter-skelter in the sea, fauna, flora, me?

Hydraulics? A worm you work, a shanty to go with, like sailors with their capstan bars?

No, there must be a code. Or – is it just that: – a catch! – you sing it, hum it – even a chord might loose the closure's hold. By chance, the wind in wires or grass, these hemlock stalks – a rhythm, a drumming with the hand, a knackers' beat, a bongo riff ... is there to be a disco strum, a ditty that will end the world?

... at least, ends our species' strut on it.

*

This paradise ... after an hour of solitude, it wears; a day – it grinds. The catch. I cannot sleep for worrying – suppose in sleep I gasp or gurgle – set it all off, the world in tatters ...what can they have devised, a trigger no one could divine – and yet, not for ever foolproof ... some fool ... Gravitational waves? a pattern known to rocketry alone: a throb? A snatch of Leadbelly? Shamanic chant of indigenes who now have disappeared, been scalped, eliminated, till one day, a log is paddled in, the fleeing warriors landed on the shore begin their song of freedom, vengeance ... might they hit upon the theme? The island rears, the whole display springs up like crocus shoots, the fuses light ... 'yah-boo fuck you' the messages shout out – the rockets go erect – the coup de grace, a blaze.... The end of the experiment, of us. The revelations, fire and blood ... afterwards – an eternity of silence, desolation....

In centuries, some creature at her telescope may see our glim, our splutter ... attribute it to physics. Not to the muse of music; still less to Santa Cecilia....

*

A wondrous invention! The island floats. Somewhere there must be a motor, a compass. It could be that. Sabrine hitched a ride on it, tied up her boat, was spirited along ... another segment of her circle done the easy way. Is this a Circe's isle, that dodges round the sea – mystifying the captains, courageous ones and not, the chartmakers: slipping up estuaries, deltas, riding on bores, refreshing around Antarctica, boiling in the plastic seas...?

Of course! – the dogs are well equipped for snow and heat, they must adapt to warmth and winds, ice, dog days – and summer nights ... a world cruise without end....

I search for signs. 'Sabrine was here....', though she was not the writing sort.

It's Yuri who shifts populations ... and he doesn't need to move. I, instead, am quite alone, and go around the globe – on ship island ... island ship....

My tale, it comes around.

*

If you don't find the motor, then of course, you drift.

How many more, I wonder – of these impotent battleships, once supposed to solve the crucial problem, now themselves problematic, written into our complicated end? No more is there a cry of 'the men refuse to eat their borshch' – though it was maggoty meat, I'm sure.... No men, no women, here. Forces of nature will prevail: still controlled from somewhere – where, who? – a threat made universal, comprehensive ... or forgotten, every cargo off the manifests...?

*

There's a function here, a 'find a friend' ... no batteries, no Chinese emporium you buy them at – but there are pedals; do a distance on the bike, cross some borders, and the panel lights.... Who shall I contact now? Julietta? Cristel?

A message jumps: 'are your former lovers friends?' No way to answer that one, naturally ... no one to discuss it with.... The island's motto.... 'Beauty above, destruction underneath'.

Destruction. You think 'chaos', but it's not. It's threat, direction, impulse but not impulsiveness. A plan, in tiny detail, made as his masterpiece by the god of death, of indiscrimination .... a universal of oblivion, the void ... generalised. This god – he left his judgment here to fester like a virus pool....

A human, I suppose, any human, corporal or above, can be His agent.

A people can consent, assent to the end of all the rest. End up obliterated with them.

Cristel, Julietta – can I see them as belonging here: the beautiful? The pacifiers, the orderers? Saviours – unlikely, that.

Maybe Sveta is the malign, the presence here. Abandonment. She shouts out to the crowds – 'my god! Omniscient destroyer – forsaken me again!'

It's so impersonal – we're told to let our Dionysian side express itself ... here for sure there is no art to hold it all in check, to give it form, a moral cast, detachment, artifice – no art, unless there's been a castaway, an indigene, a Friday, full of grace: made a dog-mask, joined in the rites, the midnight howls ... my brother. Or my sister.

We float, like death. And death we are.

Should I call Julietta, send a messenger? Revolution for two? Cristel, for cool comfort?

*

I bark, I roar.... Run up and down the beach – steel, ridged, milled for tracked carriers.... I tear my clothes – and no one hears, or sees, or cares. Without a public sat to watch, tragedy and comedy are mute – hands wrung, a piece of shtick.... The criminal, the victim – need a retribution or a pardon. The Thebans swallow the atrocity, every one of them, calmly shoo you out their sight....

The dogs back off, wait for your mood to change. There's things: the rockets; apes, dogs and me; shapes in the grass and in the cellars: what does it mean, how to represent – what isn't there? The sense, the size, the awfulness, the folly ... not felt. They're there, but not to be seen. Aesthetics? Is that the monocle you wear to see the qualities invisible? Fairies dancing in the glade...? I make myself a mask: Guro, Kwele – borrow something that has worked. Carve a shaman's staff.

Find the right mode of thought, to understand, to dramatise. Express, hint at what reality and matter can't. The science is quite evident, has created, motivated everything that's here to see. It's nothing ... doesn't mean a thing, doesn't reveal. The guillotine – an excellent device for cutting heads: science applied. It makes the emptiness some story-teller has to fill.

*

The sea is grey because the sky is grey. The water, though – look down, you see bright green ... we're snagged in algae: – the water, though – it's particulate, a *pointillisme* gone mad. I wander round – these dogs, abandoned pets – all have their courage, their self-esteem – back, restored.

I've got old here – Crusoe in reverse. He made new life, a settlement, all ready for his slave... No slaves for me – old age, perhaps. He raved, though, like I do. Invoking the invisible.

When you age, all the emotion you've repressed before comes bubbling out, a cascade of incomprehension, emotion unrelated to the real, it's taffy ... Or else, its mate, its couple, complement – is forgetting everything, reaching coffin-peace....

*

My mask is hot: I don't take it off. My staff's dead wood – I smack it at the dandelions. The bigger the monster we are walking on, the smaller do we feel – Siegfrieds dodging round the dragon, a hop, a scuttle – and we're beetling past unseen, our sting still sheathed. Our many feet don't raise a sparkle in the dust.

If there is someone here – abandoned, or wrecked, dropped, swimming ashore, survived unsaved, cast away – they'll hide.

... Not a Friday – better a Tuesday's child with far to go; and maybe take me too. Abandoned, a Marygold? I'd sooner – a Rosinette.

A boiler, seven metres tall – could house someone. I rap, I hammer with my stick, and out she runs –

Rosinette!

'A dogface,' she says, wondering. 'A lemur? Spectre?'

*

The order. It dominates everything around. The dogs in species, fish in cans. There's only me – alone, you can't be in any order. You – are you caught in the orderly?' she asks me. 'It breaks me down, how reality forms in ranks of twos and fives. You found me – but I am not a friend, nor a variety. You could have used the porthole – "find a friend".'

'Julietta – wants a modern coup,' I say. 'She was my friend. Cristel – wants a peopled place where she can be alone, and make her rules. You're exactly what we need, dear Rosinette – and ... do you find in me....'

'Nothing, Miro,' says Rosinette. 'I wanted no one, and you're him.' She laughs.

*

'I've been very careful with the food,' she says. 'We don't know how long....'

'You know the place,' I say. 'Explored ... hypothesised....'

'Oh no,' she says. 'Hardly any more time here than you. If we eat the food in cans – it's gone for good: there's no fish round – the algae suffocates. I don't want to eat the dogs – and plants here, they're poisonous....'

'You must have seen the rockets, Rosinette,' I say. 'That isn't part of us, we're innocent, but we will suffer just the same, as if the history's a species thing – the building of disaster and revenge, involving everyone in what they didn't want.'

'I never went downstairs,' says Rosinette. 'It's dark, the atoms get inside your eyes....'

'I tried to improvise,' I say. 'My clothes – I flew in from Moscow ... here, it's humid.... Maybe there's uniforms....'

'Oh yes,' she says. 'An army of them. Navy too.'

I choose a general's, with medals, unnamed stars – not as many as I'd have, back there with Yuri – but, enough.

'I still think like a shaman, Rosinette, I say. 'I can give orders – though not to you – you're not here to serve....'

'No,' she says. 'But we may stay here till we die – even if the rest dies too – some tripwire, sensor, code – a tune ... may set it off. So, do we satisfy ourselves? Each other? Or exemplify? And no one sees or knows, suggests....'

'I know,' I say. 'I've thought all that, quite unavailingly. Before arriving here I had a history profound. I know why people were afraid: maybe not enough.... First we want to escape our lives – and then we have to.

'Yuri thought big, but that's probably why he may be now in jail. We're small here, Rosinette – outside, they seem much larger, brushing us aside ... we seem naive....'

'You, Miro, seem quite crazed,' she says.

Not what I'd hoped she'd say. First, we are ourselves; then part of something quite beyond ourselves. My form of thought's exactly right for island life, with death in spades beneath our feet.... Think! As a shamanic beast, seeking its space, me, the only one to go downstairs....

'That boiler, Rosinette,' I say. 'If it was off a ship, there must have been high waves here.... Now, it seems the waters cover everything, even their own swell. They've won, they're are supreme, and calm ... a colloid....'

'The boiler was for boiling whales,' she says. 'A museum piece – dark, frightening, no dogs come in – it is my sanctuary.'

*

'Someone knows where we are,' I say. 'We're not forsaken, surely? Our friends....'

'You don't have friends,' says Rosinette, straining at the generator, pedalling hard. 'I've tried "acquaintances..." "people you recognise..." "real humans..." Someone must have blocked you off, Miro. Everybody knows exactly where we are. Anyone can want you, for anything. No one seems interested, Miro –

'Julietta.... Either her coup failed, or the sophisticates fell out with her: she's on the lam. She banked on intelligence and change – suspicion swept her away.

'Cristel told you – it's her job to know where everybody is. It's a big task – but rather trivial. Her work's not much, it leaves no trace. What are they, those outmoded two, what do they mean to you? That's old time, Miro.

'Sabrine – she understood – you have to stake your life each time the wheel comes round ... she's the success. Me – I try for something else: profundity.' She smiles and frowns. 'What's too deep for you to see.'

'We could do the history over,' I say. 'This time – get it right. We could take these arms, pledge them for the revolution – which lesson? Which is right? Party or *foco,* power through mass organisation, or the guerilla?'

'I think we can have both,' says Rosinette. 'Hypothetically. We two can reach a compromise. We can't destroy the armaments, though. We don't know how. Who would we ask? There's no one we can trust.'

'You're right,' I say. 'We've reached the end, in a single stride. Finished, no chance of development, no mode of thought, no revolutionary sensibility. Just you and me. Reaction setting in again – the island – just a metaphor: life above, death below. There's people who see their environment as a body – the clouds are breath, the river – blood, the huts – the eyes, the organs.... Metaphor – it's not much, a snack between the feasts we mustn't have. It's big as your world, a silk sack.... And then? We're much limited, Rosinette.'

'There is another way, Miro,' she says. 'We have a table here, we play our game upon it – the you and me, the black, the white – are interchangeable. Hope and despair: resignation – survival. A joust – paper lances, wooden swords. A single mind.... That's us, all there is.'

'There's lots of dope here, Rosinette,' I say. 'You take that, and you're everyone.'

'That's what they say,' she says. 'But everyone is what we already are. Everyone we want can come, spend time, pet the borzois – not touch the food, not hack paths in the garden, cut the flowers – leave everything as we have made it.'

'There's sex,' I say. 'But – I guess that isn't practicable.'

She laughs. 'No, that's the real limit you have set.'

Ah Rosinette! – my soul, my canvas and my brush.

'You know, that if you should ever leave the island, I'll not come with you,' she says.

*

You try to be a Crusoe. Make houses for the dogs, cut the dead fronds from the palmtrees, harvest the olives. You don't need do anything, but idleness is hard, much harder than what's unnecessary but virtuous. Most things the monkeys undo when they're done, or being done. I find exactly how I can live, and where it starts to fall apart – you clear the ground, you find the wires and relays – be very very careful, you might set it off, upset the balance – animals fall sick, pass it to you....

*

'Suppose,' says Rosinette, 'Yuri was wrong, and you, Miro, wrong about most things.... Suppose China, the Chinese, stay mostly put, accept short lives, eat beans and chicken wings....'

'At least I'm serious,' I say. 'I'm like those old philosophers – lead you along, pour you out more booze, you're at their banquet after all – so, you agree, reluctantly, with what they are fantasticating, and in the end, you're in their net! You've agreed to everything. 'I took you by the nose, abstractly, so it doesn't hurt – and you walked after at my pace.' The trip is all that counts – what do I care, if you agree or not? I'm in the conjuring trade, that's all! My propositions – make you into what you wouldn't want! Well then – be assertive. Try again. Another dialogue? I'm game! You don't like me, don't sympathise, don't even dislike me enough to feel hostility. You've been led on to where you didn't think, or didn't want to go.... The win is mine – there are no draws.'

'And in the end, we're stuck here on these bombs,' says Rosinette. 'If we're found – where will we go? They'll maybe change the missile settings, tow us somewhere ... and then, and then? And in the end, I, you too, realise – you're documented, I'm not. They'll take you, leave me. I won't exist for them ... and not for you.'

'I'll try to take a part of you,' I say. 'Though – we don't know where we'll go....'

I'm not convinced. Morally, taking Rosinette – that's smuggling people, so they say....

We never find the motor for the screws – it might mean it's hidden in a mechanism we don't want to operate. Maybe the motor has a motor – and, that could operate the catch ... and that could be the catch.... Without us, the dogs, the monkeys – they do well. We just eat what's in the stock of cans and drink the Doctor Pepper: life can exist without us, without humankind. Plants – sort themselves out.

The sea is getting stickier, the winds tug us, but we seem aground. I wonder, if Sabrine had an engine somewhere, to send her on when she was stuck, a stretch of nothing's much like any other stretch ... the goddam sea....

... I'm nearly round the globe, seen little, learned still less....

*

A lurch, a bump. We've hit the land. No time to gather Rosinette – I step ashore, the island disconnects – backs off, drifts – twenty metres from the shore, then more.... How they bark, the dogs! The monkeys pelt me – bottles, sour fruit.... I walk fast, then I run....

*

La peinture ne s'explique pas, on la regarde

– Renoir

'That was a big island,' says a guy I know as Folco. 'Every ship – it needs a crew. Sailors are few nowadays, but some you need. Where are your mates, your mate?'

It's true – I am alone.

'I know nothing,' I say, concealing everything. 'I know about my life, but nothing about where I've been, what it signifies, what will become of it, life ... world. I see – swirls of people, like starlings, making diagrams, da Vinci shapes of solid geometries. The wingmen – I'd hoped to be one of them – manoeuvring the fragile mass: in the flock, you need to keep your eye on seven others to keep your space, your span – if you're on the edge, it's only five or less. Then, there's the falcon, trying to direct us all, cut one out, land on it, like a bolt.'

'No,' says Folco. 'They're trying to control the whole – they've already eaten. Perhaps – they'd like to farm a herd. Your single thin birds and shitty feathers – no interest whatever.

'They don't suspect – they're not autonomous. The predators are trained, hoodwinked, blinded – they're used to the dark, these little manmade hawks.'

'You're robbers,' I say, uncertain. 'Pirates.'

He looks aware: silent. Looks seaward – nothing.

When you come ashore here, there's ultramarine, a band or coat of lapis blue on all the ranks of white houses, some with an asphodel by the door – it's unforgettable.

'If you'd hooked on to my ship,' I say, 'you'd be a big power now. But, you're right: let it go, drift – what's the use? a load of duties, then a tile dropping on your head: the end. Tall like you, Folco, your fall would bring down other trees. A big man, then a tiny coffin, like Fidel's.'

'We're black Greeks,' says Folco. 'That's what they say. Got shipwrecked, interbred, assimilated in the flesh, hybrid in the mind.'

You notice – though you don't comment – their teeth – they're filed jagged, but they're black and brown – sick sharks. Greek? Sounds to me like Cantonese....

'I'll always remember you, and Dosolina,' I say. 'Taking me in. I don't see, though – how, why, you will let me go. You're pirates – I don't care. I have no cash, I write, I don't tell tales. There's lots of money round, just fish. Here, you've found none.'

'Wait till the doctor comes, Miro,' says Folco. 'Have him check you. Then you can go.'

'When will he come?' I ask. I always ask that. I'm fine.

'He knows,' says Folco, 'We don't.'

*

My island – it was power, not worth. It's worth more if it sinks: then, it's the biggest story ever. If it floats – it's a disaster, for some day.

I've gone round the world, Even a little more.

'Let's go to the bar,' says Folco. 'Tell your story. Make your analysis. Alliances – they interest me. What happens when you ally with your best friend's worst enemy? What happens if you go to war with someone, say you were attacked, that all your allies must defend you – and they don't? Or if they do?'

'It all works out, Folco,' I say. 'It's the new diplomacy. Trade goes on, until you do accounts. Then – you switch.... Everyone's in danger – there's nothing in the system tells you what to do. Do you wait? Ignore? Panic? You're Greek, you should know how hard it is to extinguish states. Behind a state, there's a whole history of earlier states – big and little, holy empires, theocracies, assassins, cities and mountains. All those have been states, all persist.

'Trade routes even – they're a kind of state.'

'I know,' he says. 'We're not just Greeks: we're black Greeks. It's crucial, that. We had empires, dynasties....

'Trade routes – stronger than these modern states, their people doing disparate stuff, forever changing jobs, not moving round a continent, traded, but saying they're not dependent. If you don't need other people, don't travel far, far beyond your world, you don't find anything that's new.'

'Do you think, Folco,' I ask, 'we hope the world will end? All having to hustle, not knowing what is true....'

'Like going to the moon? In your big powerful ship?' he asks. 'False?'

We've been here before. A ripple wall of languages.

*

If Rosinette were here, what would she advise? Procrastinate. Stretch out the time like taffy, fluff it out like candy floss – 'you're boring, Miro, they'll get tired of you. You'll leave, end up somewhere else.'

'I love it here, Rosinette,' I say. 'I hate it because I can't get out, there's nowhere else to go.'

'Don't be stupid,' Rosinette would say. 'Everybody's been around the world – it happens when you travel west to east, the quickest way. You don't see anything at all. Remember – trade routes last longer than a frontier, even if there are no caravans.

Watch you don't get traded. You had all the power, and now –
you're just a bundle on a donkey's back.'

*

The blue houses – they're beautiful, simple – no fun to live in. If
the roofs are taken off, they look like the oldest houses anyone
has ever found, dug up.

*

'You look fine to me,' the doctor says. 'How're you going to
pay me?'

He wears a creamy suit, like Selassie did. I had a friend with
one: the modern oily cogs and rachets get it dirty in five
minutes.

The doctor is impeccable.

'I was on a mission,' I tell him. 'My chief was fired. She'd
fired me first. Bad moves: I was to be her impressionist, sucking
people in to read the ads, but really, if I can't do fiction, which
I'm truly gifted for, I'd do geopolitics.'

'We all do those,' the doctor says. 'The poetry, the warnings
of the doom awaiting.

'Trade. Think about that. It moves people. Ideas travel; plod.
Ideas – they're camels: slow but sure, and full of fat. The
caravanserai – a fine invention. There's peace in them – and if
you don't trade – exaggerate, make friends, buy drinks – you
will die out. Absorbed, assimilated, occupied and massacred.
Those bastards, whoever they may be – bring their diseases too!
If there's trade, you don't need go and steal – it's delivered to
you. If you don't pay – no treats....'

'Reflect, dear doctor, maybe you've heard,' I say.... 'The
letter to the Americans. It didn't work – people prefer their own
environment, experience, the elves and spirits in the bush, the
pub, the bed.... The world – to go around, what did I need to
know? What did Sabrine excogitate? Forget the cash, the lack of
it – to go around the world, you need not know a thing. Nothing
at all. That is the point – you come back with your brain as

smooth and meaty as a marble egg. You're clean. Receptive. Satisfied.'

'That's not entirely so,' the doctor says, taking a syringe from his bag, injecting his arm against infections, the conspiracies here that buzz around – cicadas on the spree. 'What you believe, the way you think – it's necessary, though it gums you up. It is a tarpit. Going round the world, you say – is cleansing. True, perhaps – but never quite completely so. Indeed – beliefs follow one another – it's a camel train. Ideas – they want you to take them in, put garlands on their heads and fetters on their feet – belong to you, enslaved – they then become beliefs.... Hard to be rid of – maybe, even, you don't want.'

I ponder this. 'My question is,' I say. 'When can I leave this pair, delightful as they are, dear Folco: and my love forbidden – Dosolina. As Folco says, 'Here, there's liberty and licence too. Just – leave our women folk alone – they don't want you, and we want them. That is the law. You need laws everywhere, it's hard, but even monkeys have them – lemurs, ants and bees as well – the unsung legislators of the hive and heap....'

I'm indifferent. All doctors argue so – you're doctor of philosophy, even if for you – philosophy is dead. I ask, plucking at his shirt, 'When can I go away, to somewhere else?'

'You have no destination and no craft,' the doctor says. 'You've been everywhere, seen everybody who's survived the trip, has plans for you, themselves, the universe. This, my friend – this is the end ... until ...'

'How much,' I ask, 'is your until – a till, for sure, negated as it starts...?'

'Hoho,' the doctor laughs. 'A paradox! My friend, you're wasted here – the beauty and the peace, the meagre food – earned without a massacring or exploitating. Not for you, it seems. Here – you live in truth, and beauty. Beauty and truth. They're not enough for you – a paradise would pall. Add peace, esteem, respect. Still not enough. Tradition, enterprise, equality? You call those piracy and nicking other people's good....

'What big demands you have! The planet wobbles, and the universe – a mass of gas and whirling globs – matter invisible or black, marauding, going bang and ploff without alarms ... still you cry 'more, more!'

'You know – this ends in disaster, in your death. Our bodies ought to last millennia – a lump of rock goes on for centuries – and we are pliable, we can shoot up, smoke dope, run distances, aim straight, have transplants, lose arms and legs and hop along ... And yet – the wanting: kills us young.'

'What is your price?' I ask.

'You don't know how to trade, my friend,' he says, sadness in his face, and briskness too: 'Negotiation can take years ... unto the final handshake. Remember, Miro – the Sistine hand of God, stretched out to make a deal with man .... the finger, never making it, becomes a pointing accusation, threat ... Now, there's one big God I wouldn't trust....

'When, how, do you want to go, my friend?'

'Now,' I say. 'Today. A boat, a beast. A kite, a tunnel. Out, away....'

'In a word,' he says, 'I want. My goal, my life ... Dosolina. Folco's relative, his captive – I don't ask what her status is. She is my love ... No doubt it is reciprocal.... To my love, just add a letter, "lover" it becomes....'

He looks with longing to where fair Dosolina hoes her row ... of asphodels, memorials for all who're lost at sea, or somewhere else ... like me, lost, landed at random in a place, wanting to get away from there ... and so, and so.

Ah! Asphodels ... They grow in every land and soil – I've left a score of them behind, and maybe people grieving too.

Of course – I've lusted after her – Dosolina! But – Folco's machete warned me off. She grins, she flirts ... could she want me? Or her desire – to change her life ... like me ... Does she anticipate drama? A new mode of thinking? More significance ... appearing on the culture map...?

'I'm the oven and the broom,' she says. 'The nurse, the donkey and the scold ... I feel your fantasies, like beetles on my arms and scuttling up my clothes ... what do you want, what do you offer me?'

'No transformation. Dosolina – just a ride, a little further up your road ... a private trade.....' I say.

'I'd get a better class of slavery,' says Dosolina. 'But what's in it for you, Miro, my friend?'

'I get liberty!' I say: 'Think! The good for me outweighs the bad for you. I'm sure you must believe in love – it's abstract, so we can assign to it a goodness in itself. By definition, it's desirable, you'd sacrifice your teeth to have it for a day. Whatever weight you give it – what significance – it will bear it – it's an Atlas.... Do everything for love – and once I'm off, away, I'll campaign to give you freedom too.....'

'You've got me wrong,' says Dosolina. 'I don't give much weight to love, it being maybe what ocasionally you feel, but not at all relating to what I am, to what I'm in. The argument escapes you, I am sure.... You want out! – and I'm your knotted rope of sheets, a grappling iron to get you up the wall, your limousine that takes you off to join your band – I'm the leg up that you need to start your flight.... Loyalty to the species, to the band – that's what love is, Miro, like the monkeys have. They're where we learned our love and jealousy....'

'I love philosophy,' I say, greatly impressed. 'More, even, than I feel my love for you. If I had known you were the speculating kind....'

'The Doctor, Miro – he does deals,' she says. 'He makes you offers. You take risks. Life, death or incapacity: guilt, innocence or somewhere in between. He's medical and legal, surgeon and lawyer. His trade is life, not love. Do you believe, my friend, he'll ever strike an honest bargain? You're not a chief – you are a dromedary – you'll carry his treasure on your back. What you call your freedom – will turn out "abandonment" at best....'

'I'll take it, Dosolina,' I tell her. 'Going round the world – it is the solitude we're born with, and will be our destiny in death. What you call abandonment – is tramping on. Singing a song.'

We'll slip away....

'How did you get here, Dosolina?' I ask, politely.

'I was on a tall ship. Folco came – they rocked the ship. I fell,' she says. 'Sailing on the sea is hell: it's walking on elastic high-wires – no net, no arena sand beneath....'

'Bondage is part of every life that moves, changes, recognises seasons and necessities,' I say. '"*Freiheit!*" It comes. It must! It's the movement.'

'An illusion,' says Dosolina. 'An abstraction. A "more or less", "this way or that". I don't believe you, there's no alternation, no stupid master and no clever slave. It's not about knowledge; it's power. The big terms are always present and it doesn't mean a thing. You feel them all together, love and hate, but it doesn't mean you aren't always in your cage.

'Besides – Folco isn't one you give a pill to and he sleeps, while I'm borne off and invisible. That's opera.

'He's in the bar with thirty of his gang. The sixty eyes – see in the dark. The doctor – he won't challenge Folco. Folco works for him. When he has me, the good doctor will offer me protection, that is all, and in the end – I shall be yoked, feet broken, tendons cut....'

'You must invent,' I say. 'That's what it's all about. The higher up the hierarchy you go – the more the grandees hate the stupid ones. Play dumb. They'll tire of you. Develop spots and boils. Go mad. Don't wash....'

'You're really desperate, Miro,' she says. 'You will escape, with nothing but your skin. Everything is changing here – there's a contract for a tar-pit imminent ... all will be rich, and sticky.... You're Sheherazade, you do nothing but tell tales. You want us two to steal away by starry night ... it won't be so....'

'You want to leave here,' I say. 'Not go there. There'll be a compromise. When they sleep in the afternoon we'll go – and, if my destiny was such, we'd make a pair, Dosolina. But destiny – I know, you don't believe. Nor do I – my story is about life – but just a singular one. Like all of them. The best characters on, in, earth, are mummified, they're exhibited, reappear: over and over – magi, virgins, messiahs: there's no end, they're all in stock and dusted, on the shelf, ready to be used again. It's not good, it's a curse. A limitation, an obstacle. A humanism, a humanity – hobbled at the start.... Lemurs walk like us, and wave their tails – but they can jump their height and more. We can't. Humility's required....'

'Free me, lock me up: free me, I'll escape. I'll eat your eyes, Miro,' she says. 'And cut out your lying tongue and fry it with a sterile egg ... once you've showed me the road to take....'

I ignore this, mostly.

'Compassion?' I ask, 'it's a killer. People don't expect it. They know the language and the bureaucrats – order and somehow hope. But we know we must catch the fish ourselves.

Showing it's hard, that it can't last, whatever they try to do – it's not required. Don't empathise – that door is closed. There's agencies that put up camps – that's the compassion, Dosolina. Maybe everyone gets out. Maybe no one does.... You weep for others? You expose yourself. That's all.

'Cristel wanted colour, anything but black and white – then she tottered, and was gone. Never had anything to say for on her own behalf, only told other people what to do.... Going round the world – my tales ... what did they do?'

Dosolina isn't listening. She wants out, that's all....

*

It's not at all what I had hoped. Dosolina – already she's a larger beauty, expanding, muscular and angry ... very angry; raging....

'Enough, Miro,' she says. 'You're another of those whose speciality is bullying the poor.... You call your selfishness – a toleration: tolerance. Crap! Tolerance is just passivity.

'Away go one bunch – there's another, waiting with their cash – and yours! You selfish bastard! When we're away from here – I'll cut your throat and drink your blood. Does me more good than tepid water....'

'No, no,' I say. 'The Doctor ... He will send a truck.... Folco will accept some cash for you, you'll have a better life, and I....

'The good life, Dosolina, is travelling the world, with little cash, and telling stories; colour, depth.... It takes a writer.... There's experience ... and you forget ... but memory is deep, like a cold well. Language is soft and sexy, like a plasticine; then, there is the past.... The masters ... scribes intent on monitoring their sales.... Experience transformed – the work of art flows from your pen, your fingers.... Truth, Dosolina – that is where truth starts.'

We argue on. We run on – the sun is crippling, and we find some shade – darkness comes, we're shaking with the thirst.... No one has come for us, nor followed ... and we tramp on, not far.... It's night, and cold.

'I'm off,' says Dosolina. 'There are militias, gangs, that I can join. They'll train me to take aim at guys like you.... You came around the world, thinking you'd go back to where you started from. You're wrong. The world is flat – when there is light, you'll see it's so. It's mostly sand and dust and sometimes scrub. It's hot. It's very hot. And cold. That is the start. Very soon, the limit's reached: now, comes the rhetoric. The wanting's far outrun what you could achieve. We humans know the rest – your eyes flick up, glimpsing the ethereal – but no! It is the sun, the sun, unvanquished comrade, burning us up ... flickering out....

'And Miro – you are vulnerable – I'm stronger than you seem, and you've no boss, and now ... you've made some enemies – Folco behind, the Doctor scouting out in front, both maybe looking for us....'

*

She's gone – vengeance, someone's unwanted destiny, an amazon, striding towards them....

'You're right,' I say. 'I wanted love, and what I got was truth....'

There's no one I can tell that to.

Dosolina's gone. She's right, the earth is flat, it's very flat. And yet – she's out of sight – maybe there's a curve, declivity. She could have fled before, but maybe there was – sex? Or food? Or fear? Or nothing much.... Gravity holds you while you think ... you need to be convinced before you flee – the Greeks said: 'the worse is better than the bad'.

Dosolina's decided – she'll be death: search out guilt, indifference and innocence, passivity, reaction – with her scythe she'll take it on herself to do the dirty work. The cause – it pardons anything.

Death, indiscriminate – she follows in the Master's steps. It isn't true, though, that after dirt comes clean and cleanliness: ask any chambermaid or toilet wallah. It's not so, no, not at all.

*

Not Folco, nor the Doctor – neither would be kind to me. The cash the doctor promised when I would deliver her ... gone, gone utterly.

I take the direction opposite to where she went....

*

She took the good road, to a bad end, I think.

My road – is bad. I thought there'd be more bones. The foxes hunt the rats that polish foxes' scaffoldings.

I'm lost. Still alive. What is being? I can't answer that, though it's often asked. I nearly know what being isn't, and there would be an end to it.

What I've pursued in going round – is something else. What does it, life, being, death – anything! – what does it *mean*, what does it signify? That's poetry, a fiction certainly; sometimes history, that fiction of the dullest sort....

Sand – there's up and down. It doesn't mean variety – the sameness is the up and down. Beneath me there is water – the hidden inter-continental lake, oil and water that drives your camel, drives your car, quite out of reach. I cannot drill. Find an oasis, there'll be soldiers – they can drill....

I could be shot – I'm short and dun, slink like a fox. Smell like a fox: pant, let my lying tongue droop like a fox's tongue....

No, no human skeleton here gets name or number: anything.

Should I lie down at full stretch, as if I'm striving? – or foetal: as if I've reached a goal?

*

I rest. Being. I feed, am fed. Consume, and am consumed. That is the political economy.

Do we produce too much, too many people, too much crap? The system's in equilibrium, *do ut des*. It ought to go for ever – but it won't. It doesn't. I love, am I loved? – it isn't all around, it's cancelled out. The sum – is zero ... and the smell! is putrefaction. That's what's left, our reek. I'm lucky – here, it's hot and dry: we burn up easy....

I burn.

*

'Stop fantasising', says the guy: 'Drink this!'

It's a manhattan. How thoughtful this guy is, and – how silent his approach, his dune buggy runs like silk ... the threads ... they track us back ... a fortress, a small lake, the palmtrees....

'Here,' says the guy, 'Idir' his name or corporation says, upon his smock – 'We have true communism. What you always sought – we're not the chancers here that you frequent – Sabrine and Cristel – post-civilisation types. Heroic loner-losers.

'We solve the problem that looms over you and all the rest – we live in equity, we sell the overheated wrecks that stagger in from cataclysm – serve food and water, telephones. We've engineered a change of seasons, temperatures our grannies knew....'

It's not the time to question him.

'We're mostly millionaires,' Idir goes on. 'Not that we splash the news around.'

'It doesn't interest me – not at all,' I say. 'I gave up on money when I was a child, like I did on chasing jaguars. What interests me is – did any of my loves end up within these walls? Is there a compensation for what we are, aliens on a whirling world.... Sabrine is dead, and Cristel went and never came, Sveta I didn't like and ran out on ... Julietta – she was cool.... Dosolina – settling scores, and wanting cleanliness....'

'Ah! Julietta,' says Idir. 'She made lots of cash and dropped in here – the coup went well until.... They took too much – rewards can only last so long.

'You may have opted for intangibles – love, respect, all that. Well, as you see – those are ephemeral.... We're humans, Miro – what we lost when we evolved, was the respect for bands – and for the hierarchy. We've had great men, great women too – and more are waiting – but alas ... they're human; disrespectful, and vainglorious. We bow before the strong, but then we overestimate our strength ... so, we're exploited and complain. In short, we humans are a pain. You'd never love a person of that sort....'

'Well,' I say. 'I can't dissent.'

They kill a goat to welcome me – I'm troubled by its squeals: it kicks and cries, but I've gone through some terrible ordeals.

'I'm sure you need some sex,' says Idir. *'Eat the goat, and afterwards, for modest sums – a pill and massage, that will set you up....'*

*

'Drink this....' says someone, 'and be quiet'.

He's tied me to his donkey, I'm dragged on through the sand.

No questions, no descriptions – no need to think. The hut – full of rejected things. Klébu is a scavenger. I'm not a useful find.

*

'No more babbling,' says Klébu. 'I can restore your life, that's all. Now, you must forage, like I do. What have you learned, Miro? When you were in trance – you saw the walls full of pictures, friezes – by your namesake, Mirò. Is there a clue in them? A clue to what? What have you learnt – gone round the world, and seeing everything, experiencing every sensation, feeling, every plot and fronde? Keeping cool, never the fall-guy, mostly the silent victim ... never the warrior....'

'Everything's impermanent,' I say. 'We all knew that. You use stuff up, then find a substitute or do without, or mine a star – all finishes, you do without, invent a substitute – you love, they throw you out, you die, you grow up, become bored, impotent, betrayed, traduced, sold to a slaver, buried in the cellar – earthquake, war, subsidence, or there's no room in the cemetery, not even for a cup of ash....'

'Tout passe,' says Klébu. 'That, we knew. What else?'

'I shan't tell you everything,' I say. 'My trance was luxurious; your hut and trade – less than the minimum.'

'You've earned no more; and even – you expected less,' says Klébu. 'It isn't love or stars that last, nor liberty, nor bondage. Exchange? Consumption? Tell me, Miro....'

'It's not original,' I say. 'It's mathematics. And you need a tool to access it, the silent universe. Order – you'll need – imagination. I have mountains of it.... You can't call it inventiveness ... creation of what exists already.... I leave the argument – it goes beyond my competence. My interest as well....'

'It's a joke,' says Klébu. 'Because it's something that you have to laugh at. You may not laugh, and then it falls, quite dead. It's an anomaly that happens to be true. Algorithms make a good religion – their origins obscure, a future projected, useful, crucial, but leading who knows where? Presenting answers without the means of doing something with them ... the imams, shamans, popes and priests – they understand. You don't.... Mathematics makes a good god, Miro....'

'That's casuistry, Klébu,' I say. 'It's only plausible because there's no negation for it ... and it's exactly like the other gods we've had, who've made everything, oversee it all, accomplish nothing, depart the scene ... mysteries that fill in gaps we've made.'

'It's not about religion,' Klébu says. 'You're fixated. It's about the truth.'

'Then truth,' I say, 'is self-defining. It's what it says it is.'

'So be it then,' he says.

I feel we should be experts, to continue. Or to start.

'So, going round the world, participating, seeing everything, in person or through ... all those women! Maybe you just gave them female names?' he asks.

'They were absolutely themselves,' I say. 'As I saw them, anyway.'

'They could be anything,' he insists, '– shards, places, aspirations, states of mind. Love, sex, lust! What can you have been looking for? Did you find it, find anything? Enjoy? Remember your reactions...? Don't tell me that stuff is interesting – it's not.'

'People follow,' I say. 'People, tides, the clouds. Write poetry about the animals, the reminiscences. I don't. I don't feel the need – I've seen it all....'

We leave it there.

Sabrine went round the world – all water. Spume and clouds.... 'the Neptune in the blood ... the trident – terrible!'

*

We tot some stuff. Discards, single shoes, torn underwear....
'What I'm looking for,' says Klébu. 'Is that old army, buried
here. Never found; but riches, Miro! Riches for a life!'

'Maybe they invented it,' I say. 'Give me a pen – I'll show
you campaigns and chariots, monsters defeated, princesses
rescued, animals subdued....'

'That can wait,' he says. 'And so must you....'

I could leave at any time, I don't know where I'd go. It's
eternal slavery – being in a place, no exit, no tunnel, skylight –
no door – just distance all around; unrevealing.

*

'You need help, Miro,' Klébu says. 'And so do I – alas, you are
not it. I have a plan....'

There is a little mosque, not used. 'See, in that squinch,' he
says. 'There is a hole – between the cupola you see inside the
mosque, and the cupola that forms the outer roof – there is a
little space. Enough for you. There, you'd find peace, enough to
let you rest, come down....'

The world stops there. Wait! Wait till you're ready.

'I'd say the monkeys would find you, come and feed you –
but round here – they've gone. No trees, no food,' he says.

'There's the faithful,' I say. 'But it's the same with them....'

He loses patience. But, he saved my life – what more? What
do I expect...?

'Use your maths to set you up,' says Klébu.

It's a fine experience: you lie on the rough skin of the lower
dome, as you'd lie upon a tiny world – above you is the starry
heavens – though you can't see anything at all of that. It is the
underside of the imagined universe, the old-time sky, where the
dead go, and the gods already are.

*

'These little worlds, like the space formed aimlessly, where I
was hunched,' I say. 'Bring comfort. Is that right? – they imply
that there's a universe of useless space, in history, in air,
beneath the sea, in ships' logs, in trees, in diaries and memories.

It needs a death, an autopsy to lay it out. Put them on velum, canvas, on the wall, on film – those little worlds. Do they suggest a big one that's a projection of all those? Is the small a reduction of the big? The big, is infinitely fragmentable...? Or are they all alike, like ants; no monster ant. None's needed. What would change, who cares if there's an ur-ant, immense, a mammoth.... Or – there's not?'

'I know your trek,' says Klébu. 'And you're wrong. You want to end up with individuals, all little reproductions of the big, that may or may not exist, but all having a commonality, like the squinch, the cupola. There's nothing shows that differences are variations on a theme, versions of itself of every shape and size....'

'No, Klébu,' I say. 'The little world was comforting, reassuring.'

'You enjoyed the safety of the interleave,' he says. 'The big world, though – it's not secure or conforming. Shapes are similar, they're limited, repeat. It's nothing. No significance, no meaning, no assurance ... not of anything. Nothing repeats, nothing is the same. Dead is dead and gone, nothing is reborn, renewed.'

'It gave Sabrine satisfaction, to know, to think, that there was completeness in the circle; that "going round" was something with an end,' I say. 'It left her in a tempest – the crowd swept her away. She was a failure: disorder won!'

'This is not a happy place, Miro,' Klébu says. 'You don't worry about that – you're always on the move. Here, bad things happen that are always different. You use the same words to describe it every time. It's not at all like that....'

'I can agree,' I say. 'I'm not happy here. And I've no one to describe it to, no one that waits for my despatch.'

'In your trade,' he says. 'The drama's made by someone else. You could join in, like Julietta: end up really really bad – a cold fish on the grill....'

*

Is this the end? Over there – there's mountains. Klébu takes my arm: he squeezes hard – and harder still. 'See over there,' he says. 'There's a huge pile of rusting junk. Tanks, cannons, carriers – all torn and crumpled up. We fought for thirty years – a village that was theirs, our goal; a poor abandoned place – still theirs....'

'Those carcases, they could be melted down,' I say. 'To make more tanks and stuff ... it seems this is your trade, to fight for principle, for territory – see deserts creep in, roads in disuse.... Carry on, for the seeable....'

'Don't pretend, Miro, don't do the moralistic show,' says Klébu. 'No destiny for us is written down – we tread the path, our natural one – ours since we invented civilisation – the man-bulls guarding, earth-mothers – the whole stock; and swords and spears perfected long before the wheel.... Be reconciled. The end is what you will decide, my friend. Maybe I should have left you in your dream. If you want flames and bangs and feathered friends from high, with phials of eternity ... you must invent it all.... Me – I'm a scavenger, like us all, like you – nothing is new, we use the stuff that's fallen off the donkey, resuscitate old bones....'

*

He takes me to the big green lake. 'You must calculate,' he says. 'It's not the sea, but you'll find it's as big, or bigger. Here you could end your circumnavigation – adding it on piecemeal, like Sabrine. Six countries border it – avoid the ones with wars, guerillas, a disease. You're straight, so the sex laws won't signify.... Go as far as you can. I've taught you nothing. so there's nothing you can blame me for.'

The passengers are heads down in their phones. I could call up Cristel, somewhere in the world, or floating – staking out space colonies. Post her my news – who knows?

Her message doesn't seem personal: no location – must be an ad: 'The Maghreb. Visit in your millions....'

'Dear Cristel, we never finished our affair,' I say. 'We could pretend – restart, or conclude it properly. You know how systems are – if you don't close right, you can't use them, never again. Up in the mountains – there you feel cool ... at night, at least. And there'll be the lion, like in the pic, watching over you as you sleep. You'll wear those lovely stripy robes....'

We wade out, pushing the boat until the water's deep enough to free the keel. Some people try a song. It's heavy, this boat, and riding mostly out the water, you can see it's been reduced quite bad.

*

The scientific mode of thought – none of us has it here, knows it, practises it. The monkey mode, I think – has done us bad: bands, territory, relying on the trees, the fruit – a dream.... The religious mode? I write, I could have written every word, made it shorter, more tolerant, fewer massacres, more miracles.... For polytheists, lots of homely gods mean latitude for sculptors. Longer stories, grist for the painters – makers of friezes, souvenirs.

We push off, the engine does a disco beat, and when it fails, some guys take out the oars. It's slow, so slow, and I'm like Sabrine now – 'Come on! the shore, the shore, the bands, the cheque, celebrity – another challenge....' I implore ... 'respect me....'

*

There's a hadith, says, 'most people in paradise are simple'. That sounds right. Paradise – should be a simple place. It's other places down below that need your wits, your wits will get you there, for sure. The people on the boat – not simple, not at all. Each speaks a different language, I don't speak one of theirs.... There's a shout – and everybody laughs. '*Echouf!*' it sounds like.

Bubbles sputter up, green in the green – volcanic, or the algae decomposed....? I'm in dirty clothes – the guy beside me, in spotless white, turns to me, grips my forearm, says 'charmant!' and I thank him. He doesn't mean that – he means 'shaman'. Him or me? So what? I know the axis of the world, the tree you climb – except there is no tree. There is a stubby mast.

I admire it greatly – the shamanic mode. They saw it all, what was visible, what not; what true, what false – the tricks, the recipes, inventions. Too smart to write it down. But then – what then? The shamans weren't the simple ones, for sure. They knew what everybody wants to know, and doesn't have a clue about.... They're limited. If you could speak directly to the dead – what would you say? 'Sabrine – be careful – you survived the sea, but the human wave ... watch out! No rashness, now!'

What would change?

I remember Sabrine, saying – 'Miro! – we won't capsize.'

It's true, we're down, down in the water – we can sink, we wallow: we shall not capsize. Did she speak to me? Some substance? What wisdom, emotion? If she did – it's gone, quite gone.

*

A relief: many people leave, disembark almost at once, we bob up – then, there's more and more approach. They walk through pools, puddles, of carbolic stuff. Disease?

Are they in flight? A mortal sickness? – of them, of animals, of us here in the boat? Pervasive, on the shore, the scientific mode. Or the bureaucratic one: the everlasting power.... All changes when they are aboard, they turn, become like us.

Maybe they're escaping genocide ... or they are gay ... believe the wrong things, the metaphysics skewed?

*

A squall? A storm? We see ahead, a city of the angels, skyscrapers, balloons, everybody always looking up ... people much taller than you are, live on top floors, use the stairs and you the elevator, you will never see them.... If they fall – do they shrink down? Are the ordinary ones, tramping the streets – the fallen angels? There's doorways there, lead straight off down to hell. The city rocks – rocks to a beat, and rocks from side to side – finance! – it wavers. You need a pool of carbolic to get rid of that, the smell – not sulphurous, not like the bubbles on the lake – more sweetish, something 'gone off'. Gone where,

I wonder – the flesh is there, the smell, though ... means something has departed, gone indeed.... Like me: I'm going off. I've finished going round – the other passengers are going somewhere, putting the ends together, tying a knot. I'm not....

Every country gives its share of passengers. We won't converse – some are sick, they're feverish, they lie and groan. Some bring their food – the geese.... They pull the heads, it breaks their necks.... It's hot, it's cold, it squalls – the feathers rise like soap flakes ... there's a band, some cops who take our prints, a death – the body doesn't sink, it follows in our wake ... the captains – should we elect them? Appoint them, or keep quiet? There's tough guys too.... They set up a rota – everyone has hours to row....

The guy in white beside me says, 'Relax! Disembark here, complete the circle some time soon. Don't be obsessed. I'll set you up – I need advice, your views on scientific thought....'

His house is clean. A woman, very very young, a girl – moves round us silently.

'She's mine,' he says. 'I found her. Maybe I'll sell her on, or marry her. What do you think?'

'I know nothing, Amidou,' I say. 'Travel should firm you up – instead, it just confuses. We all think in different ways – maybe it's good, and no one knows, or much reflects....'

'Oh, Miro,' my new friend says, and laughs. 'We're far beyond that now! Give me your ideas; then move on, give your impressions somewhere, see if there's an audience that's interested....'

He doesn't offer much.

He has books – they gave him all he knows, he doesn't need give back. We watch the boat move off, afar: uncertainly. 'You took the risk,' he says. 'That boat – they often sink, the poor, the crooks, eternal travellers – expelled or footloose – they all take the risk.... They come from all regimes, speaking all dialects, evading all controls....'

'Don't tell me, Amidou,' I say. 'I know. It isn't love – it's trade.' He ignores me.

'Of course,' he says. 'It's curiosity. But really, what they want, is smoothness. Homogeneity. A hope, a chance in every place.'

'I don't agree,' I say. 'The smooth. Nothing sticks: it doesn't simplify.'

'It's the pattern, Miro,' he says, infinitely sad. 'Familiarity. They risk, hoping that tomorrow will be exactly like today. Slowly, the seasons change, things improve, there's a disaster – then restoration; cover things up, sweep them away. Flowers on the grave – a stone on top, or just neglect and patina....'

The girl, Tulga, has us stand while she dusts underneath our chairs.

'I can't agree, Amidou,' I say. 'It's good that memory divides, disquiets us. When we are all your "one", all pebble-smooth, then you can forget the past. But – it's the future that's been falsified....'

'That's common talk,' he says. 'The books say that. When you've studied them – you get to where I am. I have arrived, gone right around. I am the One – infinitely reproduced, blown up, then leaking down, to human size. I have it all inside: "Spirit". They said it was outside: the muse, God, Hitler, being good, just being.... No! It's inside – if you don't find it, you must put it there. Now, say that I am wrong!'

'If I had finished – maybe I could,' I say. I wonder – where does this come from. A book, high on the shelf, a title, half covered in some mould – 'Beyond difference....' I remember, 'every word is a mask....'

Change the subject if you don't agree.... 'That red and yellow plant,' I say....

It reaches up to us – the window is an orifice, no pane – 'Hibiscus?'

'To certain kinds of birds, it's poisonous,' he says. 'Others – they love it, have the monopoly. They have resistance in their gut. They can't feed from the lake, that's obvious....'

*

The green, the water, striated from beneath with darker greens, and yellow....

*

'When it was the colour of the sky, when we were savages, and ate the fish, and threw cadavers in,' he says. 'It was grey and blue. Now, it's green – more beautiful. You must adjust.'

'What did you expect to learn from me?' I ask. 'I had no bags, no cash, no partner and no destination – what did that mean to you? That you were right? That you could make a buck by selling me?'

He's quiet. 'I'm your answer, the riposte,' I say. 'I didn't want your formula. So. There it is.'

'Not sell you,' he says. 'Support. My team. You, Miro, should be desperate ... you have no friend, no foothold, and no boss.'

There's guys outside, well-muscled friends. 'I'm not a neutral about anything,' I say. 'Impressionists are not. But – backing for the spirit – no, it's not my cause....'

I wonder about Tulga: fleeing in company, us too? – maybe I need caution, she's very quiet, too young, and too obedient....

*

I cross his room at night, to leave the house – Tulga's beside him with a fan. She shrugs, gives a little smile – I smile too, and on bare feet I leave the house, go past the sleeping guards, proceed on foot. I don't trust the boat. On, on, I walk, I'll finish going round the lake – nobody will check my distances – it all depends on where you do the trip ... the equator route is far too hot....

I see on Amidou's house a sign – 'Advice given – low monthly rates'.... Go slow ... I didn't take my shoes....

There's hills, so I don't need cross a frontier, they don't send people there, nor put up markers. I'm tired, I think of all the people met, unsatisfying talks, relationships not secure nor always wanted....

There's dawn! – there's no one following....

Who'll celebrate the finish of my enterprise? The old explorers, after years of bugs and buboes, bearers buried in termite palaces, fevers sweated out – they wrote the book, philosophised, left out the screwing ... brothels in Portugal, drastic cures for pox in Senegal....

I'll put in everything: people I've invented, prophecies fulfilled....

*

Someone ahead, she's milking goats. 'A drink?' I ask. 'I'll pay you when my story's bought.'

She lets me take a mouthful from a dipper, and she says, 'You must be going round the world! No one comes up here, unless....'

'And are there many doing that?' I ask, quite anxiously. 'And do they seek impressions, local colour, personalities...?

'Oh no,' she says. 'They want to talk of theories, ideas about the whole, and why the world is coming to an end, and who will come and take our place, how long might it take, and which of us will be the last.'

'Corine!' I say. 'Theory is dead because there is immense supply. They suffocated in a heap. You take your pick.... You hoped for something new? There won't be space....'

'The last guy here – he was a pushy type. He said it was desire that motored on, driving the unconscious in our brain, escaping our language that's within our grasp....' she says. 'We push along, uncontrolled, and uncontrolling....'

'The brain, Corine?' I say, and laugh. 'We've evolved, and still the brain is bigger than our thought. We've screwed up. Used our resources, contrived our end.... Can we escape? I think it's not desire, but doubt – love or death.... It seems they are inseparable. We vacillate, Corine – nothing's resolved, but on we go....

'Now – I'm much more earthy with this thought: I believe recorded practises are the determinant. Your position in the human structures – that's how you think, and act, and everybody does the same. That decides our potential, and the limitations of our future: – what we humans are and what we make. What we can create. The brain is bound by its creations.... It can do no more.

'At any rate, it seems to me our theories have been pondered over long ago....'

'*I have to move the animals,*' she says. '*Higher up the hill. It's cooler there, there is some grass....*'

'*This is your work, Corine?*' I ask. '*Maybe I should stay round here. You have a herd supporting you, and – it could be me as well.*'

'*Oh, they're not mine,*' she says. '*My family's ... they're very fussy: who's allowed to drink the milk, and who can court me too. They set time going backwards, back to where it froze. Now it's becoming hotter, they're waiting to see the melt, the catastrophe that happened long ago – the death of kings and monsters, start of new eras. Then, the birth of kings and monsters, the end of eras....*'

'*Your theory, Corine,*' I go on, not surprised at first there is an obstacle – '*I understand your wish: escape from power! My desire – sees power as ·inherent in all that we construct. "The spirit of the hive" buzzes with impermanence, the imminence of an end, extinction ... precariousness....*

'*The world returns to where it was before we came. It mends, patches, finds its old rhythm. Maybe – it becomes a clinker.*

'*We don't think like nature might, not naturally. Maybe mathematics is natural – but it doesn't fit with our predation, maybe desn't fit with anything at all except itself. I've been driven by desire, but going round, I've lost my interest in lust. I never met anyone who wanted to possess or be possessed, not for a minute, not by me. If you don't run, you're in bondage all your life....*'

'*Miro, all you know,*' says Corine, '*is going round the world. Do you describe it well? I doubt it. People love to hear about themselves, and you don't know much about them....*'

'*I'll need to do it all again,*' I say. '*Going around – in the other direction, a longer way.*'

*

Down the slope – a band of ragged guys with sticks. The herd is valuable to them, they drive it off....

I ought to comfort Corine, but there's nothing much to say....
I trot on down the hill – there's a city spreading out below ... a

yard with burnt-out tanks and carriers.... People with the pieces
of what's going on.

3

THE SHAFT

THERE'S LOTS of rules, lots of spies. What should I do? How vulnerable am I?

'Forget everything. We have the drill. The shaft – it's our solution. It used to be harder – now, we make up our own minds....' And Estelle puts on her helmet, counts the boxes.

'Once we find the sharp bit,' I say. 'No one will touch us.'

'Did you adopt a tribe?' she asks.

'It's on my list to do,' I say.

'I send them every night – 'I love you'. It's not so much. Do it!' she says. 'They tell you we're not on their land – it's mankind's. There'll not be room for them down there, down the shaft. The surface – that's what they lived off. They were defenceless, and there were informers. Don't be sorry for them – it's not reciprocal, and it's the cycle.'

'My family,' I say, 'some went with cows, and some went to the mines. The cows went first – no more leather.... Then the mines closed. Now – I'm the last one, digging down....'

Estelle says, 'We're explorers. We go sparing with the good stuff, don't say where we got it from, then we can go back for more. Or we could stay.... Burrow down ... down further.'

*

'It bothers me, Estelle,' I say. 'You're the engineer – but, we don't want a bore-hole. If we start the drill – the bit's tiny round: a lance. Very long, but useless.'

179

'Oh, you'll have to dig,' she says, and laughs. 'We'll find the place: it's barren here. Prick, prick and prick we go. Don't argue. The experimental method – it's the only one we have left. It stretches out our minds.'

'The tribe – they took the spirits with them when they left,' I say. I'm not convinced they could. 'Bahia. The streets they live in, they're already full, plenty of spirits there already.... The sadness! The slaving; human souls without divinity, unshipped there centuries ago, still lingering in the spirit. For the indigenes, it will seem another world.'

'It *is* another world,' she says, briskly. 'They're much worse off. But the scrub here – it tells you nothing, quite inscrutable. No spirits, and no animals... probably beneath, it's mud. We have to find a layered place ... open it up, and excavate.... Variety. The ages buried; lakes and marsh, cadavers ... an encyclopaedia of sediments. The earth is as variegated as space, except it's static. No gold and platinum rocks go whirling by.'

'They say – we should separate the mystery and the secret – two different spheres,' I say. 'Where does this lead...? Honour the mystery, keep the secret? What if we puncture something with the drill – a lung?'

'No one knows at the start where anything may go,' she says. 'We can invent new mysteries. The secret? – I think it's lost, been taken off and bartered.'

*

'They made a desert here,' says Estelle.

We lie close together in the dark. We never touch each other. Friends who tried to live in communes said there was no experimentation; they were like sea-birds, travelling continents but keeping to a life-long partner. Housework: that's what destroyed ideas ... the rages! Strange, as most people everywhere live in communes, if not communally.

I say, 'Will anyone but us come here again? The indigenous – never. Africans? Their continent's become a sand-box, an arena. They must come here, an empty useless place.... There can't be just the two of us. And the team. Whenever it arrives.

'Africans ... will they like me?'

'Don't fool around,' Estelle says. 'You mean, would you like them? Better say – if you write our venture down, or film it or whatever – will they appreciate it? If not them, then who? No one. That's your question, that's my answer. You're old-time – things don't signify unless you can make a fiction out of them. Guys coming here – they'll be workers, looking for hope. If they find it here – hope's all there is.... If they're from Africa – they have the right. Their fathers came in shackles.... What do you expect? If you can't find a way to bully them, they'll just ignore you – as if you'd never been.'

'If we succeed, Estelle,' I say. 'Or just look promising – then everyone will know. They'll come, everybody will: we'll be pushed out. The only success we could have – is failure. Total failure: sending away the team. Then us, free to leave, slinking off.'

'That's you,' she says. 'It isn't me. The future can be changed in many many languages. Some things we have to do because we're bigger than what happens to us.'

*

Somewhere on the way, the team dissolves. They won't arrive, not ever. Estelle and me – we rig up the drill, on jury-legs. It's heavy work. 'Here, here, and here,' she says, 'then over there. A kind of mystic knot, embroidery.'

We make some little holes. She's the geologist – for sure she has a plan.

Life without evil is boring – they say that. Here, it's boring but there's an expanse, a whole *maquis,* of evil.

'There's no civilisation here,' Estelle says. 'That was destroyed, when they burnt off the trees. So, we'll see what's underneath. My science will make something of what we find. Most people seek just discovery – I propose to use whatever we have found....'

'I hear you, Estelle,' I say. 'We're here alone. The team – it will not come.'

She's not surprised – I'm shocked, but not surprised.

'They say we have no permit, Estelle. We went to the wrong person, paid, and were palmed off: the wrong document. We're the illegals, maybe we're the evil ones....'

*

Did we come to find the shaft? Or make one?

We don't believe the truth – other people knew, will know, the place better than we do ... or ever shall ... or want to.

The science took us here – I didn't believe it knew. Some science we believe, but mostly – not. If we believed it all, we'd not be here.

Under the yellow fronds, there'll be a lake. Blackwater – you can't drink it, you might try to sell it. It tastes special. The shaft – it ends there, in water – abandoned there? A shaft of dark? A refuge. Or a mine.

'The shaft, Estelle!' I shout. 'There's steps! You knew that too?'

'Not steps – they're natural,' she says. 'I didn't know there was an anything ... it was the right place where there would be something. A shaft – is just the name, for nature or for man: a path. A fall, a space, accident – or an entrance.'

'The underneath,' I say. 'It awaits us; it's tradition that we end up there, the underground. Knowing what's beneath a thing – the underneath – requires a fine intelligence.... A contemplation....'

'There's no revelation,' Estelle says. 'Until you climb down, tell us what you see....'

*

We're historic, Estelle and me. The forest people, we don't know their history, so they are pre-historic. A little while – we'll be post-historic: nothing written down, but everything is known. The forest people, living in nature with no documents – they become post-historic too, when no one writes a history.

'Estelle,' I say. 'I think they were people wanting gold who dug the shaft. The forest people – they move around, it wasn't them. I'll bet the monks suggested it. You need a lot of gold for all those gods and spirits, to make them real, reproduce their images. That was a great invention, from monotheism into trinities, and then the saints ... the martyrs.'

'There's no gold here,' says Estelle. 'Though of course – they may not have known. You know by trial and error, not by contemplation. And the rocks.'

'You could live down there,' I say. 'Or hide. I'm sure they're steps, though rather large....'

'Another species may have made them,' Estelle says. 'But at the bottom – it's just dark....'

'The effort will have been for something. Things large enough to make those steps – they'd have feared no one....' I say.

'Unless it was a refuge,' Estelle says, playing along. 'A prison. Store for bows and arrows – or a birthing cell, a funeral home.... Of course, I knew the shaft was there – but there's no clue, what it was for.'

'You think it's chance. Nature, hit and miss, for nothing. But suppose there were people, living....' I say.

'They'll have evolved,' she says. 'It's sci-fi. They'd lose intelligence, and sight. Be unlike anyone we'd recognise.... Big spiders, millipedes – they have our characteristics, some of them, mixed in with theirs....'

'We must go down,' I say. 'We're designed for this.'

'I explore and find,' Estelle says. 'I finish there. Go down. You are the daring male, the purblind mole....'

'Sex doesn't enter, Estelle,' I say. 'Down – it could be gemstones – or a boiling tide.... If it's of value, it can't be realised here.... If it's death – this is the place!'

'I'll throw a rope,' Estelle says. 'But I'm not strong enough to pull you up.'

'We could hide,' I say. 'Suppose the Feds, the military cops – suppose they come ... we have no document....'

'If we're down there,' she says. 'They might just fill us in. Throw down the bits and boxes....'

'So,' I say. 'We run....'

'We leave,' she says. 'Exploration's done that way. You find a thing, give it a name, and off!'

'It's been our history,' I say. 'What you discover, could do good or ill. It's normal it does both. It becomes an obstacle – like the shaft, it starts to pull in everything, then it's world's end, the final reckoning. I expect – everything that's not resolved's been thrown down in the hole. It was you, Estelle, who found the tip, the dump where everything equivocal ends up. A few millennia – our style of life, our culture in its forms – has burned out everything – the sky, the soil, the animals, ourselves.'

'These grey-green bushes,' says Estelle. 'If I had taken biology, traditional medicine – I'd know if they might cure us.... You disgust me, but eat a leaf, or twig, maybe Eros would light upon us.... Or cure your fear. Instead – I see behind them the grey-blue, more grey than blue – of uniforms: the cops....'

'This could have been a *shoyu* pit,' I say. 'People must learn to move around, like once they did. The Africans – they must come back and settle. It's the great march, once more out of Africa, another trek to populate the world ... the move up to the northern lands, all hugger-muggering in. Places like this, destroyed, vacated: people will come and build new cities here, Seleucis reproduced, Ur multiplied – and farm the grasslands ... build walls, worship the guardians, sculpt meticulous accounts, a civilisation based on tax and *corvée,* on fermenting pits like this....'

Estelle drops in a stone – there is no sound. 'See,' she says. 'Beneath, it's soft ... or maybe bottomless.'

Tomorrow – we should leave. I remember how it was, back there.

I have my creative friend's last testament:

In this city, people create off-hand. They're more interested in shoooting up and shagging than in what their talents let them do – music, dance, quips and strips. All's memorable, all recorded, some on disc, some on tombstones, some in butter. These artists have a disdain for cash, some disdain for life as well – at least, long stretches of it – incapacitated, unselling, rehab ... They transgress what oppresses them – it comes out as love, hate, porno-torture.

People I should know – they're in everything, say 'no money, thanks, fuck off'. But – they have big audiences, big money, really big – swarming agents, thieves, suckers: – people who suck, people who suck you off.

I'm nowhere near them, their company. How do you get into their court? They like meeting reticent people, beginners, they're bears seeking trees to rub against.

I'm silent in the rough pub. The sets are very short – the bands, the sidesmen, like to booze, chat up the ladies. I met an ex-mountie – spoke of Indian women. He's met a lot: his job. Got fired for dealing – a big trade. A true story, short and lucid, plausible and monocoloured.

He didn't ask me anything. He had no scope – with jigsaw puzzles, you see a shape that fits another shape, fits perfectly, not part of the picture, but matching people set edge to edge. Shape coincides, not the design....

'I'm aloof. I write movie scripts. My friend, Jean-Yves, is in the business – a driver. They get credits, but who cares. He says, 'Your scripts are about how movies should be made – dull, specialised – the sex, too experimental, no one would pretend to try.'

'Honesty. Love. Telling what sells,' I tell him. 'That's my badge. My actors don't have lines, they follow their directions. They should be in love with each other, so there's no simulation. All life is acting – all acting is life. We see them making money, learning to dance, classical, contemp – auditioning, falling flat.

'You wobble between genres,' Jean-Yves says. 'Steak with peaches – makes you gag.'

I lay out every menu that is possible, 'Cadavers topped with cadavers, stunned flesh and forest fires ... Kings – the Weltenmantel, freak shows, then "all fall down". What else is there?'

'Pre-teens are the audience,' he says. 'Educated guys guess what it all means: you have to join the stream, go with the current – otherwise you're just anothe cracked old guy, wanting to be on the make.'

I'm desperate.

'Forget trying to meet people who aren't interested,' says Yves. 'Talk of what you see – the sadness of action, life in the deep, shells full of inaccessible meat.... The loss of being; people who have gone, been sold, not on your screen. People speaking many languages at once in a small room.'

I tell him, 'That's insipid, Yves. You have to make whole worlds, colour in the waves and trees.'

'Try one thing, then another,' he says. 'It won't matter. You're only as big as your own head.'

*

'We know people back there, Estelle,' I say. 'It's dispiriting – those millions putting themselves on show; as bargains, as presences, spirits vanishing back into their stones ... entertaining with their danses macabres.... My old friend, tormented with his dream....'

'I can't help you with your sentiments,' says Estelle. 'Enjoy them by yourself.'

'If we were beasts,' I say. 'We'd come here for a kill. There's nothing here – so one of us must go! Eaten by the other – or escaping – fallen down the shaft. Preserved in the wet and dark, then sifted out in nets – bog animals, preserved for ever in a drawer. That – would be stupid. After all, we brought some food.... We had our arguments – the last one quite definitive, with blows exchanged. It's not our fault. It's a mistake – we looked at animals that couple up for life, raise kids together – we eschewed the band, the troop – our heritage. We were quite wrong – evolution played a trick: we don't fit together, male and female. In this clearing – there is nothing but the dark. Even sin's invisible. Suppose – I'm God. Starting again. It's evident, He must have had experience first-hand of living on the earth. It's never clear, it shifts – was He a vistor, had a second house, a garden, pesky snakes.... The working time spent in the clouds.... How is the transport? There's a shift from walking in the garden to creating light throughout the universe, although in truth it's still all mostly dark....'

'Enough,' says Estelle. 'It's quite clear, God is a figment – creation came about through the first two of our species – two *sapientes*, making it all up, birth spontaneous.... God never married, that's for sure ... and now, the course is run. At the last, the fear. The Federals. Hired guns. Jail, maybe an execution here, where there is nothing; nothing but us.... And in the bushes, maybe – only them.'

'When we return, we can be separate, Estelle,' I say. 'The first two, the model couple, it's all documented – she a schemer, he – a poor sap. There's silence round the last two – even their names, Estelle, Maxime – invented by us alone.'

We lie and giggle in the dark, don't touch each other. Tomorrow we'll cover up the shaft, and leave, be separate.

*

'It seems a pity, after we have found the shaft, if we daren't go down it. We could be its guardians. Wait for the Africans. They'll know what to do, and take the risks,' I say.

'While we're on the trail of truth,' she says. 'You were right. I had a lover all along – an old watchmaker. From Campobasso, Italy – an expert in right timing.'

'That's psychology,' I say. 'Finicking, not precision. Your lover is of no account – all the time I'm with someone, you, I think of others, fantasise, explore. Not for an hour do I think of you alone, Estelle, your scientific thought, applied wisdom, the right procedure, the technological old sage, mister death the clockworker, digging down in your low field, winding you up.... I'm a dog, Estelle, a proud dog, an Afghan, Maremmano.... I don't excite: I sniff ... humiliate you for my pleasure – know your viscera, digestion, excrement.... I'm a dirty dog and proud of it....'

She sticks out her tongue at me. Claude Bernard said the normal was illusory – so, I rejoice. None of us has a fate in normality – what there lies beyond, within – he didn't say.... Maybe – 'cure, if that is what you want, but have no ideal present'. Nothing normal's here.

*

Far off, I see a lithe young man – wearing a golden bracelet, full of grace. He runs – fast. There's no one after him.

'Chico,' shouts Estelle, running towards him, pressing herself on him, close as she can. 'Chico! My loving friend, of unequalled psychological depth and sensibility! Why did you come? You needn't have – the team has disappeared, there's only you.... We're in a hole, my dear – although – the one we found, that's not the one! We haven't ventured down – or rather – Maxime doesn't dare.'

'He's right,' says Chico, flashing a smile at me. 'If he gets stuck, we'd throw a rope, but never have the power to pull him up again.'

He glances fleetingly down the shaft. 'Gold?' he asks, like they all do. 'Or cobalt? You should be cautious. If it's gold, the cops will say you're stealing it – with cobalt – they'll say it is a bomb.... Best leave it – discoveries destroyed the peoples here – over and over; not as bad as what the strangers wanted to discover, never did ... but bad the same. Beefsteaks! That was the last invention ... and burgers too – roasted on the spot.'

'Do stay!' says Estelle, hugging him. 'Our tent can hold another one for sure.... And as for me ... I'm made for holding, you can see.... You came all this way, just to say you wouldn't come...! Stay, lover, lost and found, and lost again....' And so, and so....

'Convince me!' Chico says, and Estelle shouts across to me, 'Chico's the last survivor of New Age. Such hope! Fantasy in power!'

'I know,' I say, 'I lent him money, maybe he forgot. It doesn't matter now, especially if there's gold....'

Chico peers down the hole. 'It's black,' he says. 'It could be jet. It goes with bombazine. Much out of fashion now, but then – things mostly are....'

All three – we stare down, like villagers round the well, seeing the moon down there, wondering how to fish it out. 'For sure, it's poison,' Chico says. 'For arrows. Soporific, odourless – we'll sell it to politicos – it's undetectable – a drop's enough. The problem is – we civilised guys – we let a bucket down, it floats. There must somehow be a trick to have it fill....'

Estelle looks blank, and shakes her head. 'They never taught us that,' she says.

'Suppose it spills,' I say, 'not just on me, but all of us – a suicide? Stupidity? A plot to finish off the world? The best thing – a quick sale to statesmen, and, Chico, you can pay me back....'

'I remember nothing,' Chico says. 'In those gay days – our debts melted like spring snow....'

'Those black-flies and mosquitoes,' Estelle says. 'They cluster down there – are eaten by the crows ... our successors? Shall we escape a cuddly death, as we lie here in my tent, and I tell you everything, dear Chico, everything about myself....'

'I really cannot ask so much,' says Chico. 'You know, I live by faith, not works, still less by confessions and analysis. Besides, I doubt that you have brought a pail, among the boxes piled up here.... If we cut the shit down there, it could be sold as horse....'

'And, Chico, have you seen the cops around?' I ask. 'And no, I don't mind you sleeping with Estelle – I'll hold it against her, not you. So, think, think twice before you stay....'

*

We sleep like all explorers do, naked, close together, layered like the winter wood, tobacco leaves – just like they all do, with their bearers, rivals, slaves, women left at home, men left at home ... ah memory! And after all – they're all explorers, even the guy, the TV and generator on his back.... We dream, as all explorers do, of the great Dam – some imagine they are building it, others putting the national flag on top ... some think of placing the explosives there ... we, in this tent, we think of the Dam that cracks, cement bulging out between the bricks; the turbine sheds, big enough to stage an opera, Aida, Satyagraha, Lady Macbeth – maybe all of those, a season, a Manaus.... But – in the end, it cracks, everyone is swept away, legs in the air, voices made raucous by the fear, the ducks and chickens overwhelmed with mud, vanished, gone entirely, never seen again, the cortèges too, the mourners buried by fresh cadavers, fresh mourners bury those, the coffins are split open and immediately filled with lustrous muddy bodies, and on, down the tortured brown river, joining other rivers – will they reach a sea, or make a lake, bigger than a sea, filling the sea of Aral, the Green Lake? See the torrents run and hunt, see the desire, the rush we lost ... the Paraná, Madre de Dios, rivers washed clean in the blood of the Dam.... The Dam that is no more....

*

In the morning, Chico sleeps on – young, time to waste. 'Well,' I ask Estelle, 'what did he find in you?'

'A question asked too seldom,' she replies. 'He gave me this!' And she flashes it, the bracelet, with a title, like a silent movie. 'See! It's not real gold.'

'He'll bring the rest,' I say. 'The team. To tell why they didn't come. He wears sneakers – the forest people back in Bahia can't have shone his shoes, or buffed his nails....'

'Or talked about the shaft?' says Estelle. 'I'm sure they knew about it.'

'No need to tell. If it's a poison, maybe the animals and all the rest were put to sleeping mode. Renew the universe – all will awake, start off again! *Alles leben!* Bluebeard's Castle, Beauty and the Beast,' I say. 'Sleepers....'

'How I love Chico!' Estelle says. 'You're ridiculous, Maxime. The world – not ending, naturally – but crouching down, taking off its smoky plumes, cherishing, cuddling ... Dear Chico – my beauty, my lovely sleeping one....'

'If it's a sedative,' I say. 'The shaft.... It won't be deep, it's precious stuff.... Better times will come. We'd lay him down, a Cuchulain, sleeping for millennia....'

The idea has purchase – I see that, in her depth....

It's just a thought – I don't chase ideas....

Estelle persists: 'You should recognise – Chico is good. Fragrant. Not a gigolò type, not fancy – just too good to have the common fate, ours, everybody's....'

'Our civilisation mummifies their memory, Estelle,' I say. 'Especially of the good. It doesn't kill them first. Nature does that – the nature everybody talks about and hopes will save us....'

'If only,' says Estelle. 'He'd not wake. I'd love him, and you'd not have to deal with him.'

'No,' I say. 'No complicity. Stick it out, Estelle, stick with him till he's your pustule, your smell, your reek: he's the talking head, bundled on your back. You've cut it off – it's yours for ever.'

*

Chico wakes. 'Well,' he says, naked. He's very small. 'I thought I risked everything, when I came here to tell I couldn't come.'

'I understand perfectly,' says Estelle. 'You're the soul I don't believe in, Chico. You need deep destiny ....'

'I accept it all – from you, Estelle,' he says.

It's symphonic. You feel your tears, the tears of other people too. Chico's a hero, maybe the victim, goat, as well – a double blessing for those who are still here.

'We could hide down there,' says Chico, pointing at the shaft, spoiling the climax, but it's done without a second thought. Of course, I love him too, Chico – all his team as well, although they screwed it up, and there will come, if not the cops, militias or vigilantes, guys with guns, the weapons Estelle didn't pack.

*

The team – it doesn't come. But ... There's guys, wading through the breast-high bushing – they were the team: they're not the team. There's Jota – his domed head, a cultivated mushroom.

'My parents – they were aliens,' he says.

Dear Gretian ... my shoes still filled with ash – my undeclared passion, burnt, encindered, like a forest.

Loris, Zeca – their eyes flick up – to absent crests of missing trees. I show the shaft....

'Don't touch a thing,' says Jota. 'Everything belongs to someone, not to you.'

'We *found* the shaft,' says Estelle, weeping soft....

'Oh no!' says Zeca: 'Knowing something's there gives you no title, so not knowing – means that all is property, and so, known and not....' and Loris finishes for him, 'Property is theft, so property must have its thief. And if it's not, but earned through digging, cultivating, mixing your labour with the soil – when you're dead – there's always someone with a title. Who knows who? In heaven? In a cot? Anyone – except – it isn't you.'

'If you are not the team,' I say, 'why did you come? To say that you would not?'

'No, no,' says Gretian, her body certainly beneath her clothes, quite naked: virtually untouched except by her.... 'We will prepare, protect. The cops....'

'The cops will say you stole the shaft,' Loris cuts in. 'We're here to test you, your defence. Good faith.'

'Did you bring good faith, Maxime?' asks Jota, taking notes.

'I can't be sure....' I start.

'Well, stealing's a harsh word,' says Zeca, his thin legs badly eaten by blackfly. 'Misappropriating softens it. The use you had projected, all the gear you brought to find the shaft, exploit, assay and quantify – you don't have jury legs to hold you up ... the problem is, when you're found guilty – there's no facilities to shut you in.... What does that do, I wonder? Doesn't make you innocent! We could throw you down, into the pit.... A punishment that fits....'

'Patience, brother Zeca,' Loris says. 'Stealing is proved, but there's no punishment in store. A sexual slip? That's usually between live folks, so becomes that much more grave. And Maxime – has the yellow eye ... the goat called Satan; fevered in his thoughts, unbridled in his deeds. Consider, Maxime – the intellectual, such as you are – not yet a citizen of the post-revolutionary state, although....' he pauses. 'Well, all states that are now are post- ...' He stops, goes on, 'I see you are devoid of civic sense – and then, for sure, you do enjoy the world. Self-gratification – ah, you intellectuals.... Recall – your pleasure, and its elements of brutalisation and estheticism.... You like your orgies tasteful – not in a garbage alley, but with damascene, some, enough brutality – the masks, the kudu horns – remember those...? the cuckold's pole ... your cloudy images: utopia – and madness. History, Maxime: made by and for you. Now – do you understand this desolation? Who can not! 'I *am* –

but *what* am I?' I hear you ask. Of course, to you – you're everything. Just as the animal proves superiority by eating plants – so it must reach up higher, eating other animals. This is your path – taking sex, stealing, we might say – raises you up, appropriates for you. The Man – it's written thus. The body, Maxime – always with us. Not transcended. Nature too – that *will get us in the end.*'

He rants, he rises up, he smirks. Man! His path, his aspiration, and his faults, his slides, his pratfalls and his boasts!

'Do you get bored, Maxime?' asks Zeca. 'Boredom: that enables the rubbishing of this or that philosophy? Maybe you stop before all can complete? The pagan State's enough for you – being a Master. Being your self, your *Sein,* your cock.'

'A slip, a slide in argument,' says Jota. 'And you're encysted in attempts at rape, a buzz of molestation. Pleasure and satisfaction – those should found a State.... But,' he laments, looking around, 'what we have is desolation – something has gone wrong, awry ... those states! those people! Man...!'

'We have to ask Estelle,' says Chico, speaking for the first time. 'She must be the judge.'

She's eager, not quite frank.

'He's a pig,' says Estelle. 'Never satisfied – as they say, pig-ignorant. That's not the fault.... There's much much worse. Maxime is useless at philosophy. Can't tell a higher level from the low. Doesn't grasp the history he's made himself.'

There's laughter all around. They're all the same as me – a useless lot, and self-indulgent, piggish too. The worst court to find good faith in, or culpability.

*

'If the cops come,' says Chico. 'We'll put him in the shaft. Hide him, punish him ourselves, if that is how we feel. And if he's found – better to have him tried for theft than nuisancing.'

*

'The team has gone,' I say.

We are alone, Estelle and I. 'They're still, again, the team that's not the team,' I say. 'They want to start a restaurant – no clients, but they say it is a guarantee ... of food.

'And I'm condemned, without a punishment. Philosophy – is now impractical. The good proclaimed and parcelled in a smelly envelope. My crimes – spring from convention. From unpleasantness, perhaps. Monkey peccadilloes.... Maybe a death, a disrespect – people forgive, Estelle, they laugh: they count the corpses and the motivations, why there was failure – things go on ... the monkey climbs the tree, he farts and waves his tail. How that brings the laugh....!'

'Yes,' says Estelle. 'Cover it up. Take your punishment, when you get out, you're chastened, but the truth is – you're unpleasant, Maxime. You are different – most unpleasant people don't know, try to pretend – you want to be as you are. Unpleasant. Invasive. Small.'

'Like Chico,' I agree.... 'Small.'

'It's true,' she says. 'Progress, modernity, and post – there are faults. Every fault acquires its remedy. Create the hungry – feed them. Kill – cure. The puzzle becomes solvable....'

'The shaft?' I ask. 'Finding that, experiencing its uncertainty – it's insignificant. We all recognise a shaft. The question is – where does it lead? Who created it? What consequence.... It's minor, compared with the big issues – survive or not? Let the people decide! Theirs was the choice, theirs, their bosses.... They made the fire – would they put it out? Act as a species, a humankind – or blunder on like monkeys? – what we are....'

'It's late for that,' she says. 'You being unpleasant – not here or there.'

'I don't have the powers,' I say. 'I spun the words – the cloth was full of holes.'

'What is found cannot be ignored,' she says. 'At the last – it's been put there to be found. Good or bad, it's your duty, doesn't matter if yourself is good or bad. Maxime – you could improve.'

'You said it, Estelle,' I say. 'If I act pleasant, nothing has been found. There's no duty. Now – who are these delightful people wandering through this glade – another trip to the Lighthouse cancelled? They look cross enough....'

Ladies, in fashion, a whole troop – some whooping, some chiruping, others resigned and plodding – they come closer, we see they're all keening, weeping – their hats, some with tails attached, are bouffant, they're dressed in furs, some with the scars and patches of a former scrabbling life....

'Here,' says Estelle, 'before we have to deal with these....'

She hands me a book of drawings – each page has margins dense with annotations. There's scenes finely, minutely drawn and hatched – 'North Vietnamese artillerymen', 'Russian lancers with their ceremonial pennons', 'Choctaw warriors dismounted', 'Evzones', 'Ukrainian border patrol', 'Pakistani and Indian crested soldiers, on parade'....

'They're wonderful,' I say – and 'horrible', I think.

'Sell? Give? Trade?' she asks. 'It is my gift, my talent: the drawing. A series, plaques for silversmiths.... Some time, Maxime, when I have gone, they may save your life. Already, they're my immortality....'

'All these military scenes,' I say. 'Remembering what happened to them all, the armies – the end we thought would do for everyone ... the threats, betrayals, the posing....'

'Oh,' she says. 'It is the show, the pomp, the ritual, invention.... The moment before action, or a show that's like two puffed-up birds – cranes, perhaps – leading to stasis while the rest goes on.... I don't do cops or spies or hackermen.... It's just my thing.... It's art. Or cleverness; a message you can tag on to ... a comment ... whatever suits you best.'

'It's impressive, Estelle,' I say. I'm at a loss. 'You mean I could barter these to save myself?'

'It's not for you,' she says. 'You're the only person here, that's why you get them. You can make them sing, give them life, and have them circulate – they're what has always gone on round, pictures are like solidi, rotating ... or if the shaft has silver in, somebody could strike them up....'

Maybe they could. The ladies face us now – asking what and who we are, in Russian. Estelle says, 'It's dangerous ... the shaft. I didn't know it was. Be careful – the shaft is all there is, here.'

*

'We're singers from the opera,' says Zlata. 'Empty-heads and Little devils, the contract said – but then, since there was no public, and we are really dancers, they offered us a Cherry Orchard – picking fruit. There was no fruit. We're showbiz, we do stereotypes – everybody is quite typical.... There were no people interested, and here, except for you, there are no people either.'

There's the team, that isn't any more a team, I think. But these are classy ladies, tall and scented – and how I love them all already – Zlata most of all, as she's the first, but then there is Galina, Lyubov, Tatiana and Irina, oh! and Olga too ... some weep, some kick up their heels, some stretch and some do fouettés....

'If you are models – what are you models of?' Estelle asks. 'Performers. That must be it. You can't just be furriers – maybe you're trappers? That's too bad – we're very nearly in a trap ourselves. For me, the shaft is an opportunity, hypothesis – for you, it might be a choice, a risk.'

'No, no,' says Tatiana. 'You were right first time – about the trap. The shaft's a trap – you took the door off – "flash"! You disappear, there's darkness, and you've gone and on the stage appears another travesty, and you are in the basement, trying to find a way back up.'

'Who are all these characters, Tatiana,' I ask. 'You beauties – you ought not go down the hole – that's where the devil goes, there's only one of him.'

'You're beautiful,' says Estelle. 'I wish you were my children. It seems you're not, so what's your story?'

'We're orphans,' says Lyudmila, plunged in rare fox fors, like a robin in a snowdrift.... 'Once – Ruslan, Ludmilla – then there was Ivan, Boris the awful, we had poor sisters – they went to be the Oranges, then refuge in Kitezh – but the city, not us, was invisible.... We wander, dear Estelle – too many little fathers, that's the prob. We love them all, of course, the fathers of the people; Bolshies, spies, and friends of popes; and friends of friends, and kleptocrats, tiny and huge, drunk and not sober – hunters and wrestlers, robbers and cops ... naturally, we do whatever we must. In suffering – there is glory and redemption. We love them, fathers all – but, dear Estelle, here, we're at the

end: apotheosis. Everything melts.... If only....' And they all
gather round Estelle.

'I might ... I could,' Estelle says. 'It might be destiny!
Fulfilment.... Suppose – I adopted you, my girls, my dears.
Every one – saved from the trap, the shaft....'

*

There's much excitement. What's in it for anyone? It means
Zlata's gone beyond my reach ... a kind of incest – that awaits.
And the rest? What's there for them?

States fell apart – they failed to protect, to remedy.

'The people' – they had always tried to make the states their
own – the states in turn to be made popular. It couldn't be.... In
failing, there was still a kind of victory – when states collapsed,
people were free – so the contradiction ended, of free state and
free people.

People were free, free from control, restraint – some
delighted in it. The mass cursed their own freedom to suffer,
without remedy, cursed the freedom of the few to prosper and
exploit.

And now – our daughters? And the team, that was a team and
isn't now: – my sons? Are there few people left? Or are they
bunched like bees where life is viable, spaces like this one long
deserted ... a shaft, a chute, to slide down to –

'To Potosì!' shouts Zlata – 'It's full of silversmiths – we'll
take the drawings, have them made, each of us can have a set.
We'll lodge on the Red Mountain, come back rich as hogs....'

*

'Everything that is and has been, lasts until it can defeat itself.
Nothing defeats something it is not.'

*

Our sons and daughters – my sons, her daughters, not begotten –
not by us at least – they couple up, form twos and threes and
fours.

'I don't understand a word my daughters say,' Estelle says.

'Dancers and lawyers, Estelle, they make supple slinky kids, but who would want to mix with them?' I ask. 'In the glade, the dancers twirl around, you think 'Matisse' and that is that. The lawyers – you hope to avoid that lot – that's where philosophy comes from – it stumbles, lies, and dies, and you end up in jail.'

The sons and daughters – they go crazy, wild – 'Potosì, Potosì' goes the shout.

'Potosì's sterile,' I tell them. 'A terrible place – slave souls flickering to the wick all over – dangerous too –'

'No, no,' says Lyubov. 'The drawings! We must realise them, put them on silver, not on walls....'

'You give them value they don't have,' I say. 'It will not serve you. I was given them for barter to the ignorant, to save my life. That's what art means – it's trade, there should be nothing in it that's intrinsic. You make a big mistake. You dancers – everything is in your arms and legs, and when these drop – that's it! That's art – it's life, and in most cases – death.'

They're not convinced. 'We want a ceremony!' they shout. 'A rite.'

'It always ends and starts like this,' Estelle says to me. 'No!' she tells them. 'We're not parents, this is not a garden, this is not the start, there'll be no ark, no animals, no sin – it's all been done ... these myths are binding only because they have one foot stuck in the real; the other's in your head. Mistake! We didn't father you and mother you – you ought to know, there is no father, big or little, no mother – of earth or sky....'

They caper. Couldn't give a toss. The story is convincing, what they have believed – it fits the dances and the law-courts that they know – applause and punishment, and loads of sin....

*

They've eaten all our food, and off they go – 'Potosì, Potosì!'

'Red Mountain' Marina shouts. 'Slava, Slava....' And they leave us with the shaft – it looks more black and deeper still.

We sit, alone, and further still apart.

'What can we do?' Estelle asks herself. 'Down the shaft – there won't be food. Tubers, funghi – at the most. To occupy our minds...?

'Most of what you might be – takes other people, books, documents as well – you can't do these things plausibly on your own – Jew, Arab, Slovak, Han – we could be all of those, any or none – but in one item, a person singular – it looks daft....'

'We could invent a thing we are, the two of us,' I say. 'Many identities start with ones – Buddhism, Marxism, monotheism – when there's two of you, it takes a lustre, commands a smidgin of respect. Or so you'd think – except there's schisms, sects, backsliding, agnostics, apostates.... Then there's people you'd not want to to be your second self, even less the first....'

'Whether we want or not,' Estelle says. 'We have a cult. The shaft. We're people of the shaft – we daren't go down, but it is all we have, what keeps us here, amuses and bemuses us. The mystery – and yet it is profane, and secular. It smells, is unproductive.... And I – I found it.'

'Even worse,' I say. 'Our children – who aren't ours – they didn't care. They had no theory of what it was, the shaft – it didn't bother them one bit.... It was no challenge, just a worm's hole, an empty snail shell....'

*

'This is ridiculous,' I say. 'Use your science. Find out what's down there – we'll climb down, or go away. Stasis – it does not exist.'

'You're deluded, Maxime,' Estelle says. She tries to call up specialists. Are there many? any? that would answer? She says – many are in vendettas against opponents, others have no funds, many many more are dead, marooned in ice and desert – doing projects that have been forgotten, cancelled. 'People get bored,' says Estelle. 'More and more data, information – and who cares. The end is nigh, maybe it's come, maybe it doesn't matter much....

'Science, Maxime, isn't liberal. It progresses, but you don't. It doesn't care who's doing it, if they know anything, find something, follow the rules.... Your future, identity, your sex and happiness – it's like the dancers ... science doesn't care. It needs joining on to what has gone before – like grafting apple trees – but it is quite indifferent. It is the same if you are here, or me; if we change sex, religion, if we die or live. You, Maxime, still live where there is ought and good, even if it doesn't suit you. Science doesn't bother with that stuff.'

'There's something here,' I say, reading a squib. '"A hole in the ground! This dilly's found one, wants to know what's in it, guys!"'

'Oh, that's a machine,' says Estelle. 'There's lots are miffed – they lost their animals – the last one dies ... you can't adopt....

'Look,' she says. 'Maybe this one's right: "Your problem, Estelle, your obstacle, is *him*. Not science, nothing of all that – the guy you're with – he won't go down and look. That is what holds you up. Bundle him! Give him a pacifier, give him sex, or comfort – lie to him, say he'll feel better, say there's a gift down there – but make him go! Don't risk yourself!"'

'Maybe I misled you, Maxime,' Estelle says. 'Science, and I – we're not a humanism. Science will gas you, sedate you – but you'll die whatever happens, the longer you live the more you'll regret having done nothing that you wanted, and weep alone in the midst of younger intolerant guys. If you have money left, Maxime – that's what they want, your peers – not your skin and bones ... they don't even want your skull to drink their koumiss from....'

'I agree, I'm an obstacle,' I say. 'But *you* go down the hole, Estelle. Resolve the matter.'

'Yes!' she says, inspired. 'I'd make a map – like the old geographers who made up what they hadn't seen. Illuminated.'

'Make up any animals you want,' I say. 'It is irrelevant. What is not – doesn't matter.'

'You manipulate, Maxime,' Estelle says. 'Like in unreconstructed days – manoeuvre me, and you're unrepentant.'

'No, Estelle,' I say. 'I repent. When there were many many people – one person's opinion had a force. Now there are few humans left running wild – you need a number of you to make a point....'

'In any case,' she says. 'I'm forced to follow up my brilliance ... by going down the hole myself.'

'It isn't necessary,' I say, exasperated. 'No one knows what's down there. Whatever it is, will it help us? What possibly could? Maybe ... maybe someone knows, some Intelligence. Then – it would be stupid to descend. I shall not follow you, Estelle, nor look for you. Exploration is like that. If you disappear – you're lost. The next one looks not for you, but to explore for bones – your bones. And to find what you could not.

'It's what you risk for being an original. For having an idea.'

'Make me a suit, then,' she says. 'From the bushes. Animals, small ones you find tucked away, with seams already. A protective suit. You, and your reactionary selfish unnamed friend, between you you've not made a phrase to ruffle up my skin. You're oak-galls ... I'm alone, alas – I've not been solitary....'

'I'm not anyone else,' I say. 'Not my friend, not any human concourse. You bleach me out. This here is peace. And starvation. Down in the pit, if you go down – is obliteration.'

I go looking for her protective suit, that I might make – when I get back, she's obviously gone. Down the shaft.

She never comes back, and I don't go down to look for her. There's nothing down there, I'm sure – or maybe there is her.

No one says, ever, that they've seen her again.

All discovery, creation, comes from nothing. That's where she went. It's a magnificent calling: creating.

*

'Il n'y a pas d'amour heureux....'
                                    – Georges Brassens

'We were living in the future there,' I tell Laurent and Amandine. 'Few people wandering round. A desolation – no, a devastation, like they say. People cluster where it's safe; and there's no boundaries.... We were on the edge – there, you don't discriminate, but everybody keeps their personality.... Contentious things? – they won't be settled now, injustices stay as they were. What was the point of talking anyway? We're all at everybody's mercy....' I smile, wryly. 'Estelle and I,' I say, '–

we discovered many aspects of each other – in a time of penury, you're stripped ... and then she went. I didn't search.'

They look incredulous – friends, become attentive strangers. 'It's normal here,' says Amandine. 'Just like it always was. Some time, Maxime, you'll tell us how it really was. I guess you suffered, terribly.'

'You've still got birds,' I say. It's evident. Amandine, beaked like a tern, Laurent, a carrion-seeker's stoop and flimsy legs. In the yard – a hopping cluster ... their wings – they must be clipped – hoopoes, cranes and Malabar shrikes, standing round, waiting for their mush.

'We've not much to give,' says Amandine. She hands me two cold cobs of maize. 'We're moving out.' She is downcast. 'It started going rogue round here,' she says.

'It's the attacks,' Laurent says. 'It's random: kids.... But if it grows there'll be more serious stuff. An intervention – trained guys. Standing for something, for sure it's something we'll not be.'

'Today?' I ask. It's quite a blow. 'We had some hopes – the shaft we – she – found, it could be shelter, who knows what....'

There's lots of silence here: 'The birds?' I ask.

'They'll have to forage for themselves – like we all do,' says Amandine. 'Sad.'

There is no refuge here. 'Well, maybe I can get a ride with you?' I say.

'There isn't room inside,' Laurent says. 'You could go on top, I guess.'

And so I do. There's melancholy as we leave. It has a normal look. You'd want to stay, although you know you can't. Too late, I think that maybe I need not leave. I could hide out there.... But I have left. They drop me off when we're in sight of town.

*

The town is clogged with people, every street – people with flags and badges, trying to march somewhere, but blocked, jammed solid.

'There's no state left,' says Amandine. 'It didn't work. The people! Here, they demonstrate – there is no work, so permanently they're on the march but do not move....'

'You have to do a deal with people in the gangs,' says Laurent. 'The gangs, they're like the state but harder. The street won't find you work, a place to stay. You have to pay the gangs for those – more than the tax – and you can't fool those guys....'

'I've thought about this lots,' I say. 'Making movies, or enrolling in the cops. Those are my options....' It's not true, I haven't thought about this place at all: I have no wish to stay. Better go back to the shaft – a place abandoned, nothing to fall down – no one to push you down the muddy steps....

'You'll find it's late,' says Amandine. 'These manifs – they want nothing, no new faces, no retribution, no restitution, restoration, no revolution. Nothing is claimed. Repression will come, and be resisted. It makes no odds. No change except the impossible: an operation, at the root – on time, the world, the universe.... Making it all different, intervening long ago, arriving at a different place. Somewhere we haven't reached and never will.'

'Then I was right,' I say. 'Repression or reproduction – cops or movies. That's the choice.'

'It's all the same scenario,' says Amandine, waving and crying as she and Laurent are digested by the crowds.

Laurent and Amandine – they never liked each other greatly – now they'll find that being in a couple where there's no way out, is punishing. A punishment.

At least our children might do better if they stay in Potosì....

People here – held in the perpetual manif. Me – bound in nostalgia: for the shaft.

*

Whooping it up! That's another choice. Finding a postman – they're the best companions – work's over early, what's not delivered is mailed back – tomorrow, or hidden in a secret stash ... all posties have one.

I put my bundle down, bend to do up my laces.... Then – it's gone! Stolen! A thief's mistake, I think – but it's bizarre.

Now what? Movies are a far-off plan. I investigate the cops. Are they sympa? My sort, if I should join? 'Sabena' takes my spiel – a civilian? Familiar. Maybe I was once here and lusted after her. 'I screwed it up, Sabena,' I tell her, and she writes it down. 'Everything,' I say. 'I remember you – I gave you up before I had a taste, a touch. Like you, there was Estelle.... I'd show you where I live, but I'm still looking for a place. The shaft....'

She's very young. 'The shaft?' she asks. 'And what was down it? Did you dig it out.... Live in it? That's an offence. Do you confess?'

'They say it's a mystery, what happens to us, what we do – but it's not. Each day, there's less and less of mystery and fewer explanations,' I say. 'We're like migrating birds – some have a partner and a place – they travel everywhere and still come back. But others – don't, they don't have anything, they don't go back. That's Estelle, and that's me. We weren't monogamous, like albatross, we took as kids whoever.... If I suffer – it's no one's fault. Like her. We aren't good or bad – which means we are not bad....'

It's a mistake – I over-talked.... She knows it's lies – or doubts and curiosity: the cops all know, that's lesson one, that no one ever tells the truth.... It doesn't mean the police know the truth themselves, of course....

She likes my narrative....

'A bundle, Maxime? That's what they took? This city's full of them, of bundles, every one identical,' she says. 'This place is stuck. We didn't want where we have got, and don't want what we're going to get. Forget the posties. If you want to whoop it up – I'll come along with you, we'll find a shaft and deepen it or fill it in.... Inventions and discoveries – we're tired of them – there's more and more of us, piled in the streets, nowhere to live, no work to do ... the novelties – they threaten us, it's all a trick, we've fallen for ideas of change and revelation many times.... No more!'

*

Sabena – she's my protection. She knows everything, where the best clubs are. She knows how it will end, how we'll square the cops, stop them billying us.... Of course she knows – her sphere.

'Are you arresting me, my dear?' I ask, unzipping her pistol and waving it above her head. We laugh.

'It's a ride,' she shouts, gunning her moto. 'Hold tight! We're the only ones who move!'

'Yet no one's moving down below – why do your people strike out so – water, gas, electricity they use to bully us ... and matraques – on the head and in the eye, the arse – what is the point?' I ask.

'If you can't move, you must suffer just the same,' she says. 'Change is painful. So must stasis be....'

Here's a club – down a shaft you go – there's welcomers – sequins for eyes, nipples in the half-dark luminescent....

'Don't be afraid,' Sabena tells me. 'You're trembling! Everything here – is born of will. No one can go against their will – but you can leave your brain right here....' And there's a tray, with knitted brains – like pin-cushions – you take your sloppy organ out and put in a woolly, dry, and colourful one....

'That's better,' says Sabena. 'You won't feel the difference, and when we leave – take any one, they're all the same....'

There's creatures: tall as deer, their only cover – a pussy-card, a joker or an ace....

'I recognise....' I say. 'That's Tatiana, Olga – they're the children that I made....'

'Of course they are,' Sabena says. 'You're a magnet, Maxime. Or – perhaps they are.... Listen – they'll sing to you.... The Invisible City – perhaps that was there, where the forest once had been, in the maquis, down the shaft....'

'No,' I say. 'They maybe came from there, that splendid city – but there was much much more, they knew it all, the world, and what you knew but couldn't see....'

'Drink this,' says Tatiana. 'You'll see things clear.... Forget, and drink....' She gives me a goblet, silver – incised – a scene from Spion Kop....

It's clear! All things! 'I know it all. Potosì – not the place to go, and – there is no city down the shaft ....' I say.

'There!' says Olga. 'You who love wisdom – you knew it all before you looked.'

'The others? Sisters? Where are they?' I ask – my tongue is long and thick.... 'Oh, you'll pick up lots of ants with that,' says Tatiana, and they laugh.

'Come away!' says Sabena laughing. 'I told you all you need to know! We didn't come here for the truth. Nor wisdom. Those you had – and now they've gone inside again, into your viscera, the dark, the schtum – unless I suck them out!'

'My daughters!' I say. 'They didn't recognise me!'

'You only saw them because your brains are made of wool,' Sabena says. 'The staff is paid not to recognise you – or anyone. If they recognise you, you have to be arrested. On suspicion....'

'What now?' I ask. 'I want the fun! Abandon! Fantasy!'

'Take this pill,' Sabena says. 'It makes you tell the truth. Life is much clearer so. Then – we'll see the picture show. Some shafts ... may prompt you.... Let's go down, into the members' gallery ...'

And so we do.

'Yours is no doubt a noble trade,' I say, having Sabena guide me down. 'You put truth above everything – above my innocence, above the good, the beautiful – and yet your mates are out there with matraques – billying the innocent and the stuck, immobile masses ... splitting their heads and forcing orifices – what in the name...?'

'I see you still aren't reconciled to life,' Sabena says, giving me another pill. 'It's how it is – life, is created thus. Dialectical. Try and fix it in another way – what we have now is what there is, the universe is set up so! Exactly as you see it, and the science gives you every detail, every fold, and every lug and misprint too....'

The stairs are teak, they're made for giants, the furniture is black, there's medallions – the Duce's dull and beefy face, his butcher's jaw, is on them all – the chairs are set against the wall, a peasant's gathering-space....

Sabena lets down a screen. 'Look close,' she says, I feel her body press against me, from knee to shoulder, she puts her little hand inside my smock ... the faces ... they're familiar, they could be boasters from the bar, then there's old scenes of

country life – of buffaloes, or cows with horns as long as
scimitars, of brothers in a row with knives, amazing draughts of
fish, dried and on racks, a chestnut horse with mayflowers in its
mane ... there's even dobbins ... between shafts, with round-
eyed families in the high-sided cart....

'No,' I say. 'That's not the kind of shaft at all –'

'Then wait,' she says. 'I'll have them take another lot of
pics....'

'You have suspicions, but whatever those are, Sabena, I am
innocent,' I say. 'My life's in these dull snaps. Our children; me
looking for Estelle's suit, peeling the lizards and the gourds ...
the quarrels had, planned, then overpainted.... We were on the
run, Estelle and I – the shaft was safety, mystery, our eternal
present, time out, acceptance of the greater failure all around – a
little hole, an interval, a tear in some stressed cosmic fabric....'

'We all want one of those,' Sabena says. 'And since you took
the pill, I know it's true. I knew it anyway.... You are my
indifferent lover, who's forgot his love, false, a coward; just my
type – but what you haven't said, is where the people went –
and who went down? Who were they? And – the people who
came up?'

'The only unknown character's Estelle,' I say. 'Did she go
down, or tire of waiting, run away, follow the sons and
daughters, down some other mines...?'

'No one,' Sabena says. 'No one has seen her, Estelle, not
since then. But – just tell me what I want to know. Down the
shaft – at any time – did you see light? Tell me, and you'll have
all you want, all I can give you, everything from me –
tranquillity, love, and comradeship ... a pardon too....'

'No, Sabena,' I say. 'There was no light. It was inscrutable,
the hole, without illumination. Nothing: dark – a zero absolute.
And – I want nothing. Nothing from you, my dear, let my
solitude be absolute, it is the most, the least, I ever want....'

That's what I get.

Sabena's left. My bundle – never mentioned, gone for good
or ill.... A wet brain – that, they slipped in once again, took back
the loosely knitted one, a double handful of undyed wriggly
wool.

And is this mine, my used, familiar brain? Do I have mine, the original, once more?

Sabena said, they're all the same, these brains ... or very similar.

*

'Be very very careful, Maxime,' Sabena said. 'Drifting as you do in situations extreme.... You low-flying hollander, your women had or coveted, and in the end evaded ... your children, set on perilous paths – and all with no guiding idea in your head or hand.... Your world's disorderly – a blancmange of shapelessness. You could end up guilty, end up dead....

'If you drop in on me, I'll give you snuggle room, but in time limited.... Drop down my chimney like an owl, and disappear when sooty night surrenders to the light.... You're smooth, you fall off surfaces, roll down cracks....'

She frowned and pinched my nose, quite hard – affectionately.

'I have ideas, Sabena: only – people are not central to them,' I said. 'I fear – ideas don't set a store by them, the individuals who sail around each one of us ... I want.... I think....'

'Yes, Maxime,' said Sabena sternly, as she closed my dossier, writing 'not proven' on the front. 'People who want – they sometimes get. Everyone who goes to jail has had clear aims, desires: a want – if only for a moment, but – he who doesn't want, like you – he doesn't get.'

'Yes,' I said. 'It seems I wanted something badly – the shaft. It's central to my life – but why? Why me? And what's it for?'

*

That wanting's feeble.

My secret wish, my hope – is that my daughters, working diligently – should dance and dance and ultimately become what they have aspired to be – true birds. And that my sons should strive and grow, their arms and fingers toughen up and sprout – and they become trees for my birds.

I don't tell Sabena that – not just because it is against the law, but because it shows I have a single-mindedness the cops don't have. They roil in doubt – this one or that? guilty or innocent...? a massacre or self-defence? assassination by the state...? This side that side, a fraud, ingenuousness...? Their every step is cast in spume and steam, on sidewalks before Chinese Theaters of the mind.... Footprints, pawprints, change into finger-smears ... what's concrete softens into bog. Mugshots are filed, then hung in halls of mirrors....

*

'Where's your badge?' asks this old guy. His says 'Evimar'. 'It's a courtesy, of course,' he goes on. 'But not to wear it, could be taken for a lapsus, error of taste, an insult, too.'

'I've lost my troop just now,' I say, embarrassed. 'I'm not a vagabond – just a stray.'

'Of course,' he says, 'and the cops know where you are, so everybody's safe.' We laugh.

'I'm really Doktor Doktor Evimar,' he says. 'But there's no room for that.'

'Ah!' I say, not much impressed. 'A scientist. I was close to one of those. We found this shaft ...'

'Oh,' he says and laughs some more. 'They're everywhere. No time to explore them all.'

'She thought the scientific way,' I say. 'Maybe it was always there, the shaft – or because the trees had been burnt off....'

'There's trees been growing everywhere,' he says. 'The scientific mode – will make you discoveries – too many, more than you can use. Epistemology – left far behind.... The universe – is a toyshop and apothecary's – play with some and swallow some. Play with the cat, then ride the dragon's back! That's innocence and infancy!

'But – the countryside ... the birds, the mines, the artisans ... there, yes, there you feel free. It's the cities where they go to die. There's doctors – they hold the ropes that let you down ... the rich into their grey hole, the poor – into the fiery pit.' We laugh. He goes on,

'The scientific mode – it's just hypotheses. You think there's something behind it all, that if you push on, discovering more and more – all will fit, there'll be a grand design, a jigsaw solved, like the picture on the lid that someone has prepared and drawn. And it will show you as you are, in the frame, your image sat there in the foremost row.... A graduate, your mortarboard the proof of concreteness.'

'Yes, yes,' I say: 'Exactly like that. A company, a chair for each, a comrade either side.... The destination reached – and still a life to come....'

'You never looked down your shaft?' asks Evimar.

'Of course,' I say, 'but it was dark. It was busy too, the glade – the arguments, and then there were the refugees, and we adopted every one....'

'As everybody does,' he says, 'and sent them on....'

'And then your partner goes – you're not too sad at that,' I say, wishing I didn't always blab my secrets out....

'There could be silver there,' says Evimar, 'or clay. Or iron. A plague pit, possibly, an armoury, or just a hole abandoned – go too deep, you're at the core, you've made a vent, the gases rise, the lava flows – all runs much faster than you can.'

'I understand,' I say. 'The experiment is done. Danger and nullity – then the reckoning.'

'The risks were known,' he says, 'but the benefits – a longer life, more food – were no small thing. And warriors too, protecting you against the guys next door....'

'I know all that,' I say. 'Everybody does. That's how it is.'

'It's an achievement,' Doktor Evimar exclaims. 'Can you think of any more?'

*

We could have explored some more – 'the shafts are everywhere', he says. 'There's gold and silver, but in most – boiling stone soup.'

'And now,' I say. 'I guess we wait. Maybe I'll see my daughters, two by two – on stage, the peepshow ... things like that....'

'Yes, the good and bad of it – is that you know how it will be,' says Evimar. 'But look, my friend – most vagabonds round here, they have a bundle of their stuff, photos, documents, some pills, and vodka too....' He slips me a note, all crumpled, so I don't see how much for....

'Someone will put you up – put up with you,' he laughs, and I laugh with him.

There's Amandine. But then – there's Laurent too. Where next?

'Someone with a character,' he says. 'Something you can explore.'

*

Sabena! Of course.

I wash my face, put order in my hair....

I remember where she lives.

About the author

John Fraser has lived in Rome since 1980. Previously, he worked in England and Canada.